It Could Be Forever

Léa Rebane

Sistarazzi

Disclaimer

This is a work of fiction and is presented as such, and not as a factual account. Although some of the characters are based on public figures, the opinions, dialogue and actions of those characters are purely from the author's imagination and should not be confused or associated with any actual person. Although a few portions of this novel are derived from real events and places, the author's depiction of these events, places and their timelines is purely fictional.

Published by Sistarazzi
Copyright © Léa Rebane 2014
www.itcouldbeforever.com

First published 2014

ISBN 9780646922140

Cover background picture: http://freedesignfile.com
Front cover photo: J. Reaburn
Printed and bound in Australia by IngramSpark
Designed and typeset by David Bradbury (www.dbtype.com.au)

For Mum –

*There was so much we shared together
and so much more
I'm sorry we never did.*

Acknowledgements

A few special people have shared this journey with me. I would firstly like to thank my friend Merike for her support and passion for this story. I will always treasure the late nights of analysis and discussion over Champagne. I am also glad that you came to know and appreciate David Cassidy, the artist, through this process. My "bestie", Roz Mackrill – I am so grateful you read my manuscript and shared your wisdoms with me – I didn't want to do this without you. I am blessed to have you in my life.

Merci beaucoup to my handsome French language assistant in Paris, Charles Folmard. Many thanks also to my medical adviser, Matthew Holding, who explained some rather nasty procedures – *very* thoroughly. And big "floozie hugs" to Mandy "Moo" Johns for feeding my fantasies and being there for me. You all rock.

Special thanks to my editor, Serena Tatti – you are an inspiration, and I am so very happy that through "sharing David Cassidy" we have become friends. There is only one thing left to say to you – *I think I love you.*

I have met some truly good people on this journey. In particular, I feel very privileged to have come to know David Cassidy's website manager and friend, Jane Reaburn. Our email exchanges brightened my greyest days.

Lastly, and most importantly, I would like to thank the

gorgeous one himself – Mr David Cassidy. Thank you for kindly allowing me to use your farewell quote from your final gig in 1974, and for your good wishes. I am constantly reminded of the inextinguishable love your fans have for you. On one of the fan pages on Facebook, someone had said about you, 'He has always been there for me – always.' And another defined your gift as, 'The power to define love for a whole generation of women and the longevity to awaken that in them years later.' Wow.

Thank you for being you.

Author's Introduction

After my father passed away and I began cleaning up and sorting the house I grew up in, I became transported back to my teen years. Everything from the seventies came flooding back. My hippie aspirations, the music I loved, the fashions, the music I created, what I watched on television, but mostly it was all about the music, music, music. Oh yes, and the thoughts of my first love – the guy in my head who resembled David Cassidy. I started to write frantically about all of it. And almost despite me, another story emerged and wove into my cathartic ramblings, which took on a life of its own.

This story is not what I fantasised on the brink of puberty. It is what I fantasised some forty years later for what could have been played out in my head, had I the maturity back then. I thought that females from all around the world would have wanted something along the lines of this fantasy too, or at least the fun parts. So I wrote it for my sisters of the "David Cassidy fan clan", who had their own versions of him in their heads. We certainly were a massive harem, sharing one huge burning love across the globe. And I think one could almost say that David Cassidy took the *virtual* virginity of millions of us, for he took our innocence in his stride. He was a safe prospect for us to begin our sexual awakenings with as he was just so damn *nice*. But in retrospect, that had a lot more to do with how he was being portrayed.

Meanwhile, the real David Cassidy was busy waving his penis around in the faces of his fans, according to his first autobiography, *C'mon, Get Happy*. This was a shocking read, even in my thirties, as I felt that my twelve-year-old self had somehow been cheated or violated. For many of us, the big grown up Cassidy devastated us when he admitted to liking "slutty women", when he began singing songs that told women to "get down" while they rocked him and when he asked naked women to bark as dogs as part of their sexual act for him. He may as well have sung, *Fuck Me Baby*. Was this cocky person the real David? The David *we* imagined wouldn't, simply *couldn't* do these things. We trusted him with our hearts and our developing hormones. We felt duped. Some of us had only just gone into trainer bras; this was too much to take. Could he not have been a little more dignified and less crass?

So who was the real David Cassidy? Well I guess only he would know that. And in fairness to him, I can forgive him for being human. His sharp rise to such extreme fame must have been significantly tough for him. I can't imagine anyone living through what he did and coming out untarnished and squeaky clean. My compassionate, analytical mind can empathise with most questionable things he did and truly feel for the guy. There is a side to me though, the little girl that loved him whole-heartedly, that still wants to keep *her* version of him tucked away somewhere in her head to swoon over on rainy days.

However, this story is far from being wholesome either. After all, *anything* can happen in a fantasy. To all of you who, like me, melted at the sound of his voice and would have given anything to be gazed upon by those amazing eyes, this story is for you...

Chapter 1

1974

*Like all at once I wake up from something that keeps
Knocking at my brain*

From the back seat of my father's roomy Valiant, I strained to hear the radio. *I Think I Love You* played in the background of an ad. Could it be? I thought I was dreaming. No, I had heard correctly, *David Cassidy* was coming to Adelaide. My surge of excitement was interrupted by my father trying to tell me something. *Why does he have to speak right now?*

'What was that, Dad?'

'Don't forget your piano lesson is at five today so make sure you do some practice beforehand,' he directed.

'Yes, Dad,' I groaned. Not that I didn't want to play – I loved playing music but suddenly a more urgent issue had arisen – David Cassidy was coming to town. I *had* to make plans with Brandi. Of course when we arrived home, I couldn't go anywhere until I had practised my piano pieces.

My fingers normally glided easily over the keys but on this day they kept stalling. Beethoven was dancing with Tony Romeo in my head and they kept bumping into each other. Mr Sinnet, my piano teacher, was not impressed with my performance of

Moonlight Sonata at all. He didn't even give me a new piece to practise for the following week.

'There needs to be a marked improvement on this first, my dear girl,' he scolded.

'Sorry, sir.' I made up some excuse about extra loads of homework for this period. 'I'll have it cinched by next week for sure.' I smiled sweetly in a way that I hoped looked sincere.

My dear friend in drama class, Andrew always told me, "One must always be sincere… and once you can fake that, you can achieve anything". At the time I had laughed, although uncomfortably as a part of me didn't want to think people were really like that. I shuffled Mr Sinnet out of the door with a lot of niceties.

'*Mu-um*,' I called, 'can I go over to Brandi's for a little while?'

I always asked Mum as Dad, coming from a strict northern European background, never let me go anywhere. Both my parents had been born in Sweden but my father took the role of "strict European father" to the extreme. Maybe because I was an only child. Or perhaps he tried to hang onto the threads of his culture severely, lest he somehow lose them in the "ockerism" of the land he now lived in. I didn't even want to think that it had anything to do with my bra size increasing almost monthly. *Ick.* I hated the attention my new breasts commanded. But whatever the reason, at fifteen, I felt I was still being treated like a nine-year-old. Luckily my mother tended to balance this out. I could tell her anything. Well *almost* anything.

'It's not far off dinner time and your dad needs to go to choir practice straight afterwards.'

'Thanks Mum, I won't be long.' And I raced out of the door and all the way to my best friend's house.

Unfortunately the person who answered the door was her sleazy brother, Judd. As soon as I glimpsed his greasy straw hair, my mood waned and I looked down. I hated the way he chatted me up all the time. And the way he'd always watch me with his soulless eyes made my skin crawl.

'You can come in if you kiss me first.' He grinned in his smart-arse way.

I smiled nervously; I was kind of embarrassed. I didn't want to smile at him but felt really awkward and I think it was just a defence mechanism.

Luckily his mother came to the door. '*Lisa,* come in,' she welcomed me. 'Judd, will you get out of the *way.*'

'Thanks, Mrs Goodings.' I had to squeeze past Judd.

'Brandi's in her room.'

'Thanks.' I shyly retracted from them.

Brandi sat on her bed with Tiger Beat magazines spread out in front of her. Every freckle on her face appeared deep in concentration.

'Have you heard the news?' I bounced into her room.

'What?' She looked up.

'David Cassidy's coming to Adelaide!' I announced, pleased with myself for being the bearer of this information.

'You're fucking kidding me?'

'*Brandi.*' She was such a rough diamond at times.

'Sorry. But serious?'

'I heard it on the radio!'

Brandi quickly switched on 5KA as if they would immediately play the ad. We started making all the essential plans on getting the tickets, going to the airport when he arrived et cetera, and most importantly – what to wear. No way our parents would ever let us camp overnight at the door of Allan's Music to get the best tickets, so we had to be there as early as possible. We planned to meet at the bus stop at the end of my street for the first bus of the day, shortly after dawn. Well, as long as the tickets went on sale on a school day, which they probably would. We most likely wouldn't make it to school that day but no sweat, I was a master at copying handwriting, so parental permission was already granted.

Okay, great – phase one of "Operation Claim Cassidy" was sealed. If only I'd known the irony of our plan's name.

By the time box office day came around, I had told mum of our plans. Mum was pretty cool and often let me do what I wanted, in contrast to my father. She knew how much of a David Cassidy fan I was, so I guess she figured there was no way I would want to go to school when I had DC business to take care of. And contrary to most mothers, she was actually okay with that. I loved that she was so groovy.

I planned to leave the house just before it got light, to meet Brandi at the bus stop. I couldn't sleep all night, waiting for that exciting moment to commence my mission. When that moment eventually arrived, I organised the pillows in my bed so it looked like I was still in it. I even arranged a wig sticking out from the top of the blankets for good measure. I crept quietly, carefully, avoiding any creaky floor boards, until I reached the back door. As I held the handle, I held my breath too. Ever so slowly I pushed it down and slinked outside. I tip-toed down the driveway and when I finally made it through the gate I just *ran*. As I tore down the street, I half expected to turn around and see my father coming after me. It seemed I had been successful as no figure, or Valiant, came charging along our street and I made it all the way to the bus stop.

The light was magical at this time of morning, merely

seeping into the dim grey. The withering street lights looked like glowing cough lozenges, dropped at the end of out-stretched poles. I imitated a fire-breathing dragon, as each breath from me saw mist emerging from my lips. Now that I'd stopped running, the cold picked its way through to my bones so I began jumping from one leg to the other.

Where on earth is Brandi? I kept up my little jig, waiting for Brandi and for the bus. The bus arrived first. Brandi had let me down. I had wondered whether she would chicken out. There was nothing for it but to board the bus that would take me to phase one of "Operation Claim Cassidy".

As I approached the already long stream of girls shivering along Grenfell Street, a gang of nerves punched me in the gut. *How am I going to do this on my own?* And far out – the line snaked around all the way from Francis Street at the back of Allan's Music, to Gawler Place, to Grenfell. I guess some kids were better at sneaking out in the middle of the night. So I simply joined the queue, in keeping up my duty as a dedicated DC fan.

Almost seven am – only two hours and nine minutes til the ticket sales open. Pretty soon the girls next to me and I chatted away, and I had forgotten all my apprehension. To bide the time, we even sang a few DC songs and eventually our procession started moving ever so slowly to a chorus of cheers and applause. It actually took hours though to reach around to the booking office in Francis Street. When I did turn that final corner, who should be strolling up to me smiling but Miss Brandi Goodings herself.

'Hi!' She was dripping with cheeriness, and the brash scent of *Charlie*.

'Far out, what happened to you?' I tried my best not to

show my annoyance.

'Oh shit. I couldn't sneak out. I had to go to school for a bit and then take off at recess.' She surveyed the numbers gathered for the cause, her head of auburn curls bobbing as if pleased. 'But it's all okay now, I'm here.'

'I can't just let you in the *line*.'

'Oh well, cool bananas – here's my money, I'll see you after. Thanks. *Seeya*.' And she disappeared as quickly as she had appeared.

Some best friend. I tried to console myself that at least I made the line for the tickets. And I *was* going to the concert. Eventually I reached that magical window. My voice quavered a little as I asked for four tickets to see *David Cassidy live in Adelaide.* That was the deal unfortunately, my parents had to come. I argued with my mum over this for ages but I simply couldn't win that battle. No doubt I would be the only person in the whole of Adelaide going to the David Cassidy concert with her parents. *How embarrassing really.*

When I saw Mum that evening, I excitedly told her all about the day's events. How I'd met these other nice girls, and how one of them had been asking everyone that passed whether they loved David Cassidy, and then scream, "Not as much as I do!" and it was all just so cool.

Mum said she was glad these other girls had taken me "under their wing". I was totally irritated by that comment. There was *no* under wing taking. What I didn't mention to Mum was that after I'd bought my tickets and left the line, so many boys whistled at me and called out comments, like "sexy". I think the boys of Adelaide sure were jealous of David.

Chapter 2

But be certain not to stray
Or he'll steal your heart away

The day I thought would never come, arrived at long last. Dressed in our finest Golden Breed shirts and Lee jeans, Brandi and I sat in the back of Dad's Valiant. My parents perched in the front, Dad in his suit of course. My father even wore a suit to go to the local shops. I brushed my long brown hair for the duration of the drive, hoping it might begin to resemble Susan Dey's even a teensy bit. We were on our way to Memorial Drive, where David would be performing in barely a few hours. Where else would I want to be? Abso-bloody-lutely *nowhere*.

The queue appeared endless - lucky we had numbered seats. Brandi spotted a couple of our other friends and let out the loudest whistle ever. My father gave a disapproving look.

'*Brandi*.' I elbowed her.

She completely ignored me. 'Hey! You two – over *here*.'

Adriana and Greta scuttled over. Their excitement for the concert almost oozed from their shiny faces. They didn't have tickets but had planned to just hang around and listen outside.

As the line started moving into Memorial Drive, they walked with us. We stepped up to the first ticket check and my dad showed our tickets. The guy asked if "these other two girls" were with us and Dad confirmed they were. He didn't realise they didn't have tickets. Adriana and Greta gave each other a sideways glance of cheeky thrill and slinked in. This same scenario repeated at each of the three ticket checks. My parents were still none the wiser but all of us girls giggled in disbelief. *Far out.* I knew I would be resentful for the rest of my life that Adriana and Greta got into David Cassidy's concert – for *free*.

We took our seats on a long bench type arrangement. Some pretty wild girls filled the stadium. I started to feel grateful for Dad being with us. I wondered what he thought. No one ever went wild like that for his men's choir. In fact, I had probably been the wildest at about the age of five when Mum and I sat in the audience and Dad sang a solo. Just at that miniscule pause between the end of the song and the applause, I had yelled out proudly, "That was my dad!"

These girls however, only became crazier and louder as the evening wore on. They were bad enough during the support band. Then our hearts stood still – they announced David Cassidy and the loudest unison scream I'd ever heard erupted. What the hell, we joined in too. And there he was, on stage, looking absolutely gorgeous and dancing around before our eyes – he was *real*. He wiggled away to *Puppy Song* and he sure knew how to excite the crowd. By the third song, *Preying On My Mind*, when he sang the upbeat chorus everyone jumped up onto their seats. We sat staring at each other. What could we do? We couldn't see like that. So we jumped up too. My parents stood up but didn't take it any further, thank god.

Our little group was evidently much tamer than these girls surrounding us. I wondered whether the notion of northern European girls such as me being ice queens, had some merit.

Usually I had a tendency to be quite emotive and Mum would joke that I didn't belong in the family, but at this concert I didn't see the need to act like a total loony. Okay sure, every now and then, I did swoon and gasp, like when he looked in our direction and called, "I love you!" That was just the best moment ever. And I really enjoyed listening to his voice, even listening to him talk in between the songs – at the times when you could actually hear anything above the screaming. Naturally everyone went spazzo when he shouted out, "I love Adelaide!" And everyone went even crazier when he announced he loved us so much he would do a second show the following night.

Thoughts zoomed through my head as to how on earth I'd get to that. We had a discussion on this after the show, but none of my friends thought they'd be allowed to go out to a second concert, let alone afford it. *Sucked in.* We had to deal with this bummer of a reality. I knew my father would virtually lock me in that night. *But* I could take another day off school. I had already taken the day off for David's arrival at the airport and appearance at 5KA but if I wasn't able to go to concert number two then I was definitely going to hang out at The Town House Hotel in Hindley Street. It wasn't every day DC was in town after all.

The next morning Brandi, Adriana, Greta and I met at the Pancake Kitchen for breakfast. I wrote notes for everyone from their parents, excusing them from school. After some yummy pancakes with mushrooms and sour cream for sustenance, we headed down Hindley Street to that vital corner embracing The Town House.

Not surprisingly, a dozen or so girls already flaunted there. The TV cameras rocked up too. Foolishly I said to my friends that they didn't look like they were "plugged in" so we didn't need to worry. Little did I know we were being splashed across the midday news on channels seven, nine *and* ten.

We hung out, sharing memories from the previous night's unreal concert and a small group of guys emerged from the foyer. I recognised one of them as David's real life room-mate, Sam Hyman, from fan magazines. With his coal-dark features and intense black curls, he was unmistakable. He drifted outside with a few others, perhaps members of the band, or crew. They stood around talking and after a bit, Sam walked straight up – to *me*. He told me he wanted to ask me something and beckoned me away from my friends.

We stepped into the foyer to talk. Or more like he led and I followed in a zombie-state, as my brain couldn't quite register this. None of the fans were allowed inside. Shrouded from the outside frenzy, he asked if I would like to come up to see David. He wanted to meet me.

Me? How come me?

The instantaneous shock must have created a confused expression on my face. Sam explained that David had seen me on the news footage as one of the fans outside, and asked if he'd go invite me to come up for a chat. *Those flipping cameras had been on after all.*

I completely spun out that he chose me – me, Lisa Magnusson. *Far out.* Nothing like that ever happened to *me*. I was never picked for anything. We made our way up to his suite, Sam leading the way and me trying so hard to be cool and not show my nerves.

David came up to me instantly, smiling the warmest, inviting smile. He took my hand. 'Thank you so much for coming up to see me,' he glowed, 'I'm David.'

I nearly giggled... Who else would he be? 'Sure,' I managed, 'nice room.'

That was all I could come up with. But the room was so mod, I couldn't help but gawk at it. It even had a groovy shag rug, which I made a mental note of avoiding in case I tripped on it. And it was less nerve-wracking to look at anything else apart from *Him*.

I realised I hadn't introduced myself, so quickly added, 'Oh, I'm Lisa.' I sounded like an idiot.

'Would you like to sit down?' he offered. 'Would you like a...' he hesitated, I think realising he shouldn't be offering me alcohol, '...a coffee or something?'

'No, I'm fine.' I was sure my face had frozen in a cheerful-lunatic expression.

His handsome face kept smiling at me and I became hypnotised. I think my mouth fell open a little as his soft breathy voice continued to speak. 'Thanks again for agreeing to come and visit with me. I saw you on the TV footage and you had such a nice smile that I felt I could talk to you. It's been so long since I've rapped with someone other than crew. Finding someone local is almost always impossible. I had to take a chance that you'd come up and here you are.'

I remained lightheaded and a little star struck. Okay, maybe quite a lot star struck. *Stop staring at him.*

He asked me all kinds of questions about my life and what Adelaide was like, what I liked to do for fun and what this part of the world was about. I tried to answer without sounding like too much of a dingbat, as if it were some kind of test. He joked around a lot with me which did help to relax me somewhat – at least to the level where I could place two or three words together in a semi-logical sense. But his charismatic manner eventually caused me to get into his groove a little too.

I stayed for what seemed like ages, not really caring what my friends were doing, but also not able to wait to tell them everything.

Before I left, he asked if I would come and see him again the next day, as he had to leave the day after. I must have made a gesture resembling a nod and he gave me instructions on how to gain access into the foyer, including a "pass". He softly kissed me on the cheek to say goodbye and I think I floated down to street level. The delicious softness of his lips and slight bristle against my skin had me reeling. That was *David Cassidy's* bristle that had brushed my cheek.

Once with my friends and a safe distance away, we just screamed and screamed together, jumping up and down. It seemed we were capable of that after all.

With my heart beating triple-time to *Havin' A Ball*, I set off to see him the next day. A thousand questions spun around in my head. *Does he like me? Don't be a spaz – that's not even slightly possible. Does he just want information from me? Will I really be able to convince the security that I'm meant to go in?*

We had pre-arranged the time, so when I reached the foyer door, the staff let me in straight away. I shakily headed up to the International Suite in the tiny lift. Again he greeted me warmly with a kiss on the cheek. I am not sure how I achieved it but this time we did chat and I even laughed. Probably a little too much. *What am I now – a flipping kookaburra?*

A little way into my visit, he turned to me saying he had a favour to ask me. 'I was wondering whether you might consider accompanying me on the rest of the Australian tour… Well, if you'd like to that is… But I would really like you to… And I'd be more than happy to talk to your family or parents to let them know the schedule and to assure them that you'd be my guest. What d'ya think?' That smile of his just wouldn't give in.

My head began to spin. *Would I?* What a ridiculous question. Of course I would. I suddenly didn't care what reason he wanted to be with me. Hell, *of course* I'd go.

He did push for me to bring my mother to see him before he left the next day at noon. *Hmm. What will Mum say? Dad would kill me before letting me go. But if I'm able to convince Mum, then maybe, just maybe, we could cook up some story for Dad.* So I didn't stay as long as I'd have liked but I left on the promise I would talk to my mum.

I semi-gracefully left his room, but after taking a few steps, I ran. I think I sprinted all the way to the train station and probably all the way home. My mind darted like a confined spark trying to think of the right words to convince Mum. She knew how much I loved him as a rock star. *She simply has to, has to, has to let me go.*

When I reached her, Mum knew something was up. 'What on earth has happened to you? Why are you so flushed?'

I blurted out everything at high speed and then utterly begged her to let me go. I waited in anticipation for her answer, for what must have been an eternity.

Eventually, she said *"yes"*. I was so excited I just about wet my pants. My heartbeat raced. I couldn't believe this was happening to me. *Me.* Little old ordinary "me" was going on tour... with *David. Eeeeeeeek.*

Mum and I concocted a story for Dad that involved me signing up for some kind of extensive school music camp. Mum, not surprisingly, did want to meet David the next day.

He acted no less than a charming gentleman towards her. By the way she looked at him, I began to think *she* wanted to come along too. But in a cheeky maternal way she razzed him, 'You make sure you look after my daughter.'

He assured her his intentions were honourable and that he would do everything to make me comfortable and cared for. He was just so damned charming.

I was going on tour around Australia with David Cassidy. *How on earth will I sleep tonight?*

Chapter 3

As it turned out, I *didn't* sleep that night. David had made arrangements for me to fly up the next day to meet his entourage in Melbourne. A car picked me up from home in the morning and I kissed and hugged Mum goodbye. She'd even lent me her Glomesh bag for the trip. We were both *alltför* excited. I boarded the plane, looking back and smiling at the tarmac as if I was some pop star.

At Tullamarine Airport a car waited for me to take me to his hotel. My heart did drumrolls all the way. A concierge greeted me as we arrived and asked one of his staff to take me to the suite "Mr Cassidy" had requested. The rooms making up my suite were outta sight, with long gold curtains bunched up intermittently, plush velvet furniture and a stunning view over the city and Yarra River. Never in my life had I stayed in a place such as this. *How did I land in this fairy tale?*

The bellboy asked if I would be requiring anything else. I didn't have a clue what I could possibly ask for. 'No, everything is fine.' My voice appeared to have gone up an octave or so.

'Very good, Miss Magnusson,' he answered, 'Mr Cassidy has expressed his wishes for you to make yourself comfortable and he will see you shortly. Will that be all?'

'Uh... yes... thank you.'

'Very good.' And with that he left me alone, to ponder what on earth was happening in my life.

I barely had a chance to explore the rooms when someone knocked at the door. I opened it to find David standing there with a grin, offering me a gorgeous bunch of bright pink roses. My heart began its triple beat again while my eyes blinked in disbelief. I suddenly remembered to speak.

'Oh, they're *beautiful*,' I squeaked, and quickly coughed in attempt to lower my voice.

'I'm so glad you like them.' He smiled. 'May I come in?'

'Yes, of course.'

He said he'd call someone to put the roses in a vase for me. 'So this is Melbourne?'

'Yes, I guess it is.' I had only ever been there before with my parents to visit their friends or to go to some boring Swedish Festival, but never by plane. 'I've been here quite a few times,' I said casually.

'Oh, *great*. Then you can show me around.'

Perhaps I had spoken too soon. But somehow, on some level, I felt he was onto me. Strangely enough, he didn't seem to mind. He told me he had to leave for the Melbourne Cricket Ground to prepare for his concert shortly but he had arranged a neat spot for me in the audience and oh, would I go to dinner with him afterwards?

How many times can I say "yes"?

His show was just unreal. Especially from the close view I'd been allocated. The last time I had seen him perform, I was a mere fan somewhere in the crowd, this time I was his *special guest*. I found it incredible to watch his stunning performance and hear his beautiful voice with the thought of actually knowing him. It seemed surreal. When he sang, *I'm A Man*, such a short distance from me, the strangest tingles ran through my body. They gave me exciting sensations but felt awkward at that same time – really weird. Every beat of that song pounded right through me.

Not long into it, parts of the audience began pushing to the front so forcefully that girls were being hurt. David had to stop the show. He warned he would leave the stage and stop the concert altogether if they didn't move back. They conformed for a little while but then pushed forward again. Some were carted away by ambulance from the crushing effect and their fits of fainting. This was like watching the dark shadows against the pazzaz and magic under the spotlights.

Afterwards at dinner, David told me how concerned he'd been about the crushing and how much it had affected him. A minute later he took my hand. 'But you know, I'm so grateful I have you to talk to about these things.' His hazel eyes appeared larger, as if they momentarily held the innocence of youth. 'Sure, I have my "people" but it's not the same.'

He kept true to his word and acted "honourably". After dinner he walked me to my suite, kissed me on the cheek and wished me goodnight.

A similar scenario occurred throughout the tour. Although on certain nights I wasn't able to see him for some reason. However on rare days, between interviews and escaping from hoards of savage girls that looked like they wanted to tear his clothes off, we had the luxury of sight-seeing, along with a team of security men.

I wasn't much help to him with information as I had never really thought about population numbers and specifics on native animals. Besides, this was the first time I had seen so much of Australia myself. And throughout all of it, he remained the perfect gentleman. He never kissed me anywhere except on my cheek. He had begun to call me "Beautiful" when he referred to me but he never stated his intentions. It wasn't until his last night in Australia that he told me what a wonderful time he'd had visiting our country and that this was mainly due to me. He said he would be in touch and he'd love to see me again.

When I boarded the plane from Perth airport to fly home, all I could think of was our last goodbye – the last kiss from him tingling on my cheek, his soft voice that had said such lovely things to me and his beautiful, beautiful eyes. I knew not what any of it meant, and I cried all the way home clutching one of the dried pink roses he'd given me, missing him like crazy.

The months after that ginormous experience were horrendous to say the least. I found it extremely difficult to go back to normal life. Friends kept telling me I needed to let go; it was wonderful for what it had been and I should be happy with that. I wasn't. I wanted more. I wanted more of him. I was totally bummed out and depressed, and couldn't concentrate on my school work. I was flunking every subject miserably.

Then a letter arrived for me. *Yes, it's from him!* Part of me wanted to open it carefully, saving the envelope, but I tore it open. It was a card – a simple card with a pink rose on the front. I opened it hoping for reams of words. But all it said was, "Thank you so much for being there for me in Australia. I miss you and hope to see you again soon. Love, David".

That's it? What does he mean "soon"? Is he going to come for me? Will he send for me to join him somewhere? Does he really mean "love"?

I analysed and reanalysed that little note to the nth degree. I had so many questions and so few answers. But no further answers came. After that card, I received one more "cutesy" card from him about a month later and then nothing. That damn first card had given me so much hope. I'd been lifted again to soar amongst the stars but then thrown flat onto the ground and even shoved in. My life felt like a living hell after those glorious few weeks with him. *Why did this ever happen in the first place?*

Chapter 4

Crazy little ragdoll, her hair was wild and tossed
And I put my arm around her 'cause I knew that
she was lost

After a few more stilted months, I had lost my newfound confidence and was back to being the insecure teenager I had been BC – Before Cassidy. And the worst thing imaginable happened; I found myself with a horrid boyfriend. I hadn't had a real boyfriend before and I wouldn't call this one real either. In any case, it wasn't of my choosing. I know that sounds kind of strange to say but it sort of happened by default. He was the brother of my best friend – it was Judd.

I had slept over at Brandi's place one hot summer night and we'd all slept in the lounge room under the air conditioning, including their father who was drunk. He was so drunk he fell heavily asleep, and although he lay right next to us, he didn't realise his son attempted to have sex with me.

It all happened so quickly I didn't know how to stop it. And I didn't have the confidence or self-assurance to do so. What I thought was his finger was definitely something else and in that horrible way, I lost my virginity on the lounge room floor of a Housing Trust house in Croydon; the pathetic drone of the Kelvinator air-con as my witness.

Judd wasn't happy with just that incident and kept pursuing me. Well, it wasn't really pursuing. Wherever I was, he'd be there too, and I had become such a wimp I couldn't speak up against everything he kept doing to me. I was his girlfriend according to him and I didn't want that role at all.

Judd "had me" whenever, and wherever, he could. He even dragged me into playgrounds or public toilets late at night. My parents had split up and I lived with my mother in a tiny flat. She pretty much gave me free reign – something I had thought I wanted. I was angry at Judd's parents for not acknowledging what was going on. Oh they realised all right, as they would hear me crying out in pain whenever I slept over in Brandi's room. I was angry that they didn't intervene. But mostly I was angry with myself for letting this happen to me. This was not what I would have planned for myself as my first sexual encounters.

My thoughts of what a boyfriend might be like were entirely different. He would be dreamy and gentle. He would have a kind smile and be tender with me. In my mind, having a boyfriend would be a few more steps into the cosy happiness from cuddling a teddy in childhood.

The reality that struck me was a world away from my imaginings. Judd was rough, domineering and somehow able to coax me into places I never wanted to go to, do things I found disgusting and dirty. *Why? Why am I so weak?* Maybe it had something to do with how I felt I was a loner. I always seemed different to others around me somehow… Perhaps I didn't belong in this world… I was always so honest and loyal with people – too loyal. I thought that's the way people should be. It usually turned out to be to my detriment. It seemed the world didn't reflect that back to me. I had such a keen sense of justice and fairness that I felt to my core but could not see evidence of it around me. I was always there for others but it wasn't returned. I was the friend that everyone could count on but when I needed someone, really needed someone, there was no one.

Why do I need people so much? Why do I want to please people so much when it causes me harm, when it chips away at my self-esteem? My experience of others diminished my trust in them – in everything. I really was alone in the world. There were people around me but in the end I was alone and different.

I don't exactly know for how many months this continued. I started to loathe myself more and more. And loathe Judd more and more. I detested being with him. I detested myself for being with him. One night Mum had almost passed out in the other room from drinking a few bottles of wine. I crept into her bedroom and stole her Valium pills. I took them all. I then had a shower and washed away all the dirt, the pain, the disgusting marks of Judd. I drifted to sleep with the feeling that I was finally able to let go of all of it. How good it felt to slip away... the comfort of death. I scrawled somewhere, "Imagine falling asleep and never having to wake, to the pain that will be there tomorrow".

Obviously my life didn't end there as for some reason, Mum didn't pass out completely that night but miraculously found her pills missing. She called Dad who took me to hospital where they pumped my stomach. Oddly enough, this event brought my parents back together.

A few months later, I stood at the same door of the suite David had occupied during his tour. He'd contacted me, saying his life had been "excruciatingly busy", therefore apologising he hadn't been in touch. However, when the opportunity arose to get away for a short while, he leapt at it. He was in town privately and wanted to see me.

When he opened the door, his gorgeous smile shone at me but he also looked troubled. He'd had a feeling something was wrong, desperately wrong in my life, and he wanted to check up on me.

How could he know? I broke down and told him the whole horrendous story, and how I felt so guilty for not being able to get rid of Judd. He was *still* hanging around.

David listened attentively while I purged every word. As I finished speaking, he wrapped his arms around me securely. 'Sweet, lovely Lisa... You have absolutely nothing to feel guilty about. That guy's been manipulating you. He's using you, so he's been giving you some jive to control you. Making you feel guilty is part of his sick scheme... It's just a technique that assholes like him use to control others.'

He'd listened to me in a tremendously kind, almost loving manner. But above all, he was the one person who heard me, really heard me. And without any hint of blame, promised me I'd done absolutely nothing wrong. He let me see that what I experienced had been abuse.

How could I not have seen this?

Judd was suffocatingly possessive of me. He even demanded to meet me at David's hotel, after my visit. Although I'd only told him I was catching up with a friend. David said he'd send someone down to keep watch for Judd's arrival and show him upstairs. Some moments later, an annoyed Judd reached David's room and didn't know what hit him.

David was so angry, I thought he would kill him. He told him what he thought of him and how dare he have done what he had to me. He warned that if he ever came anywhere near me again he'd arrange for someone to "deal with him". 'You know what I'm saying, asshole?'

Judd's smarmy grin crawled onto his face. 'Oh yeah? Who do you think you are – just because you're some wanky rock star–'

David grabbed him around the throat and thrust him against the wall. He stared at him so hard I thought his eyes would burn into him. 'I'll show you exactly what kind of "wanky rock star" I am if you ever go anywhere vaguely near her again.'

Judd regarded him but ultimately his eyes lowered. He withdrew. He knew he had no choice. But I clearly sensed the scorn bubbling inside him. He glared at me and split, in something significantly more than a huff.

I was scared.

David comforted me and promised me that Judd wouldn't bother me anymore. 'Guys like that are all bravado. Trust me, I've "out bravadoed" him. He'll never show his face again.'

He hugged me again and asked me softly to spend the night with him. 'I'm not coming on to you, Beautiful. I just wanna make sure you're okay.'

After phoning Mum to tell her I was staying at a friend's place overnight (well I wasn't lying), I stayed there on top of the bed clothes with him holding me, whispering, 'You're safe in my arms, I got ya.'

I had never felt so secure, never experienced such bliss.

When I woke up it took me a while to register. Once the fogginess left me, I realised I had spent the night in his arms. But he wasn't on the bed next to me.

As if he knew the moment I woke, he strode in beaming, carrying a breakfast tray. 'Good morning, Beautiful.'

'Good morning,' I returned sleepily.

'Did you sleep okay?'

'Mmmh.'

'We've got bacon and eggs, toast and marmalade, OJ, coffee and... something called "Rice Bubbles". At your service, ma'am.'

He was so bright and chirpy I couldn't help but smile.

He put the tray down on the end of the bed and came over and sat next to me. I overflowed with gratitude for him and was so happy I jumped at him to hug him. He flinched in fright at first but did return my hug. I grew to know some time later that his startled reflex was an automatic reaction from being pounced on by fans.

'How you doin', Beautiful?' he murmured.

'I'm good. No – more than good. Thank you so much.'

'It's a pleasure.' With hardly a breath, he bounced straight in with, 'Hey – there's something I wanted to ask you.'

'Yes?'

He took both my hands in his and drew me in with his radiant smile. 'What would you say... if I were to ask you to go on tour with me?'

'What, like last time?' I was confused.

'Well yeah, except this one is quite extensive. We'll be doing the USA and the UK.'

Both shock and excitement overtook me at the same time. He was asking me to go away on tour again – with *him*. I wanted to *scream*. I had to control myself as I didn't want to be found out as a hysterical fan, completely forgetting that was how he found me outside his hotel in the first place. But I didn't know what to say. His eyes fixed on me, as if longingly waiting for an answer, and I remained speechless. All I could manage was, 'Ummm...'

'I will of course look after you and you wouldn't have any expenses. I just had such a great time last time here when you came on tour. You don't know how grounding it is to have you to rap with.'

I must have appeared a little flattened by the last remark as he added, 'And needless to say… I love spending time with you.'

Thoughts whirled in my head. *What will I tell my parents this time?* Although Dad had been far more chilled since my Valium episode. I didn't care – I would simply run away if I had to.

And although I didn't consider it seriously "running away", I dug out my passport and left a note for my parents to say I was staying with a friend in Melbourne.

Chapter 5

Big silver wings flew me to the United States of America, where I was met by his people. They helped me with immigration protocols and collecting my luggage from the carousel. I visibly trembled from part excitement and part pure fear, having travelled all that way on my own but tried my best not to show it.

An official-looking guy advised that we'd head directly to David's private jet. We scurried down endless corridors and down a flight of stairs, to a black square Mercedes waiting just outside on the tarmac. As soon as we jumped in it whizzed off between giant planes, until further out, there it was – a fine looking compact jet with simply "David Cassidy" written on the side in big bold letters. They ushered me up the stairs where I entered something resembling a private hotel suite, containing plush beige seats.

David saw me and beckoned me over. He wore a groovy suit just a hint off-white, and shades over his eyes. He looked tired. In a businesslike manner, he held discussion with a man sitting opposite. I sat in the empty seat next to him. He kissed me on the cheek, put his arm around me and continued talking to the man, not moving much from his relaxed "leant back" position. I had been utterly frantic getting to this point so it seemed a bit of an anti-climax. So much for my anticipated vision of a reunion, more resembling Heathcliff and Cathy on the moors.

I didn't have much attention from him at all until he had finished his conversation with this guy and we were about to take off. However even then, he seemed a little distant, or tired. Perhaps that's all it was.

'Well, here we go,' he stated, 'would you like some Champagne?'

This was the very first time he had asked me if I wanted any alcohol. I was still a bit under age. He must not have been thinking but, *Why not?* I'd had alcohol many times before. 'That would be nice, thank you.'

David ordered the Champagne from his staff in a rather authoritative manner. Soon someone arrived with two glistening mini bowls on stems, filled with passionately bubbling liquid. I'd tasted sparkling wine before but this turned out to be quite different. It definitely wasn't sweet.

'Is it okay?' he asked. 'It's French.'

'Yes, it's lovely,' I lied, trying not to grimace. Every mouthful I took, felt like it bit me. I was determined to bite it back.

When I next looked over at David, he had fallen asleep. He'd only sipped a few mouthfuls – we hadn't even taken off yet. He sure must have been tired. So that left me to my first time glass of French Champagne to conquer by myself. We started taxiing down the runway and pretty soon that sound of the engine flared up, the one that indicated we were about to speed furiously.

I loved flying and I absolutely loved the feeling of taking off. It was like an impassioned kind of magic that thrust you into the skies, to soar. A thunderous build-up and then at one single peak all the frenzy stops and suddenly you are flying and free, unleashed from everything that lies below. Only bliss exists at such elevation. I swore no matter how many times in my lifetime I would fly on a plane, I could never be unexcited about take-off.

Unfortunately I couldn't share my excitement with David. I watched him next to me, sleeping soundly, his face serene and completely free from the worry I'd seen there earlier. It was nice to watch him sleeping next to me.

Once we were cruising, one of his staff kindly asked if I'd like something to read, or something to eat perhaps. I politely declined on the food but thought I might as well try and read something. It was going to be a long flight. The same nice guy brought me a selection of magazines. I tried to read but the French Champagne was something else. I could hardly concentrate on the words as my head kept whirling. *Far out, I'd better stop drinking this.* I didn't want to do anything embarrassing like throw up. Especially on my first flight in David's plane. I'd just *die*. I put the glass down and tried to think of a variety of things to keep my mind alert. Eventually I fell asleep next to him, thankfully without throwing up.

I woke up some hours later and a flurry of activity had sprouted around me. We were about to land. I panicked. I must have looked like Cousin Itt. *Do I even have time to fix my makeup?*

'Hey, Beautiful,' a voice said beside me. David looked much more refreshed. He must have seen the panic on my face and said, 'You've got plenty of time to go to the bathroom, which is just up there. They're all just getting a bit excited. Nothin' to worry about yet.'

I thanked him and dashed off to do my girl thing. When I returned, he was no longer in the seat next to mine.

'Prepare for landing,' I heard someone say. More scuttling around me.

I spotted David sitting in another seat, his head down in papers discussing something in-depth with the same guy as before. A nice woman came and sat next to me, where David had been. She introduced herself as Ruth. I learnt later she was David's manager. She said she'd "brief" me, whatever that meant.

'Please fasten your seatbelts and remain in your seats,' an official sounding voice announced.

My eyes darted over to David but Ruth asserted, 'We all have to remain in the seats we're in now. And put your seatbelt on.' She continued instructing me, explaining what chaos we would experience when we landed. 'There will be the usual mass of girls and trust me, this will be full on.'

I felt a bit lectured. I had, after all, seen the crowds in Australia. Some had been huge.

'We are going to have to rush David through to get him safely into his car. You stay back here with the rest. They're not going to worry about who else is here after David has gone through.'

Oh for goodness' sake, how bad can it be?

It was bad. "Full on", just as Ruth had said. David left the plane to a sound way exceeding anything I'd heard at the Australian concerts. The sound resembled a mix of high-pitched wailing birds and thunder. I peered out of the window and caught sight of the frantic mass behind a large barrier of glass. They sure as hell must have been *loud*. The thunder sound I'd heard was them beating their hands against the glass. The crowds at our airports had been nothing like this. I became worried about David.

As if reading my mind, Ruth assured me, 'Don't worry, they won't get through to him.'

I wasn't so sure. These girls looked like they had escaped from some mental asylum. I wondered how on earth David had the courage to go so near to the glass. *What if it breaks?* Soon after, the rest of us piled out from the plane into several waiting cars. David's limousine had sped off quite some time ago. I didn't see him again until much later at the hotel.

My introduction to this David Cassidy tour had been a little underwhelming. Alone in my hotel suite, I had the time and mind-space to think and he definitely had seemed different somehow. Maybe it was tiredness, maybe nerves, but he wasn't the same beaming spunk I'd always known. I caught myself out thinking that I had "always known" him. It had really only been such a short space of time. *What do I actually know about him?* Still, it was exciting to be here, and still *alltför* exciting that he had asked me to join him. On top of that, I figured he must be spending a fortune on me. I had no concept whatsoever of how much was earnt and spent in his world, compared to my little world.

I heard a knock at my door and got up to answer. A tall man poised with a huge bouquet of pink roses greeted me. He was obviously hotel staff and appeared quite senior in his position. 'Oh good afternoon Miss Magnusson, please accept my sincerest apologies, these were meant to be here waiting for you on arrival. Please accept a complimentary box of the finest quality Swiss chocolates. We do hope this makes up for this dreadful oversight.'

'Thank you. No, no problem.'

'That is very gracious of you, Miss Magnusson.' He sounded incredibly relieved. 'If there is anything I can do for you, please do not hesitate to contact me. Just ask for Gerard at the reception desk.' He put the roses, which were in an elegant

Venetian vase, on the main table in my suite along with the most gigantic box of chocolates I had ever seen in my life. He bowed to me and left saying, 'Remember, do not hesitate to contact me. No request is too much trouble – for you.' He shut the door behind him.

How strange, he'd sounded British. We were in Pittsburgh. I shrugged. *But why did he act so apologetic?* It's as if he expected me to be angry because the flowers hadn't been here when I had arrived. *Or perhaps he thought David might be angry?* I hardly thought he'd be uptight about something like that.

Another knock at the door jolted me from my thoughts. I opened it to a full on cheery-faced David. 'Hello, Beautiful!' He lifted me up and spun me around; a complete contrast to the distant, tired David I'd witnessed on the plane. 'Oh good, they organised the roses… and oh wow, what a huge box of chocolates… nothin' but the best for my beautiful girl.' He chatted to me as if his words were running against the clock and he appeared intensely happy.

My heart did a little flip when he called me *his* "Beautiful Girl". I still had no idea who I was to him. But I didn't care; here I was in a gorgeous hotel suite with my idol, David Cassidy the spunkiest guy in the world, about to spend the next six or so months with him. *What could be more perfect than this?* Yes, I was happy too – straight back at him.

We sat in the lounge section of my suite and David raved on about all kinds of trivial things. His vibe was right into nonsense and mucking around. In between all the silliness he gave me a rough outline of his, or *our*, itinerary. 'So you'll come to the all the shows… well if you wanna – and *hey*, you can watch from the wings. And uh… we'll try and get out for a meal whenever we can… More likely though, it's gonna be at the hotels we're staying in... Oh and you make sure you let me know if you needed anything, wontcha? Or if you have any questions. Um... Yeah, our first American gig's on tonight – so someone's gonna get you there – coz I gotta go hang with the sound cats... and it's always such a drag for me to be snuck in somehow... Okay, cool.'

After he'd gone my head began spinning again, nearly as much as from that French Champagne.

That night, watching the show from the sidelines entirely blew me away. He'd run past me for costume changes and steal a quick kiss sometimes, telling me he needed it for luck. I figured he was running on adrenalin – and he was hot and sweaty. However, he always looked enticing to me, sweaty or not. Seeing the show from that angle and glimpsing the enormous crowd actually reaching and crying out for him, blew my mind. It must have been such a high for him to have that kind of energy from thousands of people, directed straight at him.

After the show, we ate in the hotel's restaurant. They kept it open exclusively for us as it was much safer for him to dine with no other patrons around. He never had the opportunity to eat until quite late as he said he couldn't eat before a show. And it appeared he was still running high from it when we ate, being the super chatterbox he had been that afternoon. He asked for the second time whether I'd like some Champagne and before I could answer he called out to the waiter, 'A bottle of Dom, thanks,' whatever that meant. 'What's up?' He must have noticed a strange expression on my face.

I told him that the first time he ever offered me Champagne had been on the plane.

A realisation seemed to dawn on him. 'Oh of *course*. You're under age, aren't ya?' He smirked. 'Oopsie... It's ok, I won't tell anyone.' He laughed and continued raving on about the gig and everything else he enthusiastically conveyed to me. I don't think he even heard me saying I had about a year and a half to go.

The whole of the American section of the tour progressed in something of a routine – just about every alternate time I saw him, he was distant and tired – and then chirpy and chatty. And at every show, I watched from the side of the stage, in awe of his performances and most definitely in awe of the enormous crowds that endlessly loved him and screamed for him.

At one of the concerts, something happened that I thought would stop my heart right there and then. David had flown past me for a costume change and ran back in his dazzling black suit with silver rhinestones on the lapels and sparkling silver bow tie, completed by a glittering cane as an accessory. Parts of his suit would light up, along with the cane, when they dimmed the lights.

He offered me his cheek to kiss. 'Thanks for the luck, Beautiful,' and bounced right back onto the stage to a huge roar of appreciation. This outfit was chosen for *If I Didn't Care*, which I described as a "jazzy number". I knew practically the whole show off by heart now and hummed along to the introduction by the band. But this night, David didn't come in singing at the correct bar. Instead he started talking to the audience. *What is he doing?*

'I'd like to bring someone out on stage,' he began, 'a very special young lady.' He came back to the wings where I stood aghast and took my hand.

I couldn't speak. I tried to convey my protest somehow without words but he just kept leading me out onto the stage.

'It'll be fine, Beautiful,' he said close in my ear. Into the mic he announced, 'This is a lovely friend of mine.' Tentative cheers rose from the crowd. 'Please welcome her, this is Lisa!' He led me to a stool slightly off-centre of the stage and sat me down.

The mass broke out in cheers but although I heard the applause, I felt daggers from thousands of pairs of eyes. *Oh god help me.* Meanwhile, the musos had improvised through the intro several times and when they received the signal from him, they led into the opening bars once again. So with me sitting there, feeling like the whole world was out there gawking and screaming, David began to croon, *If I Didn't Care* – to *me*.

Man, oh man, I think it took every inch of my willpower to control myself. And it wasn't even to try and prevent myself melting from David singing to me; it had a lot more to do with not shaking and falling in a heap in front of his discerning fans. I tried so hard to smile without my top lip quivering. The dance section came up, the lights dimmed and David "lit up". I was extremely grateful that he danced *for* me rather than making me dance with him. I would have fallen for certain.

The number ended and the crowd screamed for him, even more than for the earlier songs. He spoke into the mic, looking at me, 'Thank you for coming out here,' and kissed me on the cheek.

I think half a dozen girls fainted in the front.

'Will you please thank her for me?' he charmingly pleaded. They burst into a frenzy and he led me off stage and hugged me. 'You're beautiful.' Then he darted back to give them more.

Chapter 6

It's just another dusty mile
And I've got dreams to spare and time to spend

So there was little old me from Croydon, South Australia, on this spectacular David Cassidy tour. At times I really had to pinch myself, and at other times wonder what on earth I was doing here. The whole thing would take about six months. Six months that my father now thought I spent living in Melbourne with a friend, to attend a specialised music school. As my mother and I were more like best friends, I ended up telling her the truth. After much convincing on my behalf, she did seem happy for me. She eventually realised how much I loved this trip and how excited I was to take this opportunity.

However being on the road, or in the air with David, wasn't always roses and swoons. He still acted the perfect gentleman with me but his moods were up and down like a pair of click-clacks. I never knew which David to expect at my door. Although usually after concerts, I'd be guaranteed an uplifted David. That was, when I could see him. Often after shows, I wasn't able... or "allowed" to see him. It took me a long time to work out why and what was going on. At one concert, a famous Italian actress swanned around backstage. I recognised her but wasn't sure of her name – I thought it was either Sophia Loren or Gina Lollobrigida. She was quite a bit older than David but seemed to flirt with him a lot. She had been placed on the other side of the stage to my spot and sometimes he'd go off stage on my side and sometimes on hers. I thought, but wasn't sure, David may have been flirting back with her a little too.

At the time I didn't have the courage, or the right I'd thought, to ask why she was there. But I soon learnt to be my own person. Especially as I received a great deal of respect from hotel staff and most people we encountered. If I wanted something, no matter how small or how unusual, it would be delivered almost immediately. I guess I had a certain status being in David's inner sanctum and was definitely treated as a person of authority. This taught me confidence I had never known before.

I learnt a lot about life, people and relationships on that tour. More than someone my age probably should be learning. But due credit to David, who'd been the actual one to set me off on my "road to wisdom". He'd certainly made a huge impact on my life when he stuck up for me over Judd and taught me how to recognise abuse.

The constants with us were David's housemate Sam Hyman, the photographer Henry Diltz and his manager, Ruth Aarons. All of them really neat people and they were good to me. Whenever something was up with David or I couldn't spend time with him, one of them at least would check on me to see whether I was okay.

I spent a lot of time walking around the cities of America with Sam. He was a good egg. He knew David extremely well and sometimes gave me hints on how to handle him. I think I started to pick up on this myself. I found that, although I was young, I was actually rather good with people. I was the person everyone sought to confide in and be "best friends" with. I also discovered I had a knack for working people out. I developed a strong sense of how most of the entourage felt on any given day, by their body language and the way they acted. This turned out to be a vital skill in this setting. I grew up on that tour in more ways than one. When I had left church-quiet Adelaide, I was a naïve girl but I would return as a woman – in (I'd thought) six months. And little did we know when it began, that it would be David's final tour. At his ripe old age of twenty-four.

At one of our after show dinners, David rapped away eagerly as usual. I'm not quite sure what he'd been talking about – something to do with what really mattered in the world – but he suddenly fell silent. Staring into his glass, he appeared deep in thought. He lifted his lashes to look at me. Whenever he gazed at me deeply with his exquisite eyes, he seemed to look into my soul. It gave me goosebumps – extremely pleasurable ones.

'You know,' he began, 'I don't think I've been very fair on you.'

'Oh?'

'I think I owe you some kind of explanation, a confession of sorts.'

I had no idea what he was about to say but I had a feeling I didn't want to hear it. I didn't want to hear about girls in his room, about the drugs he took. I had eventually worked it all out. His patterns had become predictable. But he surprised me.

'I'm not really this guy…' he paused, 'I'm not the guy you think you see – who comes flitting in and out, singin' my little songs and conducting this huge circus, or whatever the hell it is.' Another pause. 'Sure, I'm happy a lot of the time. Life is just one great big party. And they love me, don't they? Don't they just fucking love me? "We want you, David" they scream at me... For once I wish they would just shut the fuck *up*.' He slammed his fist on the table.

I wasn't perturbed.

'I'm sorry, Beautiful. I didn't mean to lose my cool. It's just that... just that... this whole thing is just such a crazy trip. I play a part, they play a part – but it's all just parts. It's just not my bag... It's not who I really am.'

'Who are you then?'

'The thing is... I'm not sure.' He looked at me intently again for quite a while. 'I don't know who I am. Isn't that pathetic?'

For the first time, I took his hand across the table. 'You're tired. You work so hard. You hardly get any sleep and there's this constant pressure on you. Don't be so hard on yourself. You just need some rest. It's easy to let negative thoughts in when you're run down. No one can keep up this kind of pace forever.'

He seemed appreciative that I understood.

'Besides... the drugs wouldn't be helping either.'

He stared at me like a startled schoolboy being found out for being naughty. 'You knew?'

I nodded, then smiled at him.

He came over and sat next to me, taking both my hands in his. 'Oh beautiful girl, I'm so sorry. I've been someone else with you. I've been *him*. And I haven't told you what a shining light you are in my life. I need to be more real. If only I can figure out how to do that. I don't wanna be this teen idol machine. I wanna do more meaningful things, I wanna have some freedom... I'd like to be able to take you to a movie... or the beach.' He continued to gaze at me in the most enticing way.

I think it was precisely at that moment, that night, I fell in love with him. He let me in. He let me see his soul.

'You are being real right now. And I love this guy.' I felt my cheeks ignite from my choice of words.

And then something so unexpected and almost magical happened. He kissed me. Right on my mouth. It was a short kiss but it was oh so sweet.

That night alone in my room, I realised the girl in me had left. I was no longer the excited giggly fan, heady from being spun into the world of my idol. The excitement was still there, but it was different. I just *knew* these had to be the butterflies you get when someone really special kisses you, and shares a moment with you that has some guts, some meaning.

The next night at his gig, when he sang *Could It Be Forever*, he looked straight over at me in the wings and sang me the line, *'Well I touched you once and I kissed you once and now I feel like you're mine,'* whilst grinning like a Cheshire cat.

I smiled at him and my heart beat so fast with a feeling that I was on the brink of a love affair. A love affair with the most beautiful guy in the world. He had *feelings* for me. This was *really happening*.

Chapter 7

The final show for the American part of the tour was over, and that evening a private function sizzled for the crew and entourage at our plush New York hotel, The Plaza. I walked in with Henry who placed himself in a kind of father figure role towards me, although he was as lively and wild as his long hair. When he had something to say, his words shot from him with great enthusiasm, but he also had many pensive moments of prolonged silences.

The swish room we entered purred with celebrities, separated by the swirls of waiters carrying trays of drinks through for everyone. Henry gave me a run down on everyone that had rocked up, although I knew of most of them. The line-up so far included Arnold Schwarzenegger, Alice Cooper, Micky Dolenz, Farrah Fawcett and Richard Pryor. About a hundred guests had already arrived. What I'd thought would be a more private function for those of us on the tour, turned out to be quite a show. David seemed to take forever getting there but when he did, he made his entrance in skin-tight jeans and a gorgeous leather jacket.

After some time, I started to feel a little out of place, as David appeared to be talking to everyone else except me. Henry was nice company but he wasn't David.

David eventually drew to my side, gave me a quick kiss on the lips, a look solely between us and put his arm around me. 'I hope you're not too bored amongst this circus.' Without waiting for a reply he added, 'I had no idea so many invitations went out for this. Part of the game, huh?'

'I thought you liked to party?'

'Yeah,' he almost sighed, 'I sure have partied on this journey through "teen idoldom", and some of it's been wild. But you know, it can be a drag, and I'm tired.' He did look tired. And it was then I noticed that he held a glass of soda. With his arm around me, he led me from one person to another, introducing me politely but rapping away with people about things I really didn't feel included in.

After mentally tracing numerous figures in the carpet pattern, I grabbed his attention and told him I'd head off to my suite. We had a long flight to England in the morning and I didn't want to be too jet-lagged.

'Oh.' He seemed a little disappointed but a few seconds later said, 'I'll walk you to your room.'

He excused himself and left the function with me, appearing to relax a little when we stepped out.

'I really am sick of all this.' He stopped. 'I mean, I dig the party scene but maybe when it's not such a heavy trip – when there aren't so many other pressures around.'

'What's bugging you?' I asked gently. 'Is there anything I can do to help?'

He stopped walking and turned to look at me. 'You really are lovely, you know?' he said softly, smiling affectionately at me. That moment made all the waiting for him worthwhile. 'You just being here is good for me – you don't need to do anything – just be you.' His radiance diminished as his eyes found a point of focus in the air. 'You know, I think I'm gonna quit.'

'What do you mean, "quit"?'

'This whole thing… this "machine". The whole teen idol trip. I think this tour is gonna be it. I just can't do it anymore.'

'Really? What about all those wild crowds of girls that are crazy about you?'

He laughed. 'I'm sure they'll find someone else to direct their affections… and hormones, onto. Besides, I don't want anyone getting hurt. Some of them are just so full on aggressive… *and* when they're chasing me. I have nightmares of them catching me and ripping out all my hair. And in the stadiums… so many of them are just about crushed against the stage. You can see how I keep having to stop the show and telling them to move back or I'll walk off. But they just don't listen. It's impossible to control crowds of twenty, thirty, forty thousand screaming girls. I'm really worried that someone may be seriously injured. I just feel responsible – it's like this constant heavy trip, you know?'

We continued walking slowly and he looked upward, sighing again as we entered the lift. 'And I would just like some of my freedom back. I am so sick of this sneaking around, being carted into venues like some piece of cargo in the back of a van.' He kept throwing his thoughts to me until we reached the door to my suite. 'You get where I'm comin' from, don't ya?'

I had listened to him pour his heart out and I understood, as every day I witnessed how much he went through. 'I do understand… I can see what horrible pressure you're under. You sure do need a rest, in my opinion.'

'Thank you, Dr Magnusson.' He kept looking at me intensely for a yummy amount of time. His eyes held a certain sparkle I hadn't seen before. Eventually he bowed his head and said, 'I'd better let you go to bed. I think I'll turn in soon myself.

I'm not gonna be down there for much longer.' He leaned in a little closer and I held my breath. 'Goodnight, Beautiful.'

And I got my goodnight kiss. I floated into my room.

The morning forced us into a manic rush to JFK Airport. It appeared a few crew members had partied a little too hard the previous evening, into the wee hours. I made it onto the plane even before David and took a seat by the window. In a few minutes he followed me on and sat next to me.

'Hi, babe.'

How can a simple greeting like that from him give me butterflies in my stomach? He hadn't called me "babe" before.

He leant over and gave me a kiss. 'I'm getting addicted to these.' He smiled right at me. I tried so hard not to swoon. I simply smiled back. 'Hey listen, once we're in the sky, we're gonna have a sesh on the run down for London. Sit in too.'

He was asking me to sit in on their discussion. *Far out – really?* Naturally I'd always end up hearing what the drill would be, but usually after the fact. He continued, 'Apparently, they've heard all the trouble I cause… or that my fans cause, so we're barred from staying in any hotels in London.'

'What?' I couldn't believe it.

'Yeah. Bummer, huh? They've got us on some kind of boat on the Thames.' He didn't seem thrilled.

'You're kidding me?' And I burst out laughing.

'What's so funny?'

'I can see the headlines now – teen girls jump into the Thames in attempt to reach Cassidy's boat.' It became more comical as I thought about it.

He got into it too. 'Yeah – fans hire hovercraft to reach idol's vessel.'

We both giggled together like schoolkids. Ruth heard us

and practically told us off. 'Yes, it would be funny if it wasn't so serious.'

'Ah come on Ruthie, let us have a laugh for once,' coaxed David.

I thought she should have appreciated that David was able to relax a little and not take everything so seriously.

'We've got a lot to sort out so that you, and everyone else including your fans, stay safe,' a stern Miss Aarons directed, 'but we'll discuss all that a little later.' And she walked off to take a seat. I swore I could hear her heels, even on the carpet.

'Yeah thanks… "Auntie" Ruth,' David muttered under his breath.

'What's up with her? She was a tad hard on you… or us.'

'I guess she's just doing her job… a little too well sometimes.'

The plane had taxied on the tarmac and was about to take off. 'Here comes your favourite bit,' he grinned. We gathered speed and more speed and the instant before we left American ground David said, 'Hey, come here.' He leaned over and kissed me for the duration of take-off.

That completely blew my mind. For a moment it was just him and me soaring off from the world *without* a plane.

In our little "sesh" to discuss the drill for London, one of the concerns was the constant problem of how to sneak David into wherever he needed to be. The crowds of frenzied girls always somehow grew bigger and wilder. Everyone brainstormed all kinds of silly suggestions but nothing seemed practical.

'Hey, what about dressing him up as a woman?' I chimed in.

I thought David might be appalled but he said, 'Hey you know – that could really work.'

The more we discussed it, the better it sounded. In the end

I was given the task of making up David's face. It sure suited me to take on this job; I immediately felt more a part of it all. Ruth said she'd make a few calls to purchase a realistic looking wig. They wondered why no one had thought of it before.

Chapter 8

Nothing I know beats this feeling
Of not knowing where you're going
And what you're gonna find

We had roughly two and a half months in the UK and although the end of it was tragic, the rest turned out to be unreal. No longer was I banished from being with him on particular nights, there didn't appear to be any girls snuck into the places where we stayed and no strange actresses popped-up behind stage or in the green room. I have no doubt that if David had really wanted groupies on the boat on the Thames, he would have been able to arrange it. But it seemed he didn't.

He had developed a habit of asking me, "So can I see you tonight?" As if I had somewhere else to go.

I gained more credibility with the group too for some reason. I am sure it wasn't only because I often transformed David into an exceptionally stunning female to sneak him into his shows, and the handful of hotels that allowed us entry.

Maybe a certain barrier had dropped with everyone. It definitely seemed to have between David and me. He stayed clean from drugs and even had a little *joie de vivre*, although a lot of the time he was still a bit uptight and tired. And I finally learnt to "bite" back the French Champagne that used to "bite" me.

David valued my opinion on a surprising number of issues. He even asked me what I would like to hear him sing, once he left this crazy world behind and focused in a different direction. I told him I loved hearing his voice on jazzy, bluesy numbers. I felt a bit like I had the world at my feet, along with the most gorgeous and sought after rock idol.

We did quite a few shows in London, in between travelling to other parts of the UK, and each time we made our way back to our little boat on the Thames. I called it a "little boat" but it was actually a pretty luxurious yacht. I heard a rumour it belonged to Liz Taylor. My mindset had changed so much I wouldn't have been surprised if even *she* turned up one night.

Many a night our inner circle of the entourage partied there, including of course Sam, and Henry, who played a mean harmonica. Together, we got it on – singing, jamming and just plain being silly.

Streams of David's fans lined the banks constantly, trying to catch a glimpse of him. And a few extra-exuberant ones actually attempted taking small boats out to us, or even jumped into that disgusting, murky, freezing water. The fans became much more frenzied since David had officially announced his retirement to the press. Luckily the security around our boat was top notch.

David partied along quite happily at that time. I guess it must have been a good stress release for him. He drank a little but never overdid it. And as much as he carried on in a juvenile manner with the guys, he was never far from me, and touched or kissed me often to let me know that I mattered. I enjoyed that very much.

Sometimes we'd be the last to leave the party to go to our

own separate cabins. On these nights he'd tell me his concerns and what had stressed him out most recently. He talked about his performances and what he thought he could have done better, and asked me what I thought. He still worried a great deal about the fans hurting themselves at his shows and wished he were able to control the crowds more.

I listened attentively and ached at times to soothe him, hoping my words of encouragement offered a little support. He told me it meant a lot him that I understood and he could rap with me about anything.

On one of these deep and meaningful chat nights, he walked me to my cabin as usual but said, 'Hang on, I meant to show you something... I'll be right back, there's something I want you to look at.'

I entered my cabin and hardly had time to go to the loo when I heard the door. He'd returned with some papers in his hand and an apprehensive smile. I asked him to come in and sit on the sofa.

'Have a look. Tell me what you think.'

In my hands were about five or six songs, mostly in minor keys – jazzy, bluesy numbers. 'They're songs,' I stated the obvious.

'Yep. I wrote them for you.'

Now I wasn't sure whether he meant he wrote them for me in the sense that I had said I like this style of music for his voice, or because they were love songs. I couldn't bring myself to believe the latter as some of the lyrics were so moving, so loving. One of them was entitled, *Beautiful Girl*.

'What d'ya think?'

'Well, they look beautiful. I'd really like to hear them.'

'Mmh... yeah, well all in good time. I'll sing them for you, just not tonight. They're gonna be part of the album I'll be working on when this circus is over.'

'I still can't believe you really are quitting touring.'

'Yes ma'am. I surely am. Just two more gigs to go... White City tomorrow, then Manchester and *then* baby... we are *outta* here.' His voice exuded relief in just saying that.

'Wow. The end of an era.' I thought for a moment and said, 'I feel so privileged to have shared this with you.'

'Oh baby, I'm the privileged one.' And after barely a heartbeat, 'Come here, Beautiful.' He gave me the most exhilarating, long kiss. He even tasted handsome.

I felt like spiralling off into the atmosphere, but I nuzzled closer to him. This made him nuzzle even closer to me. He kissed me again and at first I returned his kissing affectionately, but passion built within me. I wanted more and more, and I wanted to be just as close as possible to him. I didn't want this kissing to stop. My wish appeared granted by some means, as he kept kissing me and kissing me until I had feelings rise up in me I'd never known before. I think for the first time in my life I experienced what it truly felt like to be turned on.

His arms surrounded me and he caressed my back. I tried caressing him in the most pleasing way I knew how. I was so hot for him and every inch of my body pulsed with electricity. This was pure ecstasy.

My body absolutely begged for more. My nipples cried out for his touch, begging his masculine hands to touch them, to fondle them. That hand of his that stroked his guitar; I willed it to strum parts of me now. I heard myself letting out spontaneous little moans. God that kissing just owned me. His tongue seemed to explore every corner of my mouth and I loved when he thrust it against mine. I started to imagine what it would feel like on other parts of my body. I thought I was going to explode.

'Mmmh, baby,' he murmured softly, 'I don't wanna leave you but I gotta.'

What? What's he saying? Nooooooo.

He continued kissing me in between telling me he needed to go, that we needed to leave it there for now. I followed him to the door. He gave me one last smouldering kiss, smiled warmly and whispered, 'Goodnight Beautiful, sweet dreams,' and left.

It suddenly felt so cold to be alone, to be without his arms around me. *What on earth just happened?* A wave of energy seized me, giving me the sense I could do anything, tackle anything in the world. Wow, wow, *wow*. Never in my life had I known such exhilaration. My lips still throbbed from all the kissing. I fell onto my bed. Yes, I certainly was going to have "sweet dreams".

When I woke in the morning, I saw a brand new me. Something had awakened in me the night before; I had turned into a bona fide woman. I twirled out onto the weather-enclosed deck for breakfast where Henry already sat tucking into a glorious salmon omelette chef had created.

He greeted me as if he noticed my glow. 'Hey, you look great.'

'Why thank you, sir – I *feel* great.'

At that point, David appeared. He came striding in with his hands on his chest saying, 'Mmh, mmh, mmh... great, great, great.'

He sat next to me and gave me a kiss that electrified my body again. We ate breakfast together and his smile just about jumped off his face. It must have been mirroring mine.

'You two been hitting some new happy drug?' Sam strolled in, yawning.

'Yeah,' said David, 'it's called LSD – Lisa Sensation Drug.'

I giggled like a schoolgirl. He kissed me. We had our mouths full of breakfast but it didn't matter. We kept kissing. Neither of us could stop giggling.

Sam and Henry glanced at each other and chuckled. 'You two,' Sam razzed.

David tried to be serious for a moment between giggles and kisses. His face bubbled with smiles. 'Now here's the thing guys… when we get to White City, I'm gonna have to go straight to the sound check. Then I'll probably have to change there, and stay there… til show-time.' He scoffed down the last of his breakfast and focussed on me. 'And I will see *you…*' gave me a kiss, 'later in the green room.'

With that he left the table and ran back down the stairs, calling back, 'Ya better get your skates on, we gotta *split.*'

It was sad to leave our boat on the Thames. Well, I was sad. I turned around and gave it one last loving look.

Chapter 9

You got on this train when you were born
And the wheels just-a-keep on spinning

The crowd at White City was enormous. They always screamed wildly but this lot seemed to have an extra urgency about them. I somehow felt uneasy about it all but told myself I was only imagining things.

I kissed David for luck as usual each time he ran past me. Sadly, the same scenario continued here – the mass pushed forward and girls kept being dragged out from the front, right by the stage. The show had to be stopped several times. It all appeared completely out of control. Girls fainted all over the stadium and some were trampled on as the crowd pushed and pushed further forward. I had never seen so many being taken out on stretchers. One after the other they carted them out in what looked almost like a production line. David pleaded with them not to push forward and at other times sternly told them off. He again threatened to walk out if they didn't stop.

He did leave the stage at one point and came to me in the wings, sitting down firmly on a stool next to where I stood. His face contorted with stress. An assistant appeared with a towel to wipe his sweat. 'Give me *that*.' David snatched the towel.

I gently took it from him and proceeded to wipe his

forehead and around his face and neck. He didn't speak but I grasped the extent of his stress from his rock-hard shoulders and the agony in his eyes.

'You're doing all you can,' I said stroking his cheek. 'You alone can't control them.'

He dived at me, grabbing me in a hug and pressing his head into my chest. It wasn't a sexual trip, it was more like a child looking for comfort. He gazed up at me as if searching my face for answers. I ran my fingers through his hair lovingly.

'Mr Cassidy?' someone called.

'Just give me a fucking minute, will you?'

I took his face tenderly in both my hands and said, 'You can do this, I know you can. It will be okay. Everyone is onto this. There are still people out there who deserve a show.'

He nodded acknowledgement but didn't say anything or smile. He kissed me softly, transposed himself swiftly into his stage persona and ran out in his glitzy black skin-tight number with the sparkly swirls. The show went on.

Towards the end, security became concerned about David's exit. They were really going nuts out there, and still more and more girls were carted off. I wanted to go with him in his car.

'Don't worry, Beautiful. I'll be fine. See you in a bit.'

But I was out-of-my-skin worried. I watched him being raced off by security. I hoped with all my heart they'd make it through.

Later the security team raved on about how it had been the worst exit they'd ever facilitated. The car almost didn't make it. David looked ragged from exhaustion. I ran to him. I hesitated. I wanted to hold him but I wasn't sure how he would respond. He again looked deeply into my face, like a lost boy searching for answers. We both reached out for each other at the same time.

'Please go and rest,' I said. 'Go to bed. You really need some sleep. Everything will be lighter in the morning.'

We learnt the next day that one girl who'd been taken to hospital had been seriously hurt, but we weren't given specific details of her injuries. David sent her an enormous arrangement of flowers with a heartfelt "get well soon" message. He fidgeted and paced incessantly. 'Thank goodness this will all be over soon.'

His last concert in Manchester was still three days away. I could see he held this up as his light at the end of the tunnel. However the last days of the tour had an unrelenting schedule of interviews. The press hungered for any last snippets they could draw from him. David honoured his obligations and appeared in total control with each interrogation, but afterwards looked as if he'd been knocked out in a fighting ring. Luckily, each day as Manchester grew nearer, he seemed to lighten a little.

The night before his final show, we sat having dinner in the hotel and he chatted in a more relaxed manner. Unexpectedly, he reached for my hand across the table and his eyes immersed into mine. 'I can't believe there's only one more to go. I can't tell you how good that feels.'

Warmth tingled in me as I recognised a speck of happiness had returned to him.

'It'll be a whole new beginning.' An almost adoring glimmer flickered across his eyes. The butterflies in my stomach began doing pirouettes.

Far fewer fans turned up for the Manchester concert than the forty thousand anticipated; less than half. Parents concerned for their daughters' safety had returned their tickets demanding their money back. Stories in the British papers of hundreds being crushed and carted away on stretchers at his UK concerts had the country's older generation in an uproar.

Apart from the financial loss, I was quietly glad this crowd was much smaller. I hoped therefore they'd be easier to handle. The barrier to the stage had been placed well back so David remained out of their grasp. Everyone hoped this might deter them from pushing forward. It appeared to work for the most part, or perhaps it had more to do with the extra security or the knowledge of what had happened at White City. The crowd may have been smaller but they were far from docile.

This being David's final concert before retiring from touring gave the fans extra enthusiasm. They definitely didn't *sound* like a smaller crowd; in fact they may well have been the loudest yet. They sure wanted to give David their all. The concert pretty much went off without a hitch. And perhaps it was the vibe of the audience, or David's head space, but an exceptional amount of positive energy and adoration poured out to him from the stadium.

After his last number David ran out onto the field where his car waited for him, but to the crowd's elation, he turned and ran back on stage. He said, 'I love you, it's been incredible. You're not going to see me for a while, but someday I'll be back. I just want you to know how much it's meant to me.'

Oddly, this reminded me of a scene from my favourite movie, *The Sound Of Music*, where Captain Von Trapp sings a final song to his beloved Austria not knowing when, or if, he will ever return. My "captain" sang a haunting rendition of *It's All Over Now, Baby Blue* as an encore — his final song on his final concert to his beloved fans, before running off stage one last time to shrieks of adulation and frenzy. He told me later that this time as he ran across the field, with each step he felt lighter. He had been thinking to himself, *I never have to do this again,* and he felt he could finally run away from all the craziness, into a life he wanted. He thought he was free at last.

That night our inner sanctum partied well. It was just us. Nothing like the huge "who's who" back in New York. I hadn't seen David so happy in a long time. When he first saw me he lifted me up and spun me around. 'I'm free, baby!' he shouted with pure joy on his face. He laughed and hugged me. He was a different person.

We had a full on muck-up session with the guys that night in his suite and all of us felt David's exhilaration. The cats from the band jammed away and we danced and sang. David and I even sang a few pop tunes together and he looked at me mischievously. 'Hey, we sound pretty neat together. We should cut a few tracks.'

I think the Champagne had affected him a little too much.

Eventually the rest split and just he and I greeted the wee hours. David talked excitedly about his new life, his plans for a new beginning. In a sudden heartbeat, the playfulness of the evening changed when his lips met mine. We fell onto the couch kissing with full force, caressing each other.

My body lit up from his touch once again. Every inch of me yearned for more and more from him. I had never thought being with someone like this could make me so high. He had magic lips – and magic hands. I could tell he enjoyed it a lot too. When I didn't feel it against me, I clearly saw the erection he had developed in his jeans. His touching and kissing of me had more of an urgent energy. I thought at any moment we may shoot into the universe together without ever touching the ground again.

I wanted him. I wanted him to do everything he possibly could to me. My arm reached around his neck, the other around his back and I pulled him closer. He leaned over me more and more until he lay fully on top of me. I could feel so much of him and my whole body grew hotter and hotter. My breathing increased to the force of running a marathon.

'Oh god, baby,' he moaned and pulled away.

Damn – what? It was like an icy wind from somewhere had suddenly slapped me. And I felt rejected. *What's wrong with me?*

He seemed to sense my hurt and pulled me up to sit next to him and held me lovingly, kissing my forehead. 'Oh beautiful girl... please don't think I don't want you... god, do I want you.'

I felt half pleased, half perplexed. But couldn't fully believe he really did want me.

He continued, 'But not like this. My connection with you is not about the sleazy hotel trip I've been living. You mean a lot more to me than that.' He put his hand to my face and stroked it. 'I want it to be special between us.'

'It *is* special, to me. I haven't felt like this before.'

'Baby, I don't wanna... I'm not gonna... take advantage of that. I can't do that.'

I wanted to tell him he wouldn't be taking advantage of me if I wanted him so much. But instead I said nothing as I didn't want him to think I was anything like the hundreds of girls that ended up in his suite and in his bed.

'You're gonna come back to America with me, huh?' He grabbed both my hands and looked directly at me, smiling warmly. 'I know a beautiful canyon, I'd love to take you up there – have a break, you know? It's just so beautiful there, nothing but glorious nature. I'd really love to share that with you.' He thought for a moment. 'We could take a tent – go camping!' His face became animated.

'Just you, me and twenty of your closest body guards?'

'Aha! I knew you could see it too.' We both started laughing.

'Oh I don't know,' I sighed, 'I've been away from home for so long. And school – I can't continue to be away from college. My father will send Interpol to search for me soon.'

'Just stay a month or two longer…? I'll get you a nice place where I won't annoy you all the time… although I'd like to.' He kissed me playfully on the lips.

'You are so persuasive…'

'*Great.* It's settled. I'll sort out the details tomorrow.' He beamed.

What on earth am I getting myself into? And what on earth am I going to tell my parents? Also, in a few months it would be my seventeenth birthday. My parents would definitely be expecting me home for that.

The next morning he bounced straight into arranging a nice little apartment for me to stay in, not far from him. In between his vigorous phone calls and planning, a call came through informing us the girl who'd been carted to hospital in a serious condition from the White City concert had passed away. Apparently she had been in a coma when taken by the ambulance people. This information hadn't been passed onto any of us before. She'd become caught up in the crush and as she'd had a pre-existing heart condition, she had a heart attack. She died four days later in the hospital.

It was as if a huge pillar had fallen down and smashed in the midst of us and after the boom faded, a disturbing silence emanated. We sat in a vague circle staring at the floor in the centre. No one spoke.

I watched David's face. It tore my heart to see his beautiful eyes squinting, as if struggling to push away the pain. I had become a little scared of being too forward with him. Too much was at stake. I wanted so much to try and comfort him somehow.

The feeling overtook me – I rushed to him and pulled him to me. His head rested on my chest once again and I sensed his urgency of holding onto me.

No one spoke for some time. Ruth was the first. 'The press will be screaming for interviews.'

I glared at her in horror. I didn't want to see David having to endure that, but on some level I knew he probably had to.

'We're only going to do one,' she announced. 'That's all they're getting.' I was relieved.

'I need to go to the funeral,' David spoke quietly. His eyes didn't leave the floor; his pain casting a shadow over the room. The silence shattered as he sprang up. 'What the fuck am I saying? I can't go to that poor girl's funeral. It will turn into a fucking media circus if *I'm* there.'

'Just send flowers,' advised Ruth. 'I'll have it arranged.'

'No… Wait… I want to write a personal note to go with them.' Frantically he started searching for something to write on. He didn't let up until he'd found a pen and paper but sat staring at the page. 'What the hell can I possibly say…? What on earth…' He broke down and sobbed.

Somehow a voice in me took charge, 'Can you all give us a minute, please?'

Surprisingly they left us alone. I steadily walked over and wrapped him securely in an embrace. 'Hey… I got ya. You're safe in my arms.' My hold on him tightened.

As if this gave him permission, he sobbed harder. I let him release it all while I held him firmly, stroking and rocking him. Funny what you notice at times like this but I happened to notice his hair had grown longer as I ran my fingers through it. He was probably due for a cut, but I loved it extra-long. At that moment, it seemed like a shield for his tears. It ripped my soul to see this exceptionally stunning man, crying and so hurt.

He pulled away from me. 'I don't want you to see me like this.'

I paused for a moment, hoping to find words to somehow ease his pain. From somewhere I found a speckle of strength. 'What? As a human? You *are* allowed to be human you know. You're amongst friends here. No press that I can see.' My tone softened, 'It's okay baby, it really is. I promise.'

He stared at me from the short distance to where he had moved. His tear-stained face bore an expression I couldn't decipher. 'Man, you are something else,' he said through his breath. He came back to me and kissed me.

I kissed away his tears.

He whispered, 'I love you.'

♪   ♪   ♪

The British tabloids weren't kind. Headlines such as "David Cassidy is a Health Hazard" and "Cassidy's Suicide Concert" dominated the front pages of several leading papers. Requests for interviews came charging in like rounds from machine guns. The pressure to respond stressed him out immensely. He felt somehow responsible and in his head, doing what the press asked of him was a way to try and make up for the tragedy. But Ruth still insisted he only do the one, and I respected her for that.

I found the interview he did for the BBC incredibly heart-wrenching. It clearly showed how deeply the event had affected him. But I was so proud of him too. He held it together and spoke eloquently, standing firm in his professionalism. He said in no uncertain terms neither he nor his security staff could be held responsible; that the young girl had a heart attack.

The tragedy caused us to delay our return flights to America. We left a few days later than we had originally planned; not rushing off out of respect. David noticeably sunk down at this horrible time. I tried to comfort him as best as I knew how. I think he appreciated it but he didn't say much, not to me nor to anyone else. He often just sat, deep in thought. I began to feel really glad I'd agreed to go back to America to be with him for a while, to support him, or at least try.

I phoned my mother back in Australia to explain. She told me she couldn't keep up the façade for much longer and to make sure I was home for my birthday. She also reminded me that I would probably have to repeat a year of school if I still wanted to get into the Elders Music Conservatorium, as I had taken so much time off from my studies. Strangely our conversation didn't seem real. That world back there and the old me, had faded into a distant memory. And everything she told me seemed insignificant compared to my present existence.

Chapter 10

Arriving back in the USA was meant to have been an exciting new beginning. However we landed into somewhat of an anti-climax. The crowds at LA Airport, or "LAX" as David called it, enthusiastically greeted him, screamed at him and chased him as per usual. David stormed through the airport with his sunglasses on, tips of his fingers in his pockets and everyone else carrying his bags. I followed at about a hundred paces behind. No one knew who I was, thankfully. David had been quite protective of me in that regard and made sure the media didn't get a whiff of anything between us.

We were taken to the offices of David's management initially and from there, everyone headed their own way. *What a come-down — no farewell gathering or anything between us to put a punctuation mark on the crazy six months we've just shared.* I rode in a car with David and Sam. David had his arm around me but was distant. It felt full circle from that very first flight on his jet.

I eventually had to say something, hoping for a hint from him as to what we were doing. I succeeded in squeezing out one word, 'Soooo…?'

David frowned at me as if confused over what I was asking, or annoyed that I'd even opened my mouth.

'So what are we doing now?'

'Going home.'

I sighed.

Sam piped in, 'I think she means what the arrangements are.'

'We're going to our place. We can work it out from there.' He sounded irritated to have to be talking, or explaining something so trivial.

I resigned myself to the fact that I just needed to shut up and go with the flow. I suddenly became incredibly homesick. About a half hour out of LA, we drove through high wrought iron gates to David and Sam's Spanish style residence in Encino.

We hung there for the next few weeks, not really doing anything. I felt I didn't belong as David remained distant. Every time I tried to hug or comfort him, he'd push me away or walk away from me. *Why did I agreed to this and what on earth has happened between us? Is any of it still there?* I began to wonder whether what had happened on tour between us had just been for the duration of it, and now I was merely some kind of left-over baggage.

David had also developed insomnia. I guessed this must have been a result of his emotional turmoil. Often in the middle of the night, he'd go into the music room and thrash it out on the drums. He probably didn't think that when he did this, Sam and I also couldn't sleep. As I woke to his manic hammering one night, I looked at the clock. Three am. I groaned and pulled the blankets over my head. It didn't help. I became so agitated I marched down to the music room and swung open the door. Eventually he looked up at me standing in the doorway.

'Oh hi, babe – hey, would you refill my glass?'

I wanted to ask him what happened to his last slave but luckily my final ounce of compassion rose to the surface. I got him his wine and took off back to bed, stuffing my ears with as much cotton wool as I could find in the bathroom cabinet.

On the nights when we did all manage to sleep, I was usually up before the guys having my coffee by the pool. The setting overlooked their small acreage of orange trees. On the adjoining property, sheep grazed lazily on the side of a hill.

Sam wasn't far behind me one morning, dressed like he might go for a dip. 'Hey, *que pasa?* How you doin', girl?' He threw his towel on a chair.

'Do you really want to know?'

'Don't worry, he'll come good. He thinks the world of you.' And with that he dived into the pool.

Great. I hear words of encouragement from Sam but none from David. After I had read the same paragraph in the paper about three times, David emerged from the house, dark shades firmly on and a white towelling robe tied at his diminishing waist.

'Hi,' he exerted and slumped onto a lazy-boy.

I'd probably had about as much moping around as I could handle. I pulled my sunglasses down my nose and viewed him over the rims… until he realised I was staring at him.

'What?' He grimaced.

'Ok, time out.' I stood up. 'I hope you are right into the depth of your feelings and emotions right now and not quashing anything.' My eyes remained fixed on him.

'What are you talking about?' He looked as if he'd swallowed some pepper.

'Well, I just hope that all this moping around is not going to waste. If you quash your feelings, they always come back to haunt you – so I hope you are getting right into them for however long this period is. And by the way, please advise me how long it is likely to be, as I need to go back home and continue with my music studies. I can't afford to wallow my time away here by this pool, irrespective of how lovely the setting is. You can always make a time with me – if you want to – at a later date.' I wasn't speaking in an angry tone but I was firm. I was also pleased I had thought of the word "irrespective".

Sam jumped up from the pool and applauded.

David glared right at me with a face like he couldn't believe how I had just spoken to him. He gave Sam a death stare, shot up and stormed back into the house.

'That was beautiful, baby girl.' Sam walked towards me. 'He *will* come round, you'll see. He just likes playing the Prima Donna every now and then.'

'And don't you call me "baby girl" either.'

We both burst out laughing. It was a good release.

A few minutes later I heard the main door of the house shut. It appeared our "Prima Donna" had gone out without saying a word to either of us.

I nearly resigned myself to watching the midday movie but then thought I just can't do this anymore. I got up to go and ask Sam advice on how to change my return airline ticket to go back home. As I walked across the polished floor of the foyer, I heard the door again. Dressed in jeans and a white cheese-cloth embroidered shirt, a much friendlier looking David strode up to me. He took his hands from behind his back and extended them out to offer me a small bunch of loose, domestic-looking pink roses.

'Where did you get these?' I asked as I gently took them.

'I just snipped them from nearby gardens.' He smirked.

Maybe I still looked stern to him as he added, 'Yeah, well okay – I stole them'. He kept smirking.

I laughed.

He put the tips of his fingers into his front jean pockets and hunched his shoulders, giving me an almost shy look from under his lashes. 'Baby, I'm sorry... I've been a jerk...' He stopped to study my face.

'You have.' I smiled.

We both laughed and he wrapped me in his arms and kissed me lingeringly. I didn't know whether to laugh or cry – I felt as if I had my David back. I teared-up.

He put his lips to my forehead, stroking my head like a child. 'Oh baby...' We stayed nuzzled together for a glorious few moments. 'Baby, let's talk.' He took me by the hand, led me out to the pool area and sat me down at an outdoor setting. Sitting facing me, he grasped my hands. Without a word, he gazed at me for a few moments, smiling warmly.

'My beautiful girl,' he said softly, 'I've been such a jerk.' He bowed his head, his demeanour changing to serious. 'That tragedy of that poor innocent girl dying really got to me.'

I caressed his hands.

He looked up at me. 'But by focusing on all the "what ifs" and things I couldn't do a damn thing about, I was forgetting what was right under my nose.' He glanced down again. 'And what made it worse was I wasn't being very nice to you. And for that I'm ashamed.' His eyes filled with sincerity as they took mine in fully. 'Now I'm not trying to justify my behaviour but I wanted to try and explain it a little... See, if I'm down, I just shut off... from everyone, everything. I don't usually talk... about things.' A little more urgency crept into his voice, 'Now I know that's wrong. It doesn't help. But then, I'm not used to having a beautiful creature by my side who I can confide in.' He smiled a little cheekily.

I felt a surge of love for him at that point. I leaned in towards him. 'I completely understand how difficult it was for you back in England. It was a horrible, dreadful thing to happen. But without doubt you need to know that you were powerless to do anything. It was just a really, really unfortunate, cruel twist of fate. And please know that you can talk to me anytime you want... about anything.'

'I know, Beautiful, I know.' He bowed his head again. 'And I thank you for that – for being there for me.' He thought for a few moments, leaned over to me and said quietly, 'Time for healing.' And kissed me tenderly. He pulled back and gave me his gorgeous smile. 'So... you wanna go camping?'

'You mean that place you were telling me about?'

'Yeah, at Inyo Forest. I know a beautiful spot there.' He leaned in again. 'Just you and me, Mother Nature, the stars–'

'And twenty body guards.'

He laughed. 'Yeah well, I *will* organise that. We don't want anyone with a telephoto lens taking happy snaps.'

'That will end up in the paper.'

'Exactly. So what d'ya say Beautiful, is it a date?'

'When were you thinking?'

'Well... no time like the present, huh? It's not even lunchtime, we could get up there well before dark.'

'You can organise security that quickly?'

He winked. 'I reckon I might have a few contacts.'

Now it was my turn to laugh. 'Okay mister, you've got yourself a date.'

Chapter 11

We both set off to pack and I realised I didn't have any gear suitable for camping with me. I told David my dilemma and he said we could drop by a few stores on the way or I could borrow some "sweaters" and shirts from him. His pants definitely wouldn't fit me, he was so skinny. I was also a bit concerned about the weather. 'Won't it be getting cold there at this time of year?'

'No sweat – I've got some extra-warm sleeping bags to take up.' He mooched up to me. 'Although… I could always try and keep you warm.' He slid his arm around me and gave me a flash of his cheeky pout.

I playfully hit his arm and headed back to my room to gather my essentials, like makeup. A few nerves suddenly crawled over me. I tried discarding them as I tousled my hair.

Pretty soon a four-wheel-drive turned up at the house, along with a gaggle of security guys in separate vehicles. David loaded all our gear in the four-wheel and chose to drive himself. I always thought there was something sexy about a guy behind the wheel. David was sure to be the pinnacle of my theory.

Sam wandered out to wish us happy trails. 'Stay safe, have fun… and look out for bears.'

'Bears?' I gasped in horror. 'There are *bears?*

David gallantly marched over to me and put his arm around me, his other hand on his heart and looked up. 'Don't worry.

I shall protect you,' he announced as if commander and chief.

Sam leant over to me. 'I'd start worrying right about now.'

As we piled into our car, David was cool, calm and collected while I questioned frantically, 'Are there really bears…? You guys are joking, right?'

David merely grinned and didn't say a word. Sam waved us off, also grinning.

I have to say, David handled that big car stunningly. Not that I doubted he would do otherwise, but it made me realise there was so much more to him than being a rock star. We arrived well before sunset at a place he'd described as "just pure magic". It was. The scenery spun me out, being so different to the Aussie landscape. The spot he'd chosen to camp at was breathtaking in Lundy Canyon. A glorious lake stretched out to us surrounded by tall trees I guessed to be pines, and majestic mountains stood in the background like ancient guards.

I jumped out of the car saying, 'Wow,' and took in a deep breath of fresh air.

'Mmmh,' sighed David and stretched out his arms as if taking in the universe. He strolled over to me, beaming at me intently. 'I'm glad you like it.' He drew me into his arms, giving me a delicious kiss.

We both let out a, 'Mmmmh.'

'So, how are you at putting up a tent?' he asked.

'Well… I think I failed Brownies.'

I noticed that already he seemed far more relaxed. His perception of being out amongst beautiful nature perhaps resembled mine. I could be in awe of it, as if a special energy existed out there; something almost sacred.

I helped him put up the tent, following the instructions he gave, in between acting silly. My heart felt much lighter and happier, seeing him like that. I gathered we'd be sleeping in the same tent when I saw he had brought only the one. I suppose I really wouldn't have expected him to actually bring two but just seeing the one all set up, it reality hit me. This began to scare me a little. The headiness of the euphoric night of touching and kissing back on our boat on the Thames seemed eons ago. Now the time for us to make love could actually be very near.

Fuck this was starting to scare me. The pressure of how it would be... *What if it's horrible like my experiences with Judd? What if he doesn't enjoy it with me? What if the expectation is greater than the reality? What if I don't know what to do to pleasure him? Do I really want to go and do this with him?*

'Nothin' like a good fire.'

'Wha...?' I had been so deep in thought I hadn't realised he'd been collecting firewood.

He put the pile down and moseyed over to me. 'Where were you, Beautiful? You were a world away.' Before I could answer, he swept me in his arms again and gave me another tender kiss. He held me, swaying me. 'Oh baby, I love it out here, don't you?'

I tried to enjoy the kiss and cuddle but I was tense.

'Baby? What's wrong with my beautiful girl?'

I had to say something. 'Oh, nothing really.' I smiled a little. 'I guess I've just been taking in all of this nature. Sometimes when I'm in a really beautiful, remote place, I want to sit still with it for a while – almost absorb it. I always feel that special places, like this one, have an energy to them – as if it were something sacred.' I had to draw the words from my earlier thoughts and realised I was babbling.

Thankfully, I don't think he noticed. 'Yes... Absolutely. I totally agree.' He snuggled into me again, swaying some more.

'Oh man, it's so good to be here with you.'

I relaxed into the hug this time and allowed it to feel good.

'Hey! We should collect some more wood before it gets dark.' He took my hand and guided me off to find wood with him like an excited young boy on a scout trip.

We made a few trips back and forth until we had enough for the night. David started arranging it for the campfire. 'Hey babe, would you mind checking in that green bag by the car? There should be some cans in it?'

I found the bag and sifted through it. I only saw cans of spaghetti in tomato sauce. 'We have spaghetti, spaghetti and more spaghetti.'

'Great. Spaghetti it is then.'

'Is that all you brought?'

'No, baby. There's a whole box of stuff in the back of the car. Don't sweat, you won't be living off spaghetti all week.'

All week? We're staying for a whole week? The nerves hit my stomach again.

I think he read the look on my face. 'That *is* ok, isn't it? I mean, to stay a week? Otherwise it hardly seems worth coming out here. A decent time will really let us unwind, you know?'

'Yeah, sure,' I lied. I wasn't sure at all. 'Here, let me help you with that.' I began to construct the campfire alongside him.

'Okay, I'll get some paper.' He headed for the car, came back with a bundle of newspaper and a couple of gas lanterns. 'We're gonna need these at hand before it gets dark, as we won't find a thing then,' he still sounded like an excited kid.

After we had built the perfect campfire, he fossicked in his pockets for a lighter. As the blaze slowly came to life, it crackled and smelt great. 'Hey, back in a minute.' He ran off to the car again.

This time he returned with a jumper, or "sweater" as the Americans say. 'Here, let's get this on you, it's gonna get cold pretty soon, even with the fire.' He placed the jumper over my head and helped me wriggle my arms into the sleeves, dressing me like a child. It was sweet.

The pastel pink jumper had his gorgeous scent on it. I recognised it from photos in magazines so it felt weird to be wearing it, weird but nice.

'I've got plenty of jackets and coats too, so you just let me know if you're cold, okay?' He was so caring, it really softened my tension. He proceeded to make me some toast, and heat up a tin of spaghetti to go on it. I watched him do it all with flair and expertise.

'Yum. Thank you.' I smiled, taking the plate he offered me. 'You certainly are a man of many hidden talents.'

He seemed chuffed. 'Well, I don't like to brag... but I can make coffee too... if you want some?'

'I'm fine for now, but thank you.'

We sat in front of the toasty fire and ate, chatting about mundane things. But all conversations with him were fun. After dinner, he grabbed his guitar, and as I stared into the dancing flames, he played and sang sad songs in minor keys I hadn't heard before. This was heaven. And it was hard to believe this guy next to me was the same teen idol that had just been through the most chaotic, endless tour. Our existence now was so far removed from the manic screaming, the demanding press, the tearing around in a frenzy. Here we were, under a sky sparkling with stars, enjoying each other's company in simple contentment. And I was being serenaded by the same soft-flowing voice all the young girls fainted over, here in our own little corner of the world. *What could be more perfect?*

Nearby, we heard a sudden sound. And then a cough. 'Ahem... Mr Cassidy?'

David stopped playing and looked up unperturbed. 'Yes?'

'Just letting you know all is in order. We have this area securely surrounded and you won't be disturbed.'

'Yeah thanks, goodnight.'

'Goodnight, sir. And... er... miss.'

We both looked at each other and smirked. He put down his guitar. 'Isn't this bliss?' Not waiting for an answer he said, 'I love this. And I love being with you.' He reached over to me and kissed me.

I tensed again. If he felt it, he didn't let on. 'Hey Beautiful, I'm beat. How about we turn in?'

'Sure.' I kept my focus firmly on the earth I had been scratching at with a stick. I realised I had gone over and over the same pattern – a heartbeat.

He headed to the car, returning with a bucket of water and cups. 'And here we have the en suite.'

He poured a little water into a cup and took out his toothbrush. I realised what he meant and began rummaging in my bag for my own. He left me to it and disappeared into the bushes, I guessed for a wee. When he returned, he showed me where he'd packed the toilet paper and suggested I take a lantern with me if I needed to go. He offered to accompany me but I said I'd manage on my own. I never had mastered the skill of weeing in the bush very well. I had to take everything off from my bottom half, or I would always somehow wee on it. So to do this and put it back on took me a little longer.

'Are you okay?'

'Yep. Everything's fine. I'll be back in a tic.'

I was still pulling myself together as I walked back, when I caught sight of him in the flickering light of the fire, kneeling at the entrance to our tent. His eyes met mine as he said, 'I was waiting for you to go in first.'

The tent was a low "two man", a bit larger than the ones I'd seen at home. It was going to be cosy though, that's for sure. He held the tent flap open for me and I poked my head in.

Inside I saw a little lantern shining softly on a double-size sleeping bag with the edge turned down for me to get in. All over the sleeping bag he had scattered pink rose petals that seemed to glow in the lantern light. 'Aw David, that's beautiful.'

He smiled warmly and put his hand on my back. 'Go on sweetie, you go get in. I'll just be a minute making sure the fire is safe overnight.'

I did as he asked, firstly taking off my shoes and socks... and the jumper he had leant me. I folded it neatly and placed it next to the side I thought to sleep on. I left my shirt and jeans on. He came in a tad sheepishly not long after and I watched him take off his top layer also. He crawled in beside me and turned the lantern off.

Placing his arm around me he said softly, 'Goodnight, Beautiful.' He kissed me on my forehead, nuzzled into my hair and let out a sigh and a, 'Mmmmmh.'

We slept together snugly, just like that first night in his hotel room in Adelaide when he'd thrown Judd out of my life.

Chapter 12

The hill we climbed it went on forever
We reached the top of the world together

The next day we prepared for an adventure. At least that's how David described his plan for our day. This involved hiking. Before we left, he picked up a two-way radio and let security know where we were headed. When he received the "all clear" we set off. He carried something resembling a picnic basket and with his other hand he took mine. It was the best feeling in the world to walk with him like that in breathtaking scenery.

After several kilometres, a loud continuous noise emerged in the distance that I couldn't make out. It became louder and louder. We turned a corner and there it was. Before us, water crashed down from a waterfall of immense magnitude. Several streams interwove with each other. I was blown away by its size. And *sound*. We both took out our cameras and David asked me to pose for his pics. He must have taken about twenty shots, each time saying, 'Ah… perfect'.

I began to giggle each time in anticipation for his words… They made me feel a little shy.

We hung out there for a bit and then started out for "somewhere even more special", according to David. I wondered what could be more beautiful than that. As we walked, we passed several beautiful waterfalls which weren't quite as large as the first.

'That's not it,' David said each time, and we continued.

Parts of the terrain turned out to be quite uphill and David being his usual gentlemanly-self, took my hand to help me up the steep bits. Amongst the shrubs we found a pond of deepest dark-blue which transported my mind back to a school geography camp in The Flinders Ranges. When I mentioned this, David wanted to know all about the place.

I relayed our quest of climbing up the steep face of Wilpena Pound and how we'd just about slid down into the midst of it. As we'd reached the middle, we faced an army of trees that stood impossibly close to each other, and absolute symmetry surrounded us. So much so, I wouldn't have had a clue which way to go on my own and I'd held our teachers in the highest regard for once. We'd discovered a pond there, similar to the one we stood by now – an almost faultless circle of the darkest blue I'd ever seen. Simply magical. I also told him about our trek to Sacred Canyon and how I sensed an impacting energy all over The Flinders. It always made me think of the plight of our Aboriginal people and what a remarkable existence they must have had, prior to the invasion and destruction by white people.

David connected fully with everything I told him and made me promise to take him to The Flinders one day.

That took my thoughts to our relationship and what it was. *What is it exactly? Where do I stand?* I truly had no idea. He always acted the charming gentleman towards me, never crossing the line. And yet, we had both been so hot for each other. I'd also probably seen close to the worst in him, and there was a time when he had told me that he loved me. He'd shown me his inner-self as well. He always made sure I was well cared for, seemed to have my best interest at heart and talked of the future as if I would be in it.

Yet I sensed a barrier. *Somehow our relationship, if you can call it that, isn't progressing. Or are we both still at that polite stage where we are minding our Ps and Qs because we're anxious about taking it to a deeper level?* I realised, by thinking all this, I was handing power over to him. If there was one thing I had learnt from him, it was never to give your power to another person. I shouldn't be giving it to him either, although incredibly in this short space of time, something told me I could trust him with it. Still, I felt I needed to take some of it back. *He opened up to me; I should talk to him, really talk to him.*

My train of thought broke as he let go of my hand, climbed over a few rocks and announced, 'And here we are,' looking at me expectantly.

I climbed to where he stood by another smaller waterfall. The sun glistening through his hair made this scene with him in it a photographer's dream. But I didn't see anything in particular about this waterfall to make it stand out from all the others we'd passed. He put the picnic basket down, took my hand and led me closer.

'Look,' he said, placing me in front of him and wrapping his arms around me. There, before us at the base of the fall, lay a rock hollow in the perfect shape of a heart. Remarkably over time, water had trickled into the hollow to create it. David rested his chin on my shoulder and we both gazed at this precious work of art by the hand of nature.

'Unreal. David – it's beautiful.'

He turned me around to face him. 'I always knew I would

find you somewhere in the world and bring you here.' And he kissed me so lovingly. I felt weightless. He stepped back, held both my hands and gave me a look I will never forget. His heart and soul were in that look.

He smiled. 'Come on, let's have that picnic.'

From the top of the basket he'd been carrying, he grabbed a blanket and laid it out. As he opened the basket fully, I saw it was a "cooler" type and he seemed to have a whole gourmet lunch in there; ham, grapes, patés, breads, cheeses and much more. And, a bottle of Dom with two crystal glasses.

'Gosh, that must have been heavy.'

'Eh, I can handle it.' He posed like a bodybuilder flexing his muscles.

I laughed. He was so adorable. And I loved how he wooed me. We grazed on all that scrumptious food and sipped the Champagne. It was the best of both worlds; a kind of hippie thing mixed with opulence. 'I think I have a foot in both camps.'

He chuckled. 'That's probably true for me too… I do believe the French call it, *Socialiste de Champagne.*'

His expression changed and he eyed me carefully. 'I said something to you in our last days in England.'

I knew exactly what he was referring to.

He sidled closer to me, took my hand and spoke to me in words of soft flowing caramel, 'I told you that I love you… and I want you to know, I don't say that lightly.'

Goosebumps overtook my body and my eyes welled up with joy as I listened to his words.

Before I could say anything he continued, 'I kind of always had this fantasy, this dream, that somewhere amongst all those girls out there following me – there would be "the one". When I saw your face… well, all of you really… on the news footage, outside my hotel, I just knew I had to meet you. So I sent Sam down… and well… you know what happened. And when I met you, I could see you were different. You weren't one of the crazies that wanted to rip my hair out…' He laughed. 'At least I didn't think so… I could see you had substance, charm, sweetness… you were in a class of your own… and you were hot too.' A cheeky smirk appeared on his lips. 'I couldn't stop thinking about you after you'd left. I knew I had to ask you to come with me… and I was so nervous in the build up to that… I didn't know whether you would. And then, after I left Australia I was just so bloody busy that I hardly had time to even write. I jumped at the first opportunity to get back to you.'

'Oh babe… I would have followed you anywhere. But that is what I *thought* I would do back then, I didn't really know you. Now that I've come to know you, I know I would.'

The way he gazed at me continued to melt my insides. He continued, 'And that's the thing… I grew to know you too. You didn't want anything or ask for anything from me like most people do. You just gave and gave and gave. You got me through some hell back there. And then I fell in love with you even more. I think really that I fell in love with you when I first saw you but when I got to know you… oh man, did I fall deep.'

I felt my face flushing, my heart overflowing with emotion. 'I love you too darling, David.' I immediately thought my words had come out a bit corny. But I reached out for him as he reached for me, and we kissed… and kissed… and kissed.

'Baby,' he whispered softly, 'will you let me make love to you?'

'Uh-uh,' I managed.

His mouth kept devouring mine. He caressed me with his slender fingers; his touch felt an extension of the words he'd spoken. His lips continued working their magic. 'I could so easily make love to you right here and now, but my paranoia from all the touring won't let me, here where we're so exposed. I hope you understand. Let's save it for tonight?'

I was relieved as I would not have felt comfortable being "exposed" to him either, out in bright sunlight. 'Tonight,' I whispered back.

We stayed by our heart rock with no concept of time, touching and kissing. I had a sense we'd melded into one even without making love. As we left and I walked with him, holding his hand, I finally knew where I stood – right next to him.

That night by the campfire, he played his guitar again and this time he sang the songs he had written for me. I simply didn't know what to feel. I guess I felt incredibly honoured. No one had ever written songs for me before, let alone someone like *him*. They were hauntingly beautiful, with such loving lyrics. If he was determined to make this night special, he was right on the mark.

Entering the tent that night, I found more beautiful rose petals on our nest. He was such a master at romance. As he came in, he held two coupes of Champagne – perfectly chilled. 'I thought we could use a night cap.' His lips gave a tentative smile.

Perhaps he was as nervous as I was. I dismissed that thought as I didn't think it possible. We drank the Champagne in the sleeping bag, not saying much but gazing at each other and him playing with my hair. After our last mouthfuls, he took the glasses and placed them a careful distance away. He turned off the gas lantern. The door of the tent remained open with only the net fastened, allowing a view of the last flames of our campfire.

He placed his hand on my face, cupping half of it. 'I love you, my beautiful girl. Let me show you how much.'

I considered that the very first time for me. I had never made *love* before. He was loving, he was passionate, he was hot, he was commanding, he was gentle. He was so, sooo incredible.

I can't lie and say it went smoothly either. It didn't. It's really quite awkward to even describe but I suppose because I hadn't had much experience, I was quite… erm… tight. And he was just so… well there is no other word to describe it but "huge". So we didn't quite exactly fit initially. But he remained loving and patient. And he did things to me that gave me so much pleasure that I guess I just opened up to him.

We still had to go slowly as at times it hurt. He'd ask if he was hurting me and stop, touch me and turn me on more, and go on. Eventually there was no more pain, only pleasure. Such a wave of ecstasy built up inside me I simply couldn't make sense of it or what was happening to me. He gave me my first orgasm. He wanted to make sure it was good for me. I simply didn't believe anything that pleasurable was possible. To call it "pleasurable" was a severe understatement.

The experience moved me so much that I wept.

He held me and rocked me. 'I got ya baby, I got ya,' he whispered and kept telling me he loved me.

Love? I felt at that point like I worshipped him. He totally owned me.

When I woke up it took me a few moments to realise where I was. Tingles of warmth wrapped me in cosiness and the previous evening danced back into my mind. I must have slept incredibly soundly. I stretched like a contented cat – and would have been purring if I actually was one.

But an empty space lay next to me. The sound of his guitar

being softly strummed drifted to me and I smelt the enchanting scent of smoky pine. I reached around for anything resembling clothing. I had success in finding my knickers at the bottom of the sleeping bag and also found a shirt which I couldn't quite make out but thought was his.

I peeped out from the tent. There was the man who had made sensational love to me the night before, shirtless, caressing his guitar to make it croon with pleasure. Sunshine played in his hair and his face twisted in deep concentration.

As I unzipped the tent he saw me, put down his guitar and walked over. 'Good morning, Beautiful.' He took me in a strong embrace and kissed me passionately. 'Can I get you anything...? The moon...? The sun?' His skin smelt divine, just like it had the night before.

I started giggling. 'I love that you're so romantic.'

'You bring it out in me, baby.' He kissed me again and ran his fingers through my hair.

'Gorgeous David,' I said. He beamed. 'I know you do that all the time,' I gestured towards the tent indicating our previous night's activities, 'but this was so incredible for me, it was... just... just amazing. It meant so much–'

'Baby!' He took my face in both his hands. 'I don't do *that* all the time at all. This was a big deal for me too – a very big deal. Anyone can have sex on a rock tour. What we did last night was a part of my heart and soul, not just my body. Please know how much you mean to me.'

'Oh, David...' I began crying again.

'Baby...' He held me tightly. 'You are so, so beautiful.' He rubbed my back. He kissed me and kissed me more. Then, he lifted me up and carried me back to the tent.

How strange that I had thought a week at Lundy Canyon

would be too long. The days disappeared into a haze of perpetual bliss. We hiked, we sang, we made love, we visited our heart rock, we had in-depth philosophical discussions til the wee hours; we were so real with each other. I discovered that true intimacy involved revealing your soul, not your body.

Before we knew it, we were having breakfast by the campfire for the last time. We couldn't stay any longer even if we'd wanted to as David had made arrangements for business meetings in LA to discuss his next album. We had to go.

Chapter 13

All too soon the large gates of his Encino house opened for us and we drove in. A trickle of fans waited there as per usual. 'Well, back to reality,' he sighed. As I attempted to open the car door he grabbed me and kissed me. 'Thank you, Beautiful. That was the best camping trip ever.'

I smiled from my heart at him.

We heard a bang on the side of the car. 'Okay you two... jig's up.' Sam poked his head in the window.

David ignored his clowning and directed him to grab some gear from the back.

As we entered the house I noticed an impressive arrangement of deep red roses dominating the foyer on the centre table. I thought to myself, *Some slut's sent him roses.* But I said matter-of-factly, 'Someone's sent you roses,' hoping I sounded unconcerned.

'Oh really?' He seemed not to care. Maybe this kind of thing happened all the time so he'd become blasé to it. 'Would you mind having a look at the card, baby? See who they're from?'

I wasn't sure I'd enjoy this but I did as he asked. Taking the card from the envelope, I read it to myself, "To my beautiful girl, my love deepens for you every day. All my love, David". My god. I was speechless. He had always given me pink roses – these were the deepest red.

I ran to him and jumped at him, squealing with delight,

'Thank you, my gorgeous man!'

He picked me up and spun me around. 'You are very welcome, Beautiful.' Our mouths came together tenderly.

'I hope you two come up for air occasionally,' stirred Sam as he brought in a few of the bags. 'Where do you want these?' he asked me in relation to my gear.

'In my room,' said David without taking his eyes from me, and kissing me again.

And from that moment on, I took up residence in his bedroom. The arrangement of roses in the foyer felt like a monument of his love for me and now I was staying in his bedroom. Oh god, the girls back home would never believe this.

That night snuggled up in bed, he told me he had business to take care of in LA the next day for his new album – the one with my songs on it. He said he wanted me there later on in the process for the recording, but his business meetings may be a little boring for me. 'They're even boring for *me*,' he chuckled.

However he had an idea. 'How about I arrange for one of Ruth's girls to take you out shopping? You could go down to Rodeo Drive and buy some clothes if you want, or get your hair done... not that there's anything wrong with it now... but just do some girls' stuff, if you want? I'll give you authorisation on my card. Knock yourself out.' He smiled and stroked my back.

'David, I can't take your credit card.'

'Baby, I was stone cold broke a few years ago. Now I've got bread. What's the point of having money if I can't share it with the most gorgeous person in my life?'

'No David... I just couldn't spend like that.'

'Sure you can. I'll make sure that whoever goes with you is given strict instructions to go wild. Go have a nice lunch somewhere... all of Ruth's staff are great... have lots of Champagne... and then go shopping. I insist.'

'Only if I can pay you back.'

'Come here and shut up.' He kissed me. And he kissed me and caressed me... and we flew to heaven again.

Ruth assigned a younger staff member, Jan, to be my shopping and lunch companion. She had a wicked look, possibly even a glint of naughtiness in her eye. David put his arm around her and began telling her he insisted I spend up. He caught me listening so he led her away for the rest of his "brief".

They came back giggling and she stated, 'Done deal!' She linked arms with me. 'Let's go have some fun.'

David waved us off grinning, as we left through the doors.

Jan was an absolute pleasure to be around. In her vibrant manner she told me all sorts of interesting quirks about David. I felt like taking notes.

David had arranged a car for us, of course. The driver greeted us professionally and opened our doors. Our first stop was the famous Polo Lounge at the Beverly Hills Hotel for lunch. The food was delicious and we probably drank a little too much Champagne, in between giggling and playing "spot the celebrity". Jan was a cinch to talk to and very down to earth, which I really appreciated.

She suggested for me to have "the works" in beauty treatments. 'You know – get your hair done, nails, makeup – *everything.*'

I asked whether David had put her up to this.

'Well not directly – I mean he certainly didn't say anything about wanting to change your appearance but I just thought it may be fun.'

I'm not sure whether it was the influence of the Champagne, or her, or simply the mere ambience of LA, coupled with the euphoria I felt at this point in my life but I thought, *Why not?* 'Okay, let's do it!'

Rodeo Drive overflowed with designer shops. Gucci, Prada, Chanel – you name it, it was there. It all blew my mind and knocked me a bit unsteady. I had never set foot in shops such as these in my life. But I tried on *so* many beautiful clothes, they became rather addictive.

I had lost quite a bit of weight since leaving Adelaide. Not that I ever went on any crazy diet, like the *Israeli Army Diet* that Mum always encouraged me to do. I think my mum lived off apples and Fiesta cigarettes. My shrinking had occurred from the mad lifestyle, the adrenalin and more recently the physical activity. So the clothes didn't look bad on at all.

Jan sat by the dressing rooms, waiting for me to appear in each different outfit, sipping more Champagne. She would "ooh" and "aah" and make comments like, "Absolutely gorgeous on you darling".

I think I walked out of each shop with at least two items. I kept thinking David would freak out. In some of the boutiques, a few eyebrows raised as they caught sight of the credit card I handed over, with "Mr David B Cassidy" printed boldly on it. I am sure one place even phoned his bank discreetly. The woman returned with quite a different attitude and simply couldn't gush over me enough. In fact the salesgirls in all stores treated me like a star and I loved every moment of it. However my mind did have a little fear blip that this might get into the papers.

As Jan had suggested, we dropped into a hair salon. Pierre, the principal stylist suggested, 'Mademoiselle's hair is crying out to be blonde.'

Blonde?

Pierre handed me a glass of Champagne.

Blonde it is then.

Our last stop was a beauty salon where they pampered me with all kinds of lavish skin treatments, and painted my face with various forms of makeup by none other than Chanel. I hardly recognised myself at the end of it all. Jan applauded and threw back another Champagne.

On the way back, a call rang through on the car phone. David asked for me. 'Hi baby, are you having a good time?'

I told him yes indeed I was, that Jan was lovely, and that he was even lovelier for doing this for me.

'That's great, baby. I just wanted to say to have them drive you back home and I'll meet you there,' and, 'I love you, baby.'

I told him I loved him too.

Jan suggested we stop somewhere and have a coffee to sober up a bit. Well maybe she needed to sober up especially but I thought I could sure use a clearer head too before seeing David. This made us even later however and I thought for certain David would flip. I'm not sure why I thought that; perhaps I had only known angry guys beforehand, or perhaps I was thinking of my father. But nothing was further from the truth. The car slid through the large gates and ever-present fans glued there, and pulled up at the house. Our driver guided us from the car and proceeded to retrieve bags and bags of designer clothes from the boot.

David emerged from the house and asked Jan, 'So where's Lisa?' He hadn't even recognised me.

I approached him nervously and half biting my lip, asked, 'What do you think?'

I had on one of my new dresses – a sassy figure hugging wrap-around in red, falling just past my knees, with a low cut v-front. It more than showed off my hourglass figure. He stared at me and kept on staring. The expression on his face seemed one of disbelief but I wasn't quite sure whether it was positive.

'Oh, mama!' he finally exclaimed. 'Let me look at *you*.'

He stepped backwards and began checking me out thoroughly. I stood like a quivering lab rat, being examined.

'*Far out,* baby. You look like *Monroe*. You were gorgeous before but … you're a fucking *knockout*.'

'You like it then?'

'Fuck, yeah!'

'I'm sorry if I bought too much.'

'I don't care. I don't care the *least*.' He grabbed me. 'Come here, Beautiful.' And he kissed me as if he'd never let go.

'Okay, time for me to split,' called Jan as she fell back into the car.

David kept kissing me but I managed to pull away a little to say goodbye and thank her.

'We can't waste this,' David still eyed me with delight, 'we gotta go out for dinner.' He jumped on the phone to make arrangements, then ran off to get ready himself. 'I won't be long, baby.' And I happily received another kiss.

Chapter 14

Our driver took us to a little exclusive place that apparently many local celebrities favoured. Drapes of curtains flounced everywhere and little lanterns glowed discreetly on walls and pillars. It had quite a French-romantic appearance from what little I knew of style. Soft velvet booths beckoned couples to hide in them.

The Maître D led us to one in a far corner. David's security guys were dotted around but weren't too obvious to be annoying. I noticed a number of heads turn as we walked across the room to our booth, David's hand on the small of my back. He had dressed in a gorgeous ivory silky suit and looked scrumptious.

As we sat down, David requested a candle be brought for our table. The waiters cooed over us and I thought it hadn't really been long ago that I'd been lunching with Jan at the Polo Lounge where we'd also been spoilt. *What an indulgent day.* I felt over the moon *and* mars wearing a beautiful dress with David gazing at me adoringly. I had never experienced being so treasured.

'You have the most beautiful sunset eyes,' I told him.

'What do you mean, baby?'

'Your eyes… they remind me of the beauty of sunset.' *Did I just see a slight blush cross his cheeks?*

My menu had no prices so I kept asking if the dishes I

considered were okay with him. He told me to just order whatever I wanted.

His inner-rebel popped up when we ate at restaurants, as he never paid attention to dining protocols. His manners were impeccable at all times, but he usually put ice in his Champagne, ate with a spoon if he felt like it, and took no notice of the menu if he wanted something in particular.

Our first course consisted of mouth-watering stuffed caramelised mushrooms, topped lightly with a cheese and pine nut sauce. For main course, a plate each of salmon pasta arrived that actually had glittery bits in it. I didn't dare ask what they were but they didn't have any distinct flavour. The dish looked unreal and tasted great. We'd ordered the same things as all the changes David wanted to make sounded perfect to me.

When we had finished our main meals, he took my hand again and told me he'd missed holding it while we'd been eating. His half-dreamy stare fell on me once more and didn't let me go. I reflected this enamoured glow back to him. We may as well have been at home, as the rest of the world didn't exist when we looked at each other like that.

He chatted to me about his hopes for the new album and also clowned around a little. Then he said he wanted to discuss something with me. 'Baby, I know you wanna be home for your birthday and I can dig that your parents and friends would be missing you. But d'ya think you could maybe return home just one, maybe two days later?'

Far out, my birthday is barely over six weeks away. I didn't even want to think about going home now. *How will I handle that? When will I see David again?* My stomach began to stir.

'Darlin'?'

Him calling me "darlin'" snapped me out of my thoughts.

He hadn't called me that before. I beamed at him. 'Yes… darlin'?'

He laughed. 'You didn't hear my question? About going back a few days later?'

'Oh yes, that, yes… yes I did.'

'And…?'

'Oh… um… so why two days later?'

'Well…' He appeared quite pleased, almost cheeky about something. 'Well… I thought I would like to take you out for your birthday…'

My smile expanded.

'…to Paris.'

'*What?* You're serious?'

'Absolutely,' he grinned.

Unreal, how can I say anything else but "yes" to that?

As we left the restaurant to go to our car, someone snapped us. We had no idea whether it was press or an individual. We hoped for the latter. In the back seat, I rested my head on his shoulder and again became suspended in a world of magic. He kissed me a couple of times and the butterflies in my stomach made their appearances each time. His breathy voice murmured sweet words into my ear. I felt I could slide off that seat at any given moment. We eventually segued into a state of simple bliss; our heads resting on each other, his silken hair caressing my cheek.

I must have been almost in dreamland when he seemed to want to begin another conversation. 'So are you looking forward to turning twenty?'

I chuckled softly. 'You mean seventeen.'

He lifted his head and looked at me. 'Seventeen? You're kidding, right?'

'No baby, I'm turning seventeen. I thought you knew how old I was?'

He fell silent. I had seen him go through some pretty extreme emotions on tour but I had never seen this expression on his face. He appeared to be in total shock.

'Baby?'

'Let's talk when we get home.'

I wasn't sure whether he didn't want to discuss this with the driver within hearing range, or because he really was in shock. I honestly thought he knew how old I was, otherwise I would have brought it up. He had made the "oopsie" joke ages ago at the beginning of the tour, in relation to me having Champagne. I didn't think it was a big deal.

David remained stone silent as we entered the house. I followed him to the room that led out to the pool. With an abrupt flick of his hand the outside lights lit up the pool area, making it appear surreal. He charged over to the bar and poured himself a Scotch. 'Want one?'

I shook my head. I flopped on the couch like a deflated basketball. I didn't know what to think. He'd cut me off like a shard of ice. Tears bubbled up from somewhere deep inside me but I refused to cry like a little sixteen-year-old. David stayed behind the bar, drinking his Scotch, staring out to the pool.

'Hi kids, *que pasa?*' Sam bounced into the room. He saw the expressions on our faces and stopped in his tracks. 'Uh oh… trouble in Paradise? Hmm… let's see… I know, I'll put some soothing music on.'

Neither David nor I responded to him but I truly could have burst out laughing over his antics. Or perhaps my urge to laugh was triggered by my anxiety.

He strolled over to the quadrophonic system and flicked

through the record collection. 'I know!' he announced, 'how about the smoochy sounds of good old Engelbert? Here we go...'

He put on the record and soon "good old Engelbert" began singing about wanting to be released from a love he didn't feel anymore.

'Oops, wrong song.' Sam immediately flicked the needle onto the next track in his madcap manner. 'Sorry about that folks, the sound problem... er track problem has now been rectified.' He grinned, looking pleased with himself.

I don't think David found him at all funny but I had my hand in front of my mouth to hide my smirk.

'And no thanks again...' Sam sighed, 'no wonder I feel unloved.' He raised the back of his hand to his brow in a dramatic gesture.

I appreciated him attempting to lighten things up but it wasn't working, at least not for David. He was just so intense at times. And fast as a feral cat, he sprang from behind the bar, flippantly commented to Sam that he wasn't funny and took his stance behind the sofa where I sat. He placed his hands a little too firmly on my shoulders and shaking me, demanded, 'How old does she look, Sam?'

'Hey!' I protested at his roughness.

'*Sam?*'

Sam raised an eyebrow, pretending to sum me up. 'Well right now she looks like she's about a day or two into the "hot mama" stage of her life.' He winked at me.

I didn't know whether to feel complimented or offended.

'*Sam,*' David screeched, 'will you be serious for once.'

Sam wiped his face as if wiping the smile off. 'Okay, seriously?'

'Yes, fucking *seriously.*'

'Oh I don't know, probably around twenty-three right now?'

'But before this new hot look?' David kept pressing.

'Oh fuck David, I don't know… I never really thought about it. I guess if she's under twenty-one then you shoulda found that out beforehand.'

'She's sixteen man… fucking *sixteen* years old.'

That was it. I'd had it. I jumped off the sofa and yelled, 'Yes I'm fucking sixteen years old. And I'm old enough not to put up with you two talking about me as if I wasn't here… as if I was some fucking horse you've just bought and found out I'm not suitable to ride or something.' I realised how bad that sounded as soon as it fell out of my mouth.

Embarrassment flushed over me. I ran out of the room and to bed – in *my* room. I tore off my new dress (carefully), flung myself on the bed and let out all my tears. My fun day of indulgence had just turned sour and my perfect fairy tale began crumbling before my eyes. I felt alone and empty.

I heard a soft knock at my door. 'Who is it?' I called out, as if I didn't know.

'It's me baby, can I come in?'

'Hang on a minute.' I draped the sheet around me so I wasn't exposing anything and tried to quickly eliminate any mascara streaks or evidence of crying. I made him wait a few moments. 'Okay,' I called.

David entered sheepishly, not knowing what to expect I guess. His face lit up a little when he made eye contact with me. 'Can I sit down?'

'Yeah.'

He sat on the edge of the bed, still looking coy. 'I always seem to be apologising to you.' He looked down, his long lashes casting shadows on his cheeks from the bedside lamp. But I didn't say anything; I actually didn't know what to say. 'So um... I'm sorry,' he offered quietly.

I was so mad at him for the way he had been carrying on in the bar room but I couldn't help noticing how attractive he looked in this light, damn him.

He then surprised me. 'Look, I came here to apologise and... well I *am* apologising... and I do wanna talk to you about it all... but... baby... you are such a distraction... you look so fucking desirable lying there with the sheet draped around you... you really are Monroesque... and I just can't help feeling... I just can't... oh fuck...' He grabbed hold of me so passionately and kissed me with such force, I liquefied completely into that kiss and embrace.

We both knew how much we wanted each other. I don't think either of us wanted to argue. But something didn't sit well with me. I had flashbacks of Judd and not wanting to have sex. I pulled away. He appeared confused.

A wave of thought grasped me and suddenly it became clear. I did want him; I loved him. But it didn't feel right for me to simply abandon myself into the throes of passion when we hadn't sorted out what was wrong in the first place. Maybe being a guy, that didn't matter so much to him – but it did to me. He was so striking, so tempting, but I knew I had to be true to myself.

I took his hand. 'I just can't do this right now.' I looked down. I didn't know how he would respond.

His energy changed as if a realisation swept over him. 'I understand, Beautiful,' he said lovingly, 'I really am very sorry...'

'Can we talk about this in the morning?'

'Sure baby, sure. Anything you want.' He paused. 'Would you like me to leave you alone or can I hold you in my arms tonight?'

I hesitated for a moment, then said, 'Stay.'

Chapter 15

We both woke up early. I don't think either of us slept very well although I enjoyed the comfort of him lying next to me. The old "rule" for successful relationships popped into my head about never letting the sun go down on an argument. I thought normally this would have been good advice but I'd been exhausted from it all the previous night to talk. I didn't want to have an in-depth discussion when I couldn't think clearly.

When I turned over to face David, he had his eyes wide open. He bent his head towards me and smiled a little as if unsure of what to say or do. If that's how he felt, then I felt the same. I rested my head on his arm and he stroked my shoulder. We lay like that for a long time.

Eventually I broke the ice. 'Still love me?'

'Oh baby, come here.' He pulled me to him and kissed me tenderly. 'Of course I do.' After a few moments he sighed. 'I really need to get a handle on my moods.'

Yeah, well he wasn't going to get an argument from me on that one. I didn't say that though. I said, 'Maybe we should both say what we felt about last night.'

'Yep, yep… that's a good idea.' He sprang to attentiveness.

'Do you want to go first?'

'No baby, you go first.'

I wasn't quite sure whether that was politeness or a cop out.

But I began, 'Okay… I just wanted to let you know that I didn't feel good about a few things that happened last night.' I glanced at him.

He'd developed a wanting-to-please puppy look. 'Yes baby, I'm listening.'

'Well… firstly, I didn't like how you shook me–'

'Oh hey listen baby, that was–'

'You'll get your turn in a minute.' I smiled. 'I also felt like you'd rejected me and that the two of you were talking as if I wasn't there. That upset me.'

He looked like he wanted to start explaining but I gestured to let me continue. 'But at the end of the day, this is who I am. I am sixteen going on seventeen…' We both chuckled and I felt like breaking into song.

I continued, 'And I never pretended to be anything else. I never lied to you and I never tried to deceive you. I guess I just presumed you had some idea of my age. But anyway, I am still the same person. *C'est moi.*'

'See? You just… you're so… I think sometimes you're more mature than I am. And you have such wisdom and confidence that I never even entertained the idea that you'd be so young.'

'But baby, you gave me that confidence. I was pretty hopeless beforehand. I let people walk all over me. You helped me to become a stronger person… and I will always be so grateful to you for that. I can't imagine what my life would have been like without your… care and concern. Don't you remember the wimp I was?'

'You were never a wimp,' he spoke softly. 'I never saw you as anything less than charming and… well… it just never occurred to me how young you are… When you'd told me ages ago that you had two years to go to drinking age, I suppose I was thinking in American terms.'

I must have looked confused, so he added, 'It's not eighteen here like for you Aussies – it's twenty-one. And even when you said you needed to go back to college – I'd forgotten *that* meaning is different for you too.'

'But I'm still *me*. I'm still the same *person*.' My voice became unsteady, 'I thought you didn't want me anymore, just because I'm a few years younger than you'd thought... I was scared...'

'Oh, sweetie... of course I want you.' He took my hand. 'I know you're the same person.'

He gazed at me deeply with his beautiful eyes. 'And all I can say again to you is express how sorry I am, really sorry. I certainly didn't mean to make you feel rejected, or shake you in a way that frightened you – I would never do anything like that. That's just so...' he put his hand on his heart, 'just so against my inner being. I was just in shock baby.'

He bowed his head, his long lashes again falling against his cheeks. 'I don't think I'm very good at these things called relationships. I know I need to learn. I've been living in this crazy world that's been all about me and I tend to forget that I'm hurting someone else's feelings. And it especially hurts me when I realise that someone is you. I never ever wanted to do that to you. Please give me another chance – please help me learn to be a better person. I promise I'll try much harder to manage my moods, to be more aware of your feelings. I need you just so, so much... and I wanna be there for you also. Can you forgive me?' He searched my face.

'I love you, David. You've brought so much happiness to my life... and meaning. I just want you to be happy–'

'*You* make me happy.'

'Please just be my gorgeous David that I spent a week of

bliss with at Lundy Canyon. Be the David that belongs with me at the heart rock.'

'I *am*, baby. That person is foremost who I am.'

We looked at each other with such depth, such realness. That moment seemed to be a stepping stone to a different level of closeness between us.

The spell was broken by a knock at the door. 'Breakfast anyone?' Sam chirped. 'I think the paper might interest you both too.'

Worry instantly sprang onto his face.

I put my hand up. '*Uh*,' I directed cheekily, 'composure, yes?'

He smiled. Then leant in to me and murmured, 'I love you, my beautiful adviser,' and our lips drew together effortlessly. 'I suppose we'd better go see what Sam's got for us.' He hesitated. 'But please do kick me if I ever get out of line, okay?'

'You got it.'

He put his arm snugly around my shoulders as we stood to go. On the way out of the room, he shook his head and muttered, 'Sixteen. Huh. Un-fucking-believable.'

Sam had laid out a simple but mouth-watering breakfast for us on the table.

'Aw, that's sweet of you Sam, thank you.' I cuddled him.

'Don't thank me yet,' he joked, 'this could be equivalent to the Last Supper.'

'What are you going on about?' David grimaced.

Sam threw the paper on the table. 'Not quite front page, but page two.'

David snatched the paper. He practically turned white.

'What's wrong, baby?' I put my hand on his arm.

He didn't say anything but handed me the paper. The pic

snapped of us looking very into each other on our way out of the restaurant dominated page two. The headline stated, "Retired but not too tired for a hot date". I read the article out loud, 'Supposedly retired teen idol David Cassidy was seen out in downtown LA last night with his latest love interest. The unknown young lady appeared to be one of Cassidy's numerous staff... *staff?* I shrieked, '...who accompanied him on his latest tour. Cassidy had announced during the tour it would be his final. He wished to retire at age twenty four. "I'm tired," Cassidy had announced to the British press... blah, blah, blah. Oh yes and of course they had to make mention of White City.'

David and I both sat stunned. His brow creased as concern crept onto his face.

'Why would they think I was your staff, for fuck's sake?' I'd begun to swear a bit lately.

'Baby, they just make up whatever they want. And you have no idea how ruthless they can be. I have a horrible feeling that they're gonna go for you now too. Oh god, I hope...'

'What?'

David appeared more than worried and he and Sam exchanged glances.

'*What?*

Sam spoke, 'If your age gets out, David will be fried.'

I looked at David and I think he tried to hide all expression from his face. Now *I* was worried. 'Oh baby, I'm so sorry.' I didn't know what to say to try and comfort him.

'Ah, darlin'... it's not your fault, sweetie.' He enclosed me in one of his arms. 'I just know how these guys operate. And if they smell blood, they don't let up until they get it.'

'But they won't find out. How will they know how I old I am? I sure as hell won't tell them.'

'Baby, trust me… they have ways.' He looked defeated.

'*But…*' Sam joined in, 'at least they don't know exactly who she is yet. Let them think she's staff. Ruth certainly isn't going to let the cat out of the bag.'

David sat staring at nothing for a while. He turned to me. 'Darlin', I need you to stay here, to not go out anywhere. They can't know you're here. There've only been a few hangers around lately but this could flare things up. The media will start sniffing around no doubt. Just lie low for a while. Can you do that for me?'

'Sure,' I sighed. 'Where do I have to go anyway?'

'Oh, baby,' he rubbed my back, 'I really wanted you to come to the studio with me… when I lay down your tracks.' A mix of frustration and sadness filled his beautiful eyes.

'That's okay babe, I'll hear them on the record.'

'Order in anything you want… just do it through Sam or me… okay? It's just for a few weeks really. Then we go to Paris,' his face lit up, 'it won't matter then.'

'What do you mean?'

'Oh… nothing,' he smirked, '…just that we'll be outta here.'

Chapter 16

Those last weeks in the Encino house weren't exactly thrilling. I read a lot, started writing a journal, hung around with Sam, and on the odd occasion Jan would drop over to say "hi", or more to the point, share a few bottles of Champagne with me. David also asked me not to go outside by the pool as choppers sometimes flew over to take snaps. By the end of my confinement, I well and truly had cabin fever. The only good thing in all of it was David telling me to ring Mum whenever I wanted. At least I had the chance of some decent heart-to-hearts with her about what was going down for me and how our relationship had progressed. Thankfully she understood and was therefore more comfortable about making excuses to Dad. I do believe I sensed a little excitement in her too.

David spent long hours in the studio cutting his new album, or "my album" as he called it. He wanted to complete as much of it as possible before we left for Paris. As that day drew nearer, my excitement grew, but the thought of going back home afterwards dampened the thrill a little... or sometimes a whole heap. Not that I didn't want to go back home – I was hanging out to see everyone again – just that I didn't know when I'd be with David again. Every time I tried to talk to him about it, something would come up or he'd change the subject. I didn't know what to think... *Perhaps he doesn't want to acknowledge it, or think about us parting?* I truly had no idea.

The night before we were to fly out from LAX, David promised he'd be home early to finish packing. A bit after seven, he rang in from the studio. 'Hey baby, I'm really so very sorry but I really wanna do some overdubs and a few extra vocal lines so we can wrap this up – you know, before Paris. I've got some really wild cats workin' with me and we've just bounced some tracks – it's sounding unreal. I'll be home as soon as I can, I promise... Don't worry about dinner – I'll organise something – but please wait for me, huh? And we can still have dinner together. It'll be late but... I gotta go... you understand baby, don't ya? Sorry baby, I gotta go.'

Bummer. I had to wait even longer for him. I did wonder whether his request for me to not make dinner had anything to do with my lack of skills in the cooking department and he couldn't stomach anything I attempted anymore, or because he wanted us to have something special on our last night in LA. I wanted to believe the latter but wasn't terribly convinced.

I watched the clock. Each hour felt like three... eight pm... nine pm... ten pm... As it got close to eleven pm, I thought I'd go to bed. Right then he arrived, followed by a swarm of kitchen staff who charged in with the gusto of catering for a royal banquet.

'There's my beautiful girl.' He came and wrapped me in his arms. 'Hang on...' He scurried off again, this time returning with a bouquet of deep red roses.

'Oh wow. Baby – *thank you.*' Their rich colour smouldered with love – I adored them.

He looked pleased and held me ever so tightly while his lips played with mine. 'Paris tomorrow, baby!'

'*Yes,*' I shared his excitement. 'But the roses?'

'What?'

'I can't take them with us.'

'Sure you can.' He twirled me around. 'Besides, we can get some more in Paris. It's gonna be *great*.'

At almost midnight we sat down to the dinner prepared for us, accompanied by a little Dom naturally, but not too much as we had to be at LAX by six am. I had no idea how we'd manage this. David rapped happily about his day at the studio and being thrilled at completing the album. It reminded me of how he'd chat to me at our late night dinners on in his tour. Now he was much more down-to-earth. Or perhaps I thought that as since then we'd grown closer through loving each other.

The alarm buzzed in agony way too early. I slapped my hand on it to shut it up. David merely groaned. Neither of us were morning people. I put my head back on the pillow for a second and a quick realisation jolted me just in time to not fall asleep again. I forced my head up, my eyes still shut. I gently shook David. He grunted.

'Baby, we have to get up,' I coaxed in the hope of gaining some camaraderie. '*Baby*.' I nudged him harder. He lifted his head a little and his eyes opened slightly but no further than tiny slits. His head fell back onto the pillow again and his mouth fell open.

Not fair. I didn't want to get up on my own. It would have been so much easier to accomplish if he did as well. Still, I dragged myself out of bed and put on the light. 'Wake up, sweet prince,' I called to him. 'Yoo hoo! Mr *Cassidy*.' I jiggled him again. 'Come on, will ya? *Paris* is calling.'

That put a grin on his face and he pulled me back onto the bed on top of him, kissing me.

'Hey, we haven't got time for that.' I pulled away from him

and stood up. 'Get up, sleepy head.' I was well and truly awake now.

'Just one more kiss?' he pleaded with his eyes still closed.

'And then you'll get up?'

He nodded.

'Okay then.' I leaned over him to kiss him and he pulled me back onto the bed.

'I lied.' He smirked, and rolled around with me, fondling me. We both couldn't help indulging in a little playfulness which continued into the shower. Now we definitely needed to compete with the clock. I quickly shoved a few last minute things in my suitcase. It was far fuller than when I'd left Adelaide – I had no idea how the hell it would shut.

Sam passed the doorway and saw me struggling. 'You need *Super Sam*.' He came in and told me to sit on the case while he zipped it. 'Another damsel in distress saved by…. *Super Sam* – tada!'

His bright state was a tad too much for so early in the morning. But his vibe gradually stilled. 'Hey, baby girl… it's been great getting to know you.'

'Yeah, I feel the same. Thanks for all those walks around America.'

'You know,' he spoke a little warily, 'and tell me to shut up if it's not my business… but I just wanted to say…' He inhaled a little air and let it escape. 'You might find him a little difficult at times… He has well and truly lived this "teen idol" life where he's had everything thrown at him and everything on tap. I guess you can't really live through all that without it affecting you. So he can be a little self-focused occasionally… well maybe a lot. But he does love you. In fact, I think he loves you a *lot*… and I know he'll be loyal to you. He's a good guy.'

He gave me a slight punch on the arm. 'I know you'll be sweet, baby girl.'

I smiled up at him and he gave me a hug. 'I told you not to call me "baby girl".'

David returned, looking more alert. 'Hey! You movin' in on my girl?' He began play-boxing him.

I observed a genuine happiness in him that definitely wasn't there on tour. And I knew he was going to miss Sam. Hell, even I was going to miss Sam – and LA, and this weird existence in this gorgeous Californian house. It felt utterly weird to be going home. Well, nearly home… next stop – *Paris*.

Chapter 17

You hang on tight with all a-your might
As if your heart's ignited

Naturally David brought a security crew along but he wasn't overly concerned about Paris. He said the French were rather low-key with the whole teenage idol trip, and nowhere near as fanatical as the Americans or the Brits, or Aussies. Our flight wouldn't be a problem either as we were travelling first class, so he didn't think it likely the teeny boppers would be in there.

'Maybe some older women might fancy you too,' I teased.

He smirked and asked if I'd protect him.

First class was like flying in a mini presidential suite with your every whim catered for. I tried acting sophisticated, hoping my efforts at least fell on "cool". And prayed no one noticed my mouth falling open from amazement.

David leant closer as the engines started roaring and we pashed deliciously for take-off again. *These take-offs are becoming just more and more enjoyable each time.* Once in the air, he looked at me over the rims of the sunnies he still had on and said, 'I'm lonely'.

'What are you talking about?'

'I'm lonely, baby. Why don't you come over here with me?'

He was being wickedly cheeky, but the seats certainly were wide... So I joined him. He was super skinny anyway, and with me being much thinner too now, we fit quite snugly. The air hostesses acted nothing less than polite towards us but I did think that secretly they were annoyed. Maybe I irritated them more, being his companion. I can't imagine what they thought as David sure was being naughty with me. Luckily the partitions gave us privacy. I don't quite know how we managed it but on that flight between LAX and CDG, I joined the "mile high club". I didn't ask David whether he was already a member as I didn't want to know the answer or details.

As we approached Paris, I bubbled with excitement. David stroked my cheek. 'Seeing you so happy does me good.'

'Look, baby, *look*,' I almost shouted as I spotted the Eiffel Tower.

When the plane landed everyone clapped. David told me it's a French thing. In the airport, escalators in tunnel-like tubes transported us to another world. I was so keyed. Not only was I in Paris, but I was there with my love; the one and only David Cassidy. And where else would we be staying but The Ritz. I had no idea until we were on our way. A car took us there directly, followed by the rest of our security entourage in another.

'Nothin' but the best for you, darlin'.' He kissed me.

My heart jumped with sheer joy. *Can I possibly be any happier?*

The Ritz was simply too stunning for words. Unassuming from the outside, except for the rows of flags announcing its presence on the side of Place Vendôme. But on the inside... *ooh la la*. The *maître d'hôtel* greeted both David and me, telling us we could go straight to our suite and everything would be taken care of.

'*Merci, monsieur.*' David nodded.

Hearing his sensual voice speaking French just about made me giddy.

The *maître d'hôtel* clicked his fingers and a swarm of staff sprang into motion taking our bags, sorting out paperwork, and providing us with information leaflets on the hotel and Paris attractions.

We walked through gold and blue hues of grand décor – *très* gorgeous. Our suite looked like something fit for Marie Antoinette. I discovered later it was modelled on Versailles and the bed was a replica of the Queen's itself. On a grand centre table with a marble top and gold scrolled legs, a bottle of Dom Pérignon chilled in an ice bucket. A card reading *"Bien Venue"* leaned against it. Next to it arched the biggest arrangement of deep red roses I had ever seen.

We faced each other in delight. 'Well here we are,' announced David.

I walked up to him and put my arms around his neck. 'I love you so much. You are the best thing that has ever happened in my life.'

His gaze deepened. 'I feel exactly the same, *ma chérie.*' And he kissed me so passionately I thought I'd lose my footing – even though I now stood on solid ground. He then threw me gently onto Marie Antoinette's bed.

For our first evening in Paris he'd organised dinner in a private dining room. As we were about to dress he said, 'You always look gorgeous babe, but wear something special tonight... for our first night in Paris?'

I certainly had a lot of stunning designer dresses to choose from, courtesy of my darling man. I chose an off-the-shoulder cream dress, flowing with femininity and complimented it with a shimmering necklace and matching earrings. I dressed in a separate room of the suite and when I had finished, including makeup and hair, I glided in to show David, twirling as I entered the room.

He sat in one of the high-backed maroon chairs with gold leaf trim, wearing a blue-grey silky suit, with a striking electric blue shirt. I could have eaten *him* up for dinner. His eyes darted up from his magazine and the expression on his face made me blush. His face lit up and he walked over to me, kneeling before me.

'Oh baby, I am not worthy.' He gazed up at me with his captivating eyes.

'Don't do that,' I protested and dropped to my knees to join him.

He kissed me with engulfing tenderness, holding me like a precious bouquet. I'm not sure what it was about him; it's as if a different energy had overtaken him. It wasn't only that he now appeared more light-hearted and happier than I'd ever seen him, but he had a certain intensity about him – a delicious, loving intensity. I felt I was falling even deeper in love with him. *But of course... we are in Paris.* He stood, swept me up in his arms and began to carry me.

'What are you doing?' I asked but he just smiled. He carried me all the way to the elevator with me kicking my heels and laughing.

A sparkling white grand piano stood near the entrance to our private dining room. It seductively invited me to play as we walked past but I didn't dare. Dark blue velvet drapes held with gold ropes framed our dining room and the ceiling's centre featured a glistening chandelier. Tall slim glass doors opened onto a quaint balcony overlooking a private garden. This view glimpsed the very last embers of twilight. Everything looked picture-perfect. A charming waiter seated us and David beamed at me from across our table. He looked perfect too.

'Hungry, Beautiful?' he asked softly, viewing the menu.

So many sophisticated sounding dishes to choose from and I hadn't a clue what any of them were. 'I have no idea what to order.'

'Baby, don't sweat it.' He studied the menu a little more and then suggested, 'Can I order for you?'

I'd heard of this concept of guys ordering for you but never thought I'd dig it. Still, this was David, we had quite similar tastes and I trusted him. 'Sure, why not?' It felt nice in a way to let him take command like that.

'I think we should have *une entrée, un plat principal et un petit dessert* for this special occasion.'

'What special occasion?'

He smiled at me as if I was a lost child. 'Darlin', it's been your birthday already for six and a half hours in Australia.'

It was nine pm in Paris. I had forgotten about my birthday completely. 'Oh wow. You're *right*. I can't believe I forgot. Yep, well okay… three courses it is then… you choose.'

He did and he chose well. For *entrée* he selected a caviar dish. I had never eaten authentic caviar before – I felt *très chic*. In between the *entrée* and main they brought us sorbets. For our *plat principal* we had *Coq au Vin* which practically glided onto our forks and into our mouths. David didn't normally eat meat or fish but he hadn't been as strict lately. Needless to say, we drank Dom to accompany the food. David requested a decent break before looking at desserts which my stomach appreciated as it resembled an over-expanded balloon already. But I didn't want to miss out on dessert either, especially not at The Ritz.

He took my hand from across the table and beamed another beautiful smile at me. A new sparkle shone in his eyes. He didn't say anything but simply gazed at me with love in that sparkle. Seconds later, I heard the sound of a violin. At first I thought I heard enchanting music in my head but it got louder and louder, until the player himself wandered into our dining room. The tune sounded incredibly familiar. Then the realisation hit me – it was the main song David had written for me, *Beautiful Girl*.

He saw the recognition on my face and chuckled warmly, squeezing my hand. 'I wanted to arrange something special for your birthday.'

'Oh babe, what a lovely thing to do. This is just *so* beautiful. Thank you so much for doing all this.'

We listened to the violin singing sweetly and I applauded when the player finished. David joined in too. The violinist nodded in appreciation and carried on playing. I listened for a few seconds, trying to pick the second tune... and then I connected. It sounded quite different on violin but it was *Could It Be Forever*.

David started singing along, '*Well I touched you once and I kissed you once and now I feel like you're mine.* Do you remember when I sang that to you from onstage?'

I felt my eyes tearing up. 'Oh baby, do I ever. That was such a beautiful, memorable thing for me.'

'Anyway, as I said before, I wanted to do something special for your birthday–' he put his hand up to silence me as I tried to thank him again, 'and I wanted to get you something.'

He reached into the top inside pocket of his jacket. 'Something not only for your birthday but to acknowledge us.' He looked at me in a kind of half-mischievous way, peppered with anxiousness – and reached his hand across the table to me. In it was a small black box.

I gently took the box from him and told him he had done so much for my birthday already in bringing me to this beautiful place, in bringing me to Paris. I gazed down at the elegant box he had offered me. It was made of black velvet with a gold trim. A clasp at the top opened the lid into two sections like wings opening up. I opened it. A dazzle hit me like lightning – from the shimmering ring inside. It cradled a solitaire marquise cut diamond. It was *exquisite*. The most beautiful ring I'd ever laid my eyes upon. While I sat staring at it, I hadn't noticed David had knelt before me. My eyes must have been as big as an owl's and my heart pounded so loudly I was sure he could hear it.

'Darlin',' his gaze deepened, 'you have come to mean the world to me.' He sighed. 'I must have gone through this a thousand times in my head but now I'm still not sure of what would be the right words, right now.' He gave me a look of intense warmth and said simply, 'Will you marry me?'

My head began to spin and honest-to-god my whole life whooshed before my eyes like a movie reel on speed. My heart leapt into a dance – soaring with a flight of birds, accompanied by a kaleidoscope of colours. And as if someone had suddenly turned off the music, an instant surge of quiet hit, before a million thoughts crashed through my mind all at once.

So there it was on the table. I was being offered the part of Mrs David Cassidy – a lifetime role. I would have given my eye teeth for that chance a few years ago. No, I probably wouldn't even have dared to dream of it. And now it lay before me. I didn't know what to do. *I love him, that's for sure. But is he sure he really wants this? Is he still concerned about my age?* Part of me recognised I was still quite young. *So I've been on one rock tour*

*- what else do I know of the world, of being grown up? He thinks
I am wise for my years and looks to me for advice, and I just make
it up as I go along. I guess some of it has made sense. Oh gosh, I
love him so much. But is this the best thing for me, for him, for us?*

The twinkling ambience of the romantic room started to
filter into my awareness again and there he was before me. 'Oh
boy,' he tensed, 'I can't believe how nervous I am.' He coughed.
I realised I was taking a long time in answering him.

I took his face in both my hands and caressed his cheeks.
'Beautiful David,' I took in every inch of his stunning face,
beaming at him with love, 'I do love you so.'

'But it's not enough?' He looked so unusually vulnerable.

'No... *No*. I mean, *yes*. Yes, of course it's enough.' I became
apprehensive about what to say – I didn't know what I wanted
to say. After a few more moments of silence I concluded,
'Maybe... I'm just a bit... scared... just a little bit.'

He stroked my cheek. He took my hand. He took control.
'Come and dance with me a little bit then.' He led me to a
corner of the room.

'But there's no music now?'

'Sure there is,' he smiled, 'in here.' He put his hand to
his chest. He drew me into a dance hold and swayed gently
with me; two steps one way, one step back, two steps one way,
one step back, while we slowly turned. The lights somehow
magically dimmed. We were completely in synch, mirroring
each other. Our rhythm swiftly became autonomous, my head
lay on his shoulder, his rested on mine, and he crooned softly,
'*When I fall in love... it will be forever...*'

We stayed swaying in our rhythm for a cosy length of time I
didn't want to pass. He had definitely relaxed me but also made
me realise how exceptional he was, how much he truly meant to

me. He had a beautiful soul. 'Baby?' I reached to him.

His head was still on mine and he seemed in a dream state. 'Mmmmh?' he made this soft sound without opening his eyes.

'I just want to know one thing.'

'What's that, baby?' he murmured from a depth in his throat.

'You're not feeling pressured to marry me because of my age and that we've slept together?'

He stopped swaying and stepped back to look at me directly, placing his hands on my shoulders. 'Is that what you're thinking? That I would marry you to somehow save my reputation, or your honour?' He laughed. 'Baby, not even I am that crazy to do something like marry someone for any of those reasons. Don't you think I'm sincere? I *love* you. That's why I want to marry you. I… I just feel like you're my *other half*… I've never met anyone who has made me feel that.' His eyes filled up like sparkling pools.

I looked up at him and my head swirled again. But this time in a gentle way, like a boat rocking and turning with ease, being held in the protective vastness of the ocean surrounding it.

My heart reached out to him. 'God I love you, David. I must have had a sanity break. I do want to marry you – so much.'

We both had tears escape from our eyes. He held me tightly, so incredibly tightly. And I held him just as tightly back.

Chapter 18

When I woke up in our divine suite, I was inches away from his face, his breath. He slept deeply. It warmed my soul to watch him like that, to see him so peaceful. My mind drifted to the girls who thought he was lovely – if they could see him like this, they would think him a hundred times more so.

As if he'd felt I'd woken, he opened his eyes. A smile emerged on his lips. 'Mmmmh... good morning, my beautiful fiancée.'

'Good morning, handsome.' I kissed him. I rested my head on his shoulder and we made plans for the day.

'We can take a car and look at some sights,' he suggested. 'And for tonight I've organised a private boat for dinner on the Seine. Is that okay, Beautiful?'

'Mmmh. It sounds heavenly,' I sighed.

'And,' he sounded more awake, 'I wanted to talk to you about some details of our engagement.'

Details? Far out, this actually is happening. I hadn't been dreaming after all. 'Sure babe, what in particular?'

'We-ell,' he half sat up, 'I was kinda hoping you'd say yes,' he smirked cheekily, 'so I took the liberty of booking myself a ticket to fly back to Australia with you.'

'Really?' I threw my arms around him, completely thrilled. I had been worried before the previous evening's events about when we would part. 'And what if I'd said "no"?'

'Oh, I could've always cancelled,' he shrugged, '...or tried to be more convincing.' We both laughed. 'So I thought I'd do the right thing and ask your father for your hand.'

'*What?* Just the thought of that halted my laughter and twisted the pit of my stomach.

'Sure. Don't you think he'd appreciate that?'

'Umm, yes… well… I don't know… um…'

'Don't be uptight about it baby, it'll be fine.' He smiled reassuringly.

'Far out. You don't know my father.' I panicked. 'I don't know that you're ready for my father.'

'Ha, he can't be any worse than *mine.*'

'Oh, god.'

'Come here, baby.' He kissed me softly. 'It'll all be sweet, you'll see.'

I simply could not for the life of me imagine this scenario. I had been traipsing all over the world with him but now, David Cassidy was coming to downtown Croydon to meet my father. *Unreal. Oh god help me.* I presumed he meant at the house. Not that it was the best scenario either.

'Umm… where do you wanna – er, I mean – want to meet my father?'

'Well… how about at your place? That'd be good.'

'Oh.'

'Darlin', what's wrong?'

I looked down and fidgeted. 'Well, it's just that… just… our house…'

'What about it?'

'It's just so… ordinary.'

'So? And the problem is…?'

My eyes met the floor again.

'Baby, the last thing I want you to do is to worry about

taking me to your house. Don't think that I've always lived like this. You should've seen some of the pads I've shared, or just bunked down in for a bit. This lifestyle is not what I'm used to. It's not what I value. A house is a house. It's the people that make it, not the bricks and mortar.'

'Yeah well, ours isn't so much bricks and mortar either, but cladding.'

'*Baby*. Please… Stop this.' He held me. 'I don't care whether your family lived in a teepee at Ayers Rock. In fact, that'd be great. I'm not gonna care – please believe me.'

'Okay, okay.' But I still felt awkward. After all we'd been through, thinking of bringing him home to meet Dad made me think of him again as *the* David Cassidy and somehow I had gate-crashed into his world. I had absolutely no imagination available to me on how he and my dad would come together. I had to phone Mum.

My thoughts were interrupted by a knock at the door. David got up to answer. I heard a male voice and David saying "thank you". He returned with his attention immersed in a paper he'd been given. He appeared concerned. After reading it thoroughly, he looked up at me. 'Well, looks like they know.'

'What do you mean, honey?'

He told me the paper was something called a "telex" sent from Ruth to our hotel. She was informing him of an article that talked about me and had transcribed most of it into this message. The headline read "We Think He Loves Her". David had been right in suggesting the press would be ruthless in sniffing me out. They had apparently spoken with some of the entourage from his tour, and consequently found out I had accompanied him throughout. And that I was the "special friend" he'd brought out on stage to serenade at one of his concerts. Comment was made that, "Cassidy didn't surface from Lisa's room during most of the tour and after its conclusion took her back to his home in LA".

We sat staring at each other. David maintained a neutral face. I couldn't tell whether he was really flipped out or not. Eventually he said, 'Isn't it great how you can trust people?'

'Yeah. People never cease to amaze me.' My focus froze into the distance.

'Mmh. God, I hate people.'

'Well at least they didn't say anything about my age.'

'Hmph – probably only because they didn't know,' he scoffed.

'And they *lied*. You did *not* spend all your time with me in my room.'

'Yeah, well... that's hardly surprising.' He was deep in thought for a few minutes and then announced, 'Well, we'll just have to do a press conference.' He looked at me. 'How do you feel about that?'

I remained lost in what he'd said. 'What...? Um... what do you mean, "we"?'

He took my hand. 'We could announce to the world together that we're engaged... Actually, that'd be good...' his demeanour brightened, 'I'd *love* to announce it to the world.'

I suddenly felt like a rabbit trembling in the spotlight. 'Yes but... why... why do I have to be involved in this?'

His laughter gurgled from deep within as he swung his arms around me. 'Because, my gorgeous baby, *you* are the woman I'm gonna marry. We're a team now.' He stroked my hair and murmured into my ear, 'Let's discuss it over dinner tonight, huh? Let's make our wedding plans and then decide what we'll tell the press?' He kissed my neck. 'How does that sound?' He placed soft effervescent kisses right in the crease of my neck. 'Hmmm...? Oh baby... mmmmh...' I never got to answer those questions.

When David had expressed his insistence in asking my dad for my hand, I knew I needed to phone Mum and fill her in on everything. After that telex had come in from Ruth, I knew I had to do it quickly. If I wanted to be fairly sure of her answering the phone, I would need to phone late at night when Dad was in bed. That wouldn't be until about lunch time in Paris. That was doable.

I gulped some courage and dialled the number. She answered thank goodness. 'Happy birthday, darling!'

'Yeah Mum, thanks. Listen, I have to tell you something... We're in Paris Mum–'

'Yes I know that, darling.'

'And we're coming back to Australia–'

'Yes I know that, darling.'

'Will you listen to me, Mum? *Yes*, we are coming back to Australia but the both of us will be coming back–'

'Oh that's nice.'

'Mum, will you *listen*? Both of us are coming back because David has asked me to *marry* him.'

The line fell silent which was extremely unusual for Mum. Eventually she asked, 'Well what did you say, darling?'

'I said *yes*, Mum, I said *yes!*' And we both started crying.

I pulled myself together enough to tell her that David has this crazy idea he wants to see Dad to ask for my hand. Mum thought it was nice of him. 'Yes Mum, but what about *Dad?* He doesn't even know where I've been for the best part of the year.' Another silence on the line. '*Mu-um.*'

'Well darling, please don't be mad but he does know a little bit. I had to tell him some of it. I told him while you were in Melbourne, David had been there, you got to know each other and he asked you to go for an all-expenses-paid trip to America. I said understandably Lisa would think that too good an opportunity to miss, so she went. So the initial blow has been dealt. I'm sorry, darling.'

'Oh, *Mum.* I love you! You're *wonderful.*'

I don't think she expected that reaction but I was so glad that at least Dad knew a little so it wouldn't be a total shock. The best part was, if he was *alltför* angry he would have cooled down by the time we saw him. My mum could sure spin a story, bless her.

Chapter 19

I guess I had never really thought much about Paris. It had always seemed to me like it might be lovely enough, but I just didn't think I'd ever go there. And I definitely hadn't known how perfectly pretty it was. If anything, I probably would have presumed it to be a bit posh. But now being immersed in her, I found everywhere you looked, your eyes fell in love. It was obvious the French were extremely proud of their leading lady. Paris simply oozed feminine energy, an energy that encapsulated *amour*.

'I seem to recall another great night when we were on a boat together.' He smirked at me.

I was tucked under his arm after a glorious dinner, gliding down the Seine. The stars in the sky merely couldn't compete with the sparkles of Paris reflected in the water. Every scene we floated past was *parfait*; the gothic spires of Notre Dame, the couples dancing on the bank to an accordionist, the ornate figures of Pont Alexandre III staring down at us mere mortals.

'I'm not so sure that was a great night.' I smirked back.

'Oh?'

I softly said in his ear, 'There was something unfinished that night.'

His smile returned and he nestled a little closer. 'Let's finish that tonight, sweet darlin'.' His breath tickled my ear.

I rested the back of my head onto his arm and was

mesmerised by this magic man. I sighed. I felt so high being with him. High on love.

'So I was thinking,' he continued in his soft flowing caramel voice, 'once your father gives us his blessing…' he glanced at me cheekily, 'which I'm sure he will… I think it'd make sense for us to be married in Australia.'

I didn't speak a word. I hadn't actually given any thought to the "hows" and "wheres" at that stage. I just stared at him.

He continued, 'Well, I've looked into it and it seems there'll be less bureaucracy and red tape for us to go through if we marry in Australia instead of America. We'd have to put the papers in pretty much straight away though as we need to wait a month – maybe a little longer because of my citizenship. Then we scoot back to the USA and it'd be a done deal. We'd be Mr and Mrs.' He beamed at me.

'Gosh, you've really done all the homework, haven't you?'

'Well, of course. You weren't planning on having a long engagement, were you?'

'Oh, David. You make my head spin.' I laughed. 'Have you also worked out what we should say to the press?'

His demeanour became more businesslike. 'Well not exactly *what*, but I thought about how the best way to go about it might be. I don't think doing a press conference in Australia would be the wisest move. I don't wanna alert them to our presence there. Instead, I thought we could write a press release announcing our engagement and I'll ring Ruth and ask her to release it in America. That way she can tell them we're away on vacation but not reveal where. Then, when we go back, all married and everything…' a smile flickered across his face, '*then* we can do our press conference.'

I gazed at him and adored his organisational skills. None

of the dingbat guys back in high school could organise a bus ride to beach if their life depended on it. I told him this and he chuckled. 'Darlin', that's not me at all. I've never been good at organising… but unfortunately in this lifestyle, I've had to learn to be strategic when it comes to the press.'

'Regardless, you are very sexy when you are commanding.'

'Oh, yeah?' He looked pleased. 'Well come here, baby.' He grabbed me and our mouths met eagerly. I loved how my heart missed a beat or two at the touch of his lips.

We pulled up at the bank and an accordion player came on board. He started playing *La Vie en Rose*. It had such a profound effect on me my eyes welled up with emotion. The realness of everything hit me precisely at that moment. I was in *the* Paris that had featured in so many films, artworks and novels, and in which many a starry-eyed lover had written songs of their breaking heart. But I was with the most gorgeous man in the world, who also happened to be the man I was about to marry. *How can I be so blessed?*

Our boat glided forward and a million sparkles sprang to life on the Eiffel Tower. Pure magic.

Chapter 20

You can feel my heartbeat too
I can see you feelin' me

The incredible chemistry between us astounded me. He would only have to slightly touch me or call my name and a superbly delicious tingle would develop between my legs. More often than not, this grew into a fire only he could put out.

When he wasn't chasing me for a little nookie, I was chasing him. My body always responded to his touch, so easily. His voice too always turned me on, especially when he leaned in close to murmur something. He told me I had the same effect on him. I'd catch him looking at me frequently with hunger in his eyes. Plus he seemed to have an erection most of the time we were together.

I'm not sure whether for me, this insatiable appetite had developed because of the raw chemistry between us or because I felt I could trust him more than anyone before him, and through that trust my sexuality felt safe to fully awaken. I suspect it was a bit of both. I had been totally disgusted by sex in the past, now it was such euphoria. I had always been asked to "show my tits" by both boys *and* girls, I suppose because I was quite well endowed from a young age. And there always seemed to be a penis popping up somewhere with a demand of "touch this" or "suck this". All of it had grossed me out. Now being with David; he'd allowed me to develop my own natural desire for him. He had never tried to coerce me in any way and by being so loving and caring in the bedroom, my inner sex goddess felt secure in rising to the surface, and even go-go dancing on the table.

I thought about how he had been so generous with his gifts and how he'd taken care of me, and I very much wanted to do something for him for a change, especially on our last day in Paris. I didn't have the money to lavish extravagant gifts on him, so I agonised over this. Then it came to me.

'Babe, do you mind if I take the car and go and do a bit of girl-shopping by myself?'

'Sure honey, I'll organise for one of the boys to go with you.' By "one of the boys" he meant a security guy.

'Really? I don't think I'll need security.'

'I'm not gonna have my future wife wandering around Paris with just a driver. I'm sure you'd be okay but I wanna make a hundred per cent certain.' He drew nearer and put his arms around me. 'I wanna take care of my baby.' He kissed me softly with those lips of his. 'Let your fiancé take care of you...? Huh?' He kissed me more.

'I'm not the one who's famous.'

'Oh don't worry, you're gonna be.'

I hadn't thought of that concept. I shrugged it off. I really didn't think so.

'Won't you let me take care of you, Beautiful? Otherwise I'll be worried.' He nuzzled into my neck.

What could I say? I really didn't want a guy coming with me to where I planned on going but it seemed like I had to give in.

'And...' He walked over to the writing desk and grabbed his

wallet. 'You're gonna need this.' He slipped his credit card into my jeans pocket. I thanked him and our lips met lusciously. This would make it even better. I knew exactly what I was going to do with it.

Before setting off, I asked at the concierge desk to speak with a female staff member, made a few enquiries and set off with my male driver and male body guard. First stop – lingerie shop.

My eyes coyly examined all the pretty lacy things and slowly widened. I had never even thought of stepping into a place such as this before. A flush crept over me seeing all the risqué little numbers. They looked like they belonged in a burlesque show. Still, this little girl had grown up and was getting married. Half of me still couldn't fully believe it. And I intended to make my future husband very happy on this last day in the city of love.

At this frilly little shop, I chose a bra and knickers in innocent ivory lace, with a shimmery-soft matching overlay. Then a cherry and black corset winked at me. The bright cherry half-bra cups beckoned to be touched, to take pleasure in their silky satin. The corset came with an option of suspenders to which you could add black silk stockings with a seam running up the back of the leg. I took the additional option. Oh, and one more bra and panty (as he would call them) set caught my eye. These were whispery-sheer black and purple. The bra featured little holes so the nipples could peek out, surrounded by a soft rim of black fluffiness. I discovered the same concept applied to the panties. *Ooh*. I decided to also purchase the matching high-heeled slippers. I don't think I ever would have dared this kind of shopping in America on David's card. *Can you imagine?*

My next stop was a beauty salon that specialised in very

personal waxing. I asked for a heart. After that, one more stop for a few little accessories.

When I returned, I found my honey sunning himself by the pool. He lay on his stomach with his eyes closed. I tip-toed up to him, picked up the sun lotion and without saying a word, started massaging it onto his sun-kissed back. 'Mmmh,' he moaned, 'that feels so good. I know that touch... Didn't I meet you when I did my concert here in Paris last year?'

'Oh, *you*.' I slapped his back.

He laughed and rolled over. 'I knew it was you babe. No one else has such a sensual touch.' He grabbed me and I enjoyed the feel of his smile through his kiss. We settled happily into kissing and cuddling on his sunlounge, until he remembered my outing and asked what I'd bought.

'Come upstairs and I'll show you.' I took his hand and led him to our suite. I sat him down on our giant bed and told him to wait. He had the cheekiest smile as he said he couldn't. I was beginning to think he could read my mind. I firstly put on the most innocent set. As I re-entered the room he looked more than impressed.

'Oh, baby! Come *here*.'

'Ah, ah, ah,' I wagged my finger at him, 'just for looking, not touching.' I winked whilst doing a catwalk stride.

'No fair!' he called out as I left to change into the next one. I put on the corset, suspenders and stockings. I added the heels. This time his mouth fell open. 'Baby... I'm *speechless*.'

I paraded up and down for him but still wouldn't let him touch. 'Patience, honey.' And off I strutted to change again. I thought the holey number might blow him away but I hadn't expected how much.

'*Fuck.*'

That was it. That's all he could manage. The expression on his face was priceless. I certainly hadn't seen *that* in a magazine. After a little while he uttered, 'Far out, whatcha doin' to me? You're gonna *kill* me.'

I walked over and sat down on the bed next to him and all he did was eye me up and down, his mouth still half open. 'Good,' I chuckled, 'I was hoping you'd like them.'

'*Like?* Oh, baby I... I... Fuck. You sure have surprised me... uh... in a good way of course.' He began to grin. 'That's gotta be the smartest thing I've ever done – giving you my card. Each time you come back, I'm just a whole lot happier.'

'Well...' I twisted the end of my hair coyly. 'That was my intention… to make you happy – and that's exactly what I'm going to do. Wait here.'

I walked off and he looked like he had *no* idea what to expect now. I returned with a few of the accessories I'd bought – a bottle of massage oil and some feathers. 'Lie down, big boy,' I commanded.

His look of amazement slowly turned into the kind of pleasurable grin a panther would develop when he knows he is about to catch his prey.

♪ ♪ ♪

Our last night in Paris, we dined in our suite. We'd spent the whole afternoon in bed and were both too, dare I say "shagged", to care about getting gussied up for dinner. So I put on a skimpy nightie and he a silky dressing gown, and we ate dinner like that. We sat next to each other at the table, spoon fed each other, giggled a lot and touched each other a lot.

Eventually we fell onto our huge Marie Antoinette bed

for the last time. David exuded loving energy and caressed me tenderly. He kissed my mouth and our tongues began their wet dance. 'Beautiful girl?' he murmured in my ear.

'Yes, gorgeous.'

'Will you marry me?'

'I already said yes, darling.'

'I know, but say it again.'

'Yes… oh *yes*.' I pulled him closer to me and his grasp on me tightened.

'I love you so much.' His lips explored my face, my neck.

'Oh god, I love you too.' My body responded to his touch by thrusting towards him. He lowered himself and his tongue found my nipple. I squirmed with delight. Our hands simultaneously reached further down each other's torsos, moving slowly in feathery touches. We exposed each other's most pleasurable places with ease.

'Talk to me, baby,' I begged him.

'What, sweetie?' he breathed.

'Talk to me. Tell me what you're going to do to me… I love hearing your voice.'

'Oh, sweet baby, I'll do anything you want me to do to you… how about you open your legs for me a little?'

I wriggled against him and did as he asked. I felt his erection pulsing against my thigh. I needed to touch it and gently ran my fingers along the tip. He quaked with pleasure. Slowly he moved his hand between my legs, where I already felt a burning tremor for him. With the tip of his finger he traced around the heart I had there now.

'I'm gonna touch you,' he whispered, 'I'm gonna touch you a lot, baby.' He slipped his fingers inside me. 'Oh, darlin'… you are so wet… is that for me, baby?'

'Uh uh.' I licked his neck. 'Just for you.'

'Oh baby… that's so good… I'm gonna want to stroke you… really softly… like this…'

My insides screamed from a knife-edge of pleasure, and ached for more. I had his glorious cock in my grasp and I fondled him. 'I want you… I need you inside me…'

'I haven't finished touching you yet,' he purred.

'Oh god, *baby.*' In a beat I expected to be catapulted into the heavens from sheer ecstasy. He continued caressing me, his fingers wet from me, gyrating around my clit. His stroking of me kept going and going, ever so gently, like bubbles of pure rapture. I couldn't hang on, I needed him. 'Baby… *please…* I want you…'

He teased me with his fingers for a little longer, then murmured, 'Turn around baby, I wanna have you from behind.'

I would have done anything he asked at that point. I rolled over and arched my back.

'Oh yeah darlin', show me your gorgeous ass… god do I want you…' He entered me and I gasped with euphoria. He ground into me, shifting from tenderly to intensely, deeply. His movements gave me a feeling of leaving this world for moments and then returning to the delicious realisation of what he was doing to me.

Oh god, what *was* he doing to me? I had to plead with myself… with the universe… *something…* to not explode. We managed to continue for a sassy length of time and at a point, the energy became more urgent, our need more immediate.

'Come with me, darlin',' his voice pleaded from somewhere deep in his throat. 'Come with me, darlin'.'

My body obeyed him and together we soared, crying out for each other in the strongest tremor of elation. I felt his last thrust

– so deep, so complete, so sating. He flung his arm around me and I clutched onto it with all my remaining strength. Time stopped and so did our breaths – until we crumpled onto each other, panting in unison.

He held me firmly and turned to look deeply into my face. 'That was amazing baby, you are amazing.'

I watched his soulful eyes, my heart over-filled with love. 'My perfect lover,' I whispered.

'What was I saying before this…?' his face sparkled with warmth, 'that I love you? Baby you own me.' He reached for my mouth with his and we merged again through our unrelenting passion.

I woke in the middle of the night to an empty space beside me. My eyes stretched themselves open and surveyed the room. A small lamp on the writing table emitted a soft glow over the velvet furnishings. David sat there, naked, slumped over a piece of paper on the desk. The back end of a pen rested on his lip, his face deep in concentration with his hair hanging over it in a perfect frame.

I scrambled my way off the big bed, grabbed his robe and walked over to him. 'Aren't you cold, baby?' I asked as I placed it over his shoulders.

He turned around and gave me an adoring smile. 'Thanks, Beautiful.' He pulled me onto his lap and gave me the full attention of his sunset eyes. 'You wanna know something?'

'What, gorgeous?'

'I'm crazy in love with you.' He wrapped me in his arms and held me snugly.

'Oh baby, you are so yummy… I am so in love with you too.'

We kissed each other indulgently through our smiles.

I didn't want it to ever stop. I was truly becoming addicted to him. Eventually I asked, 'What are you doing here in the middle of the night?'

'Believe me baby, it was really hard to leave you there in bed, really hard. But words kept going round and round in my head for the press release. I had to come and write them down. I hope I didn't disturb you.' His voice cooed so softly and lusciously I was mesmerised watching him speak.

'You could never disturb me.'

A look of half cheekiness, half satisfaction swept over his face.

'What do you have so far?'

'Okay.' He cleared his throat and explained this was for Ruth to say. 'Mr Cassidy... no... *David* has advised me that he is delighted... delighted...? Maybe there's a better word, baby? Anyway – delighted to announce his engagement to Miss Lisa Magnusson. The two have been seeing each other for a few years–'

'Ahem.'

'Well it is... *almost*... anyway... for a few years, and are currently taking a long-overdue vacation together. Mr Cassidy and Miss Magnusson will give a press conference when they return to America in approximately one month's time. What do you think, baby?'

'That's it?'

He seemed deflated. 'Well... yeah... um, what else should we add?'

'I'm sorry honey, I didn't mean to criticise...'

'No, no, that's okay.' He rubbed my back. 'Tell me what you think.'

'Well I don't know exactly what else to add but I wondered

whether it isn't a little short? Still, I don't know about these things really.'

He looked troubled.

'No baby, forget what I'm saying. I think it is straight to the point. Maybe though, if you didn't want to sound so formal by saying "delighted", you could say something like "extremely happy"?'

'See? That's why I'm marrying you. Not only are you beautiful, but smart too.' He kissed me again. 'Oh and maybe I should add something like "Miss Magnusson accompanied him on his final tour recently"–'

'Come on, enough… come to bed.'

'Okay honey, you got it.'

We snuggled into each other once again, told each other we loved each other and fell blissfully asleep in one big heart-warming embrace.

Chapter 21

David phoned Ruth to dictate the press release but asked her to hold off until we were in Australia and gave the clearance to send it out.

We had our last glimpses of beautiful, ornate Paris in the grey light before dawn. I mouthed *"Au revoir"* to my beloved Tour Eiffel as we whizzed past in our car, and nestled into David's arm around me.

We had a seven hour stop in Singapore which we idled away in the first class lounge. Somehow David arranged it so we could have a shower together. Apparently this was a huge no-no. But he managed it. The design of the shower was an experience in itself. It was certainly big enough for both of us and caressing sprays of water hit us from all directions. They were cosy hot. David held me as we soaked up this luxurious feeling. 'I've missed you, darlin',' he murmured against me. 'I've missed the touch of your skin on mine.' I reached up to him for our mouths to meet.

We mooched away the rest of our time at Changi Airport over bubbles, making plans for our nuptials. David said his people had conducted a little research and apparently a few private islands were available for hire off the coast of north Queensland. He thought that might be the perfect setting for a romantic *and* secure wedding. It made my heart flip to fully think about it.

The time whizzed as we immersed in discussions and each other. We heard our flight called and gathered our gear to go to the gate. The authorities in Australia had been informed of our arrival ahead of time so they could take the necessary measures to steer us through customs privately and securely. David already put his hair up under a hat, wore dark glasses and walked snugly next to me to avoid any chances of being recognised.

We boarded and relaxed into our generous first class seating. Next stop – home. I could hardly believe I was going home after all this time, *and* bringing David with me. What a journey it had truly been.

Initially we flew into Sydney International to go through immigration procedures – both of us feeling quite anxious over whether we'd make it through without the public recognising him. It had been bedlam here on his tour. Though having the security guys gave us a little comfort, and the airport officials moved us through quickly so we weren't out amongst it all for too long. But we had more than a few jitters. The disguise and hanging closely onto each other seemed to work well, luckily.

I purposely didn't tell my family and friends exactly when we'd arrive in Adelaide as we thoroughly wanted to avoid any attention. David thought we should take a low key hotel which could accommodate the security entourage as well, so I'd booked The Haven at Glenelg in my name. I signed in at the desk while David hung back.

As we entered our nice, quaint room I didn't feel like unpacking. I didn't even feel like visiting my parents. For some reason I worried about my two worlds meeting, as if they would magically disappear into thin air, cancelling each other out somehow. But I knew we had to go. All too soon our car, followed by two cars of security, rocked up at the house my father had built.

My parents were expecting us. The door opened and my mother stood there. Without warning a surge of emotion gushed from me. I fell into her arms blubbering like a little girl. I had experienced so, so much in the time I'd been away and seeing my mother completely flushed it all out. My tears arose from deep within, blended with joy. They didn't really belong to any particular emotion, or thought. They were just very rich and wet.

David stood back a little with affection on his face, watching Mum and me embracing. I snapped back to this vital occasion and stumbled over a few words acknowledging him to her. He told her warmly how happy he was to see her again. I hoped Dad hadn't heard.

At the entrance to the lounge I saw him. The man that was my father. I approached him apprehensively. David hung in the background next to Mum. In an instant he grabbed me and hugged me so tightly, I thought I would break. He wasn't one for words, my father. In fact he said nothing. He didn't have to, his hug and tears said it all – *I've missed you, I was worried about you, I'm glad you're home safe, you've grown up too quickly, you'll always be my little girl; you are so precious to me.*

His tears drew more of mine but I untied myself from his grip. I knew we were at the pinnacle of angst for this meeting. I turned to David to beckon him forward. 'Dad, this is David,' I almost whispered. I stood still as stone.

David smiled charmingly and offered his hand. 'I'm so very happy to meet you, Mr Magnusson.' He leaned forward.

My father hesitated before he shook hands, casting a critical eye over him with a look on his face indicating caution –

sprinkled with a smidgeon of approval, I'm sure.

They shook hands. 'Yes, yes, nice to meet you too.'

I sensed my mother recommencing breathing again, along with me.

'Please sit down,' my mother offered, 'let me get some coffee.' She almost applauded as she waltzed off into the kitchen. I sat next to David on the sofa. My father gave a certain glance as I took David's hand.

'How was the flight? Who did you fly with?' Dad began the small talk.

He and David bantered away fairly smoothly. Dad asked all kinds of strange things about America and raved on as usual, telling him which parts he had visited and liked. David remained ultra-polite and acknowledged everything my father bored him with.

I waited until Mum came back to the room with her Pyrex pot of percolated coffee, before commanding her to sit down and offering to fetch the rest of the goodies from the kitchen. She protested, telling me I didn't know what to bring out but I told her I'd be fine and work it out.

'Don't forget the jug of cream,' she called to me as I reached the kitchen.

Dear Mum. She would always say a coffee table is not complete without a small jug of cream. It had to be a little crystal jug of course. She had gone to the trouble of baking a traditional Swedish sweetbread, *Lussekatter*. Ooh, *yum*. The kitchen oozed the sweet spiciness of saffron. She had also made Dad's favourite – honey cake. I brought them both onto the coffee table to hums of appreciation from David.

'Mrs Magnusson, you really didn't have to go to so much trouble.'

'Oh yes I did,' Mum insisted, 'and please call me *Emma*.'

David leaned in closer to her and said quietly, 'But I'm so glad you did, Emma.' He winked at her and they both chuckled together. It was lovely to see.

'Well?' Mum stared at me expectantly.

I had a moment of confusion. 'Yes of course Mum, the cream jug. On my way…' I fetched the dainty little jug, along with Mum's wide rimmed cups smothered with roses that sat precisely on their matching saucers, all ornately trimmed with gold.

'Here, let me help you,' David offered, giving me a flash of the private connection between us that made me tingle.

'Will you two stop already,' Mum interrupted and I felt instantly guilty for having a private moment with David. 'Let *me* do it.' I then realised she had meant for us to stop helping. I giggled. 'What's so funny?'

'Nothing, Mum. Nothing at all. Thank you for doing all this for us.'

We all sat there as easy as apple pie, chatting about everything yet nothing in particular. I caught a glance from David I recognised as a sign he'd like some time with my father.

'Hey Mum, let me help you with that thing in the kitchen.'

'What thing?' She looked puzzled.

'You know – that *thing*.' I tried to convey to her I needed to drag her away.

David pursed his lips, trying hard not to smirk. I think Mum got it. She followed me in any case.

In the kitchen we just about pushed our ears through the wall, trying to decipher the conversation between them. They made some more small talk, out of nerves I suppose. I found it incredible to think of David being nervous in there with my dad. Hundreds of thousands in a stadium – not a problem, but my dad – a definite problem.

As if night had fallen in a stroke, all fell silent. David eventually spoke but he was speaking so quietly, we couldn't make out what he was saying.

We heard a cough to clear his throat and out came the words, 'May I ask for your permission for Lisa's hand in marriage?'

Mum's eyes grew huge. They had to be mirroring mine. We stared at each other through either sheer thrill or terror, I had no idea which. We waited for a response, just about jiggling up and down through the tension.

Nothing from my father.

'I promise I will care for her and protect her for the rest of my life...' we heard David's soft voice again, 'I will take very good care of her.'

Oh *come on*, Dad. This was *killing* us. I could only imagine how David felt.

Eventually he spoke. He mumbled really. I don't think he could quite bring himself to say "yes" but he did mutter something in the affirmative.

Clearly David wasn't going to let the opportunity pass. We heard him get up from his seat, presumably to shake my dad's hand. 'Thank you, Mr Magnusson. I can't tell you how happy you have made me. I give you my word that Lisa will be more than well cared for.'

Mum and I took that as our cue to go in.

'Congratulations!' My mother beamed while swanning over to David.

'Thank you, Dad.' I hugged him lovingly.

I slinked over to David, squeezed him and whispered, 'Well done, you.'

'Phew,' he whispered back close to my ear, 'I've broken out in a sweat.'

'We need some Champagne,' Mum announced. 'Go and get some, Dad.'

'No, it's really not necessary,' I protested.

'Nonsense, go bring some. How often does our daughter become engaged?'

Dad toddled off to where he kept his stocks of wine, if you could call it that, in the shed fridge and I dreaded what he'd return with. As I suspected, he reappeared with a bottle of Starwine. *Oh god, no.* I looked at David apologetically. He patted my hand. Dad popped the plastic cork and all too soon, one of the cheapest sparkling wines in the world poured into my parents' delicate crystal coupes.

Mum proposed the toast simply, 'To Lisa and David.'

'Yes,' Dad contributed, 'all the best.'

I gazed at David in this sweet, sour moment as we sipped the bubbles that ran up the stems of our shimmering glasses. David remained immensely well-mannered in not making a face over this horrid sweet liquid. I think I behaved a lot more transparently, although I didn't actually say anything. I thought they had graciously accepted David, so I should just keep quiet.

David spoke of our wedding plans and that most likely we'd rent a private island with a resort off the coast of Queensland. 'Naturally we'll make all the arrangements for you both to be there.'

Dad enquired when that would be and David thought in around a month. 'We'll submit the paperwork as soon as possible.'

Dad raised his eyebrows, no doubt to the speediness of it all. 'And then?'

'Well,' David paused to look at me and take my hand, 'we go back to LA.'

'Oh dear,' Dad sighed, 'when are we going to see you then?' he asked partly of fate, then observing me. 'Hmm... yes, we won't see you after that. That's going to be a question, that is.'

David tried to reassure him, 'Please don't worry – we will come back and visit. And we can arrange flights for you to visit us at our home.'

Our home. What a concept. A kind of fairy tale aspect to all this still swirled in my head. I looked over at my Prince Charming and he certainly was that, sitting discussing things with my father... *my* father for goodness' sake.

Mum lightened the ambience by saying Brandi had been frantically ringing every day to see whether I was back yet. I smiled, just imagining our next conversation together. Mum said she and the "girls" had wanted to hold a welcome back party for me.

Dad asked me if I wanted to unpack.

Oh dear. 'Umm... I'm staying with David.' My eyes lowered.

Dad raised his eyebrows – again. But I felt he put that on a little. Right on cue the phone rang, thankfully. Mum jumped up to answer. It was Brandi. I cheerfully trotted off to take the call, although a trickle of uneasiness nudged me in leaving David with my parents. I promised myself I'd be quick.

After giggling madly between sentences with Brandi, I returned, hopefully with a resolution to appease some of Dad's angst. I told them about the girls' party they'd planned, 'They want to hold it here. So I thought I'd stay at home... um... I mean here, that night for the last time?' I looked to David.

'Of course, sweetheart. That's lovely of them to do that. Of course you should stay here that night.'

A warm glow wrapped around me as if to signal that all the fragments of my life were connecting into a precious work of art.

It was settled. We would finalise the details over the next few days.

Arriving back in our hotel room, David took a few steps and plonked straight onto the edge of the bed. He looked weary. He yanked off the tie he'd gone to the trouble of wearing for the occasion. Although he had insisted, it now looked like a noose he was happily rid of. I stood behind him and massaged his shoulders, his lush hair danced on my hands.

'Mmmmh, that feels so good baby… thank you, sweetie.'

'So you haven't changed your mind after meeting the future father-in-law?'

'Not a chance,' he asserted with his eyes closed, his head to one side as if he could hardly hold it up.

My fingers kneaded deep into his muscles to release tension. He was as floppy as a rag doll, allowing my hands to manipulate his body. Eventually he put his hands on top of mine and stroked them. With his eyes still shut he pulled me onto him and we rolled together like a carpet unravelling on the bed.

'Oh, baby,' he sighed and I think that's when we both fell asleep.

Chapter 22

Those five weeks or so in Aussieland flew as fast as a whirly-whirly across the Nullarbor. We put in our Notice of Intended Marriage immediately at the Births, Deaths and Marriages office, or "Hatch, Match and Dispatch" as it was commonly known.

Back in the seclusion of our car, David paused a moment to acknowledge this step. He looked at me in the intense way he does at times – that makes the world stand still, that commands attention for some deep longing in his soul. He spoke in soft words powerful enough to penetrate me, 'I can't wait for you to be mine,' and kissed me tenderly. I cried.

He made arrangements for Sam to fly to Australia as his best man, and also for Henry. From his family he only invited his mother, organising everything including the best seats on the plane for her. I patted my nerves over meeting her, being the most important person in his life, although he assured me she would love me. *Sigh.* He also phoned Ruth to give her the go-ahead with our press release.

Next on the agenda was my girls' night. I told David my concerns over my girlfriends attending the wedding, as they were his fans. He told me not to worry, that he knew how to handle them. I was worried.

'Darlin', I think we should just all get together sometime

before the wedding… So they can get to know me a little as a person.'

'But where on earth could we have this little gathering?'

'Baby, surely there's gotta be a low key place somewhere… where people won't notice, or care?'

My mind was blank.

Then it hit me – *Where does one go where people are too icy to care who's around? The Swedish Club of course.* David laughed when I told him.

I hated leaving him to go to my parents' house for my party. We enjoyed a lingering kiss in the car park that somehow still didn't seem long enough. He waved me goodbye as the car ascended to street level. I set off early to begin the task of sorting and packing up my room but knew it would take much longer than just one day. I remembered I needed to go to my old school at some stage also to finalise everything there. *And* I had to find a dress somewhere in which to be married. So much to do and on top of it all I developed bride butterflies. Not that I worried about getting married – just for everything to go smoothly.

Funny that on the night when David asked my father for my hand, I hadn't even thought to pop into my old room. When I did, I nearly went into shock. There over my bed, a gigantic replica of David's face hit me so hard it took my breath away. I stared at it as if in a trance. His hair glistened in the sunlight and his exquisite eyes pierced into me. The expression on his face looked sincere, yet perhaps a little tentative – but as if he would smile if I moved closer.

His unmistakable handwriting jumped out from the bottom right hand corner. It read, "Hope all your wishes come true! David".

I fell to my knees. I began crying and laughing at the same time. *Who was the girl who had lived here? Where is she now? How could this possibly have happened in my life?* The man I would share my life and dreams with, had been towering over my bed all this time.

Looking at his face there now, I recognised I had absolutely *no* idea who he really was back then. I had totally made him up in my head. I'd thought he was the perfect man – only I had no idea what that truly meant. He *is* the perfect man but he is so much more than I could have ever possibly imagined. "Hope all your wishes come true!" *Oh David, if I'd only known… oh god, what a beautiful soul you are… thank you…* I released the tears that begged to not stay within me any longer.

When the last drop of sentiment had fallen from my eyes, I stood up. The pretty pink mirror I'd sent away for through Dolly Magazine rested on my bedside table – I caught a glimpse of myself. I had grown up.

Again I sat in my parents' lounge, this time waiting for my friends to rock up. It was Dad's choir night so this was definitely going to be a "girls only" event. Before long, the tiny lounge spilled over with giggles from my *alltför* excitable girlfriends; Brandi, Greta and Adriana. Even though I had talked to Brandi on the phone a few times since being back, I wanted to wait til this evening to tell them all my big news. But I also adopted a little anxiety, as seeing Brandi made me think of Judd and I hoped with all my being I would not have to see him during my visit or that he wouldn't cause any trouble. I pulled her aside with my concerns. Luckily she said he had taken off to try and dig for gold or opals, or something, and he'd be away for about six months at least. That put me at ease.

My closest group of friends gathered around and wanted

to know everything about David of course, and the tour, and everything we'd been up to. They fired questions at me like shots at a duck in sideshow alley.

'Geez girls – *calm down*... Okay, okay, I'll answer everything... well *mostly* everything.' Screams and giggles erupted. 'But first I have something to tell you.'

'Oh shit, now what've you done?' Brandi directed every freckle on her face onto me.

'Weeell,' I smirked cheekily, 'David and I... are engaged.' I extended my left hand for them to see my beautiful ring.

I swear the next sound was as loud as Wembley Stadium. They just about screamed the roof off. We hardly noticed Mum parading into the room with a gigantic *Smörgåstårta* – Swedish sandwich cake.

'I see you have told them the news then,' she stated dryly.

'You knew?' Brandi puffed up.

Mum glanced back at her as if she obviously knew everything.

'You sly fox.'

'Now don't be cheeky and have some *Smörgåstårta*.'

'Thank you, Mrs Magnusson,' they chanted in unison.

'And have fun.' Mum winked at me as she left the room.

I felt a connection with her at that moment, as cosy and warm as the pyjamas you wore as a child. But I knew she must have been also thinking this would be the last girls' party she'd be supervising, and that would make her sad. Before my melancholic thoughts engulfed me completely, my friends grabbed me and squeezed me, making squealing sounds over my gorgeous engagement ring. I have to say the attention was lovely and I knew they genuinely cared, but I began to feel as if I didn't belong in their world anymore and started to miss

David like crazy. *Then again, do I really belong in his high flying world either?*

'Ahem,' Brandi caught my attention, 'so we all got together to get you a little something. And now that you've given us your news, it's even more appropriate.' She grinned fully and presented me with a gift, wrapped up in a display of guitars, treble clefs and staves of music.

I thanked her and carefully opened it. Inside was a funky, long loose black T-shirt. It had "The One" printed on it, in bold white. Now it was my turn to shriek. I loved it and I loved their intended meaning of it.

'Thank you! This is *so* lovely. I love you all for doing this.' And I began to cry. They surrounded me in one big embrace. The crying became contagious. I seemed to be doing so much of it lately.

'You're going to be *Mrs David Cassidy*,' shrieked Greta. That set everyone off again – okay, including me.

'And you're all invited to the wedding,' I announced, to much elation. 'Just do try and behave.'

'How on earth do you control yourself around him?' queried Adriana.

I gave that question some thought, then said, 'I *don't.*'

We all screeched with laughter. It was so neat to feel like a teenager again. We ate the spectacular *Smörgåstårta* and Mum even let us drink a little Starwine. I told them all about the tour, the celebrities I'd met, how we'd stayed on Liz Taylor's yacht on the Thames, how lovely Sam was, the shopping spree on Rodeo Drive, how David had led me out on stage, our romantic camping trip, Paris, the proposal, simply *everything*. There was so much to tell and they hung on my words perched at the edge of their seats, and made "ooh" and "ah" sounds in between. I really felt as if I was the celebrity instead.

Brandi apologised for interrupting but asked if she could watch the weather as she had a volleyball game on the next day. While she focused on the TV, Greta and Adriana continued to interrogate me with every fine detail from my time with David. Suddenly Brandi screamed, '*Shut up* everyone. *Aaaaaargh.* Look at this!'

We all turned our heads toward the television and the monitor gleamed with the photo snapped of David and me outside the restaurant. The news was on and it appeared the press release had reached far and wide. The screen changed, showing the presenter.

'*Turn it up,*' yelled Greta.

'Miss Magnusson accompanied Mr Cassidy on his final tour throughout the United Kingdom and United States of America. The couple are currently on holiday in an unknown location but expected to return home in a few weeks' time. In other news today–'

'Oh my god – they were talking about *you*. On the *news*,' shrieked Brandi.

I matter-of-factly explained the press release David had phoned over to Ruth announcing our engagement, but inside I was thrilled to bits.

'The whole world knows you're engaged now,' announced Greta.

I guess she's right.

Chapter 23

A love there is no cure for

The next day I couldn't wait to get back to the hotel to see him. Only one night and yet I had missed him incredibly. As I opened the door to our little room, he was just coming out from the shower. A white hotel towel snuggled around his hips, his bronze skin glistening with droplets of water. He looked irresistible.

'Hi, Beautiful,' he greeted me happily.

'Oh hello, *handsome.*' I ran to hug and kiss him.

'I'm still wet you know,' he warned me with a wicked grin.

'I don't care. I missed you *so much.*' I grabbed him and he returned my eagerness by wrapping his arms around me ever so securely.

He would sometimes tell me how much he loved it when my adoration for him showed, and it definitely gave me the highest thrill to know how smitten he was with me. I think it took me a significantly long time to fully realise exactly how much I meant to him but when I did, the feeling was unreal.

'Let me look at your beautiful face… I missed you too.' His lips played with mine in small teases and then his mouth captured mine fully. I dissolved into his arms.

'You know what I did last night? I watched TV.' I must

have looked perplexed as he added, 'It was *so* good to *just* watch TV and do nothing. It's been so long, I can't remember the last time I had time like that to myself.' He bent his head down and peeked up at me a little coyly. 'I did miss my playmate though.'

'*Playmate?* Is that all I am to you?'

He gave me another delicious kiss, pierced his gaze directly into my eyes and said, 'You know what you are? You're my best friend, my playmate, my lover, my fiancée, soon to be wife and the mother of my children – *you* are the owner of my heart.'

My eyes completely filled with tears hearing that. It was some statement. I felt so much love for him my heart could have burst through being over-filled. I put my hands on his cheeks and held his beautiful face, the tears escaped from my eyes. He went to comfort me and I stopped him. I spoke and sobbed at the same time, 'I can't believe what a beautiful human being you are. And how very lucky I am to have you. I never knew it was possible to love this much. I will love you forever, my darling Sunset Eyes.'

His eyes became watery also. 'I know that I'll love you for at least that long, if not longer.'

He enfolded me in his arms once more and we made love in a way that found us crying together from the high of connecting through genuine love. It was the most incredible thing I have ever experienced and will never forget. It brought us even closer, if that was at all possible.

Chapter 24

The leaves of life are falling down around you girl

I needed to finalise paperwork at my high school for leaving, and to clear out my locker. David instructed a security guy to accompany me. I thought that might be a little weird but he insisted. When we arrived, the security guard was the least of what was weird. Everyone acted so differently, strangely towards me. Only a few said "hi" in a normal way. Some kids I'd shared lessons with appeared skittish and awkward talking to me, some just kept right away and pointed and stared. Others were rude, even mean. As I cleared out my locker, one girl strutted up and spat at my feet. *What the hell have I ever done to her?* But within me I knew this had to do with who I was about to marry. I started to appreciate the guy being with me. Goodness knows what they would have done if he hadn't been there.

I walked past my old music room and heard a class practising. Part of me longed to be in there with them, even if Miss Nord did have a spaz attack at times. I was going to miss her outbursts even. I knew I had to leave my hopes of continuing with my music studies at the conservatorium behind me.

Music had been a part of my life since I could remember. It was as much a part of me as breathing. *And now I haven't picked up a guitar or cello, or tinkled on the piano for… how long? Well, since I've been hanging around in David's world.* There was a hunger in me for music that hoped somehow I could continue playing, but I definitely didn't want to do that with David. No way would I be another Linda McCartney. Perhaps I did need to leave it in the past after all. I was about to become David's wife and something told me there would be quite a bit in that role to keep me busy.

I turned around to look at that magical place, the transportable building – our music room, one last time. This had been my sanctuary to escape to from other tedious lessons. I sighed and in my head wished it, and my fellow music students, "farewell".

Back in our little hotel room, I relayed to David how strange the visit had been and how people had treated me. He kept apologising and I kept telling him it wasn't his fault. I suppose neither of us could have guessed how some people may react to our engagement. And we had no idea how the rest of the world would either.

I arranged for us to meet my girlfriends at the Swedish Club. Interestingly, this coincided with ABBA landing in Sydney for the commencement of their Australian tour. The crowds waiting for them at the airport were a few thousand strong, with one young girl already trampled as they touched down. Luckily she was okay. The tabloids printed simply, "They're Here!" as ABBA mania had grown so huge no further explanation was needed.

As we entered the club, David's security in tow, the television screen showed the hysteria under commentary that held them up as "the biggest thing ever". David watched through his dark shades.

'Do you miss all that?' I whispered to him.

'They can have it,' he responded – a little too eagerly, I thought.

We sat in a dark corner of the club and I really didn't think David needed to bother with the shades. My people weren't known for being overly gushy, no matter who you were. Frankly, it was even a little surprising for them to have the ABBA coverage on at all.

Pretty soon my friends appeared at the door so I jumped up to sign them in. 'Now please hold it together, will you? He's just a guy after all.'

'Yeah, just about the hottest one in the world,' retorted Brandi.

'Sssh!' Greta told her off, 'that's not *helping*.'

'*Girls*,' I warned, like a ventriloquist through my teeth as we reached the table. I made the introductions. David stood up to greet them and smiled charmingly of course. He offered to get drinks but I butted in, thinking it may work better for him to have a little time alone with them.

When I returned, I found only him doing the talking. I think they were too afraid to utter a word. I had never seen Brandi so quiet in my whole life. David talked about Australia and what he loved about it, and about meeting my "lovely" parents. I'm sure they would have preferred for him to rap about touring and the rock world. Although I hoped his subjects and manner might relax them a little. They all made agreeable noises on how lovely my parents were. In fact they nodded and agreed with everything he said like little marionettes.

As I sat back down next to him, he gave me a peck on my cheek. One of my friends gasped. I felt my cheeks warming. David continued speaking, 'And of course the best thing about this country was meeting your gorgeous friend here.' He put his arm around me and gave me a sensual glance. I hoped to god no one would make a squeak. 'So you're all coming to our wedding, yes?'

They nodded in unison.

I felt the need to jump in a little and help. 'I thought I'd be a little radical and not have bridesmaids or anything but just a "best woman"... if you would do me the honour, Brandi?'

Brandi let out a sound like puppy being released from its cage and rushed over and squeezed me.

Adriana piped up, 'How rude of us, we should be *congratulating you.*'

That finally brought them around into a form of normality and everyone hugged everyone, with words of acknowledgement and thanks.

David laughed. 'Oh and I gotta say – I *loved* that T-shirt you guys bought Lisa.'

They giggled and looked a little embarrassed. But the conversation slowly became easier and we spent a little longer together, discussing mainly the wedding.

David turned to me with a twinkle in his eye and said in his breathy voice, 'Darlin' I'm a little beat, what say we turn in early tonight?'

Everyone instantly fell silent, listening to every syllable he spoke and waiting for more. I knew he was playing with them.

So I played along too and raised an eyebrow saucily. 'You read my mind, baby.' And gave him a little sensual kiss on the lips.

'Fuck me!' Brandi stared at us.

'Excuse me?' said David.

Brandi turned fully crimson realising what she had said. 'No... I didn't mean you... I meant me... oh fuck.'

David smirked. 'Well it's a very nice offer but I'm engaged to your best friend here so I don't think I can take you up on that.'

Brandi nose-dived onto her arms on the table as if that might make her somehow invisible. Everyone else laughed wildly.

David put his hand on her back. 'I'm sorry Brandi, I'm just teasing you. Please don't feel bad. I do swear occasionally myself.' He could hardly stop laughing as he patted her back.

Brandi eventually surfaced and mustered some composure. 'Blimey David, you'd be better off saying "stirring you", instead of "teasing you". Geez, how much can a koala bear?'

David got it and laughed even harder. 'Ah, okay Brandi – I was just *stirring* you. Can you forgive me?'

'I'll think about it.'

'Fair enough.' They chuckled together. It was neat to watch them gel.

Brandi found her glitter-wings in the part of "best woman". She raced around town with me looking at dresses and helped search the Yellow Pages for a celebrant. When I simply didn't have the time to go somewhere or do something, she'd go for me.

A few security guys were never far. I still had difficulty in getting used to this but began to acknowledge I needed them too. At least most places we went to were not like my school where they knew me. I could still manage anonymity as not many in the world knew where the future Mrs Cassidy currently hung out. Brandi even helped with buying our wedding rings as David and I really didn't want to chance that. She and I acted as David's eyes and reported back each time on what we saw and liked. Then David and I made the decision together. I sometimes wondered whether the jewellery store staff thought Brandi and I were lezzies.

A wave of dread crept closer and closer to me, as so much needed to be done in so little time. Apart from finding the rings, the right dress, shoes, earrings, accessories et cetera, I also needed to find time to sort through my stuff at my parents' house. Plus fill in official documents and general last minute things to take care of. *Where is the time going?*

The dress gave me a big brain-ache. *I don't want a traditional bride's dress but what else can I have?* Eventually, through many discussions with Brandi, I became enthusiastic over searching for a feminine, romantic, more or less gypsy-style dress. Something maybe Stevie Nicks would wear. We scoured through shop after shop but nothing at all resembled my vision. Brandi reminded me of a little shop in town, downstairs in one of the arcades – Fata Morgana. *Yes.* That sounded promising. They were right into that kind of style.

My eyes widened as soon as I descended the stairs – not due to the dim lighting, but through finding the first shop with racks of dresses in the design I had pictured. This little boutique was funky; like a romantic dungeon. I didn't think I'd be *alltför* radical and go for a black or dark colour – a soft pastel would be just the thing. I found about seven to try on and made my way to the change rooms while Brandi, and the guys, waited.

I absolutely loved the first one I tried. Made from a gorgeous ivory chiffony material with whitish feminine swirls, it had been created into a midi length dress that flowed in numerous layers. Each layer fell softly on an angle creating a flouncy, jagged hemline. The sleeves were apparently called "Camelot Sleeves". Brandi called them "candle catchers". I needn't have bothered trying on all the others, this one really was perfect.

When I floated out of the dressing room with it on, Brandi gasped, 'It's fucking *outta sight*. David's gunna *love* you in that. You look like you wunna be unwrapped.'

'Gee, and here was I thinking it was romantic.'

We both cackled.

I was determined to pay for this on my own, without David's card. It just didn't seem right to have him pay for the dress. I looked at the price tag – *$220*. That was more than either of my parents' weekly wages. I had a little in the bank but nowhere near that much. I didn't know what to do; this was exactly the right dress. I *had* to marry David in this. Then it dawned on me – I would sell my cello and guitar.

Chapter 25

Do dreams come true, well if they do, I'll have you
Not just for a night, but for my whole life through

Sam, Henry, David's mum, and an assistant he organised from Ruth's office, were due to arrive on the same flight at 14.35, at Brisbane Airport. And our troupe from Adelaide – my parents, the girlfriends, David and me, and not forgetting the security guys, would meet them. Our plane was scheduled to reach Brisbane half an hour earlier, so we could easily link up and fly to Cairns, where a private plane waited to take us to our luxury island booked out exclusively for the wedding.

My dad lapped this up completely. I did hope he wouldn't embarrass me by liberating any souvenirs from the plane. I hoped the girls would behave too. My thoughts shifted onto our American guests. *I can't wait to see Sam and Henry again but what will David's mother think of me? What will she think of my parents?* I prayed Dad wouldn't flirt with her. As we taxied on the runway, these plus a million other thoughts and fears stampeded through my head.

'Where are you, Beautiful?' David's voice purred beside me.

'Huh?'

'You seem a million miles away,' he said softly against my

cheek. 'Come here, baby.' And he kissed me as we thrust into the skies.

My girlfriend gang chatted away at a thousand words per minute during the flight and were still going when we landed. Mum and Dad just looked through absolutely everything they could get their hands on. I am sure the first class section of Ansett had never seen such a menagerie.

David had arranged for our guests to be brought into the lounge in Brisbane when their plane landed. I was as jittery as a jumping bean. I could not relax at all. Brandi yapped away in one of my ears while Dad showed off his knowledge on air traffic controlling.

David had darted off to the loo, I thought. But a figure behind dark shades with hair tucked under his hat, began making his way towards me with an ice bucket of Dom and a bunch of glasses. I rushed over to him. '*Darling*. Why are you carrying all that for goodness' sake?' I grabbed several glasses from him and placed them on the table.

'Eh, I need the exercise,' he grinned solely at me, 'the guys are bringing the rest.'

I looked and sure enough, the security guys paced in single file; two bringing an ice bucket holding a bottle of Dom each, and the rest carrying the glasses. I could almost hear the incidental music from an episode of The Partridge Family as they marched.

David popped the first bottle, poured glasses for everyone, swept to my side and took my hand with his free one. He gazed at me adoringly, raised his glass and said, 'To my beautiful bride to be. We're on our way darlin', I love you,' and kissed me tenderly on the lips.

Everyone applauded and shouted, 'Cheers!'

I wanted to say something profound to him in return, something poetic. But before I could think of anything, I caught sight of Sam entering the lounge in the far corner. I practically shouted, 'Look darling, *Sam's* here. Sam's here!'

A half pout, half smirk formed on David's lips. He paused for a moment and then said, 'I only hope you're gonna be half as excited tomorrow when you see *me* waiting for you at the altar.'

Everyone laughed.

And there they stood before us – Sam, Henry, David's mum and the assistant, Julie. David immediately rushed over to his mum, gave her a kiss and put his arm around her, leading her to me. I tried to smile warmly without the help of oxygen.

'Mom, this is my Lisa,' he said in an almost hushed tone, his eyes sparkling.

'I'm so very happy to meet you,' she greeted me in her own soft voice. She had the same charming manner as David and I could see him in her eyes. She was truly beautiful.

'Oh Mrs Cassidy... sorry – *Ward...* I'm very happy to meet you too,' I fumbled. I had to stop myself from curtseying.

She smiled graciously at my awkwardness. 'Please, call me Evelyn.'

I offered my hand to shake hers but she hugged me. She *hugged* me. I was ecstatic.

David took charge and introduced everyone to everyone, and I heartily squeezed Henry and Sam. Sam winked at me. 'See? I told you it would all turn out okay.'

As we arrived in Cairns, they informed us our chartered plane would take us to a place called Mission Beach, from where we'd be transported by helicopter to the island. David became annoyed that he hadn't been informed of this and threw a few angry words at the pilot. I think he must have been tense before the wedding. I wrapped my arms around him and told him quietly it didn't matter if we had to change to a chopper; the main thing was we were all together and this was going to be the best thing ever. I gave him a few baby kisses around his neck and ear.

He began to smile. 'I'm sorry, baby, I guess I just want everything to go smoothly.'

'It will honey, I promise.'

He brought his lips to mine. 'Mmh, that makes everything better.'

'Come on, there's an island somewhere out there waiting for us.'

David and I boarded the first chopper flight to the island, along with my parents, Evelyn and two security guys. Due to the small number of seats, the others in our party had to wait for the second run, followed lastly by the remainder of security. Approaching the island, it stood out like a heart-shaped green jewel that had been dropped into iridescent aqua water. David squeezed my hand. Our day was really close now.

Upon arrival the shiny-cheeked staff presented us with delicate jasmine bouquets and demitasses of aromatic tea. They showed us into a luxurious outside lounge area, where we sank into gigantic futon type cushions on rattan lounges while waiting for the others.

The whole island was exclusively ours, with seven villas to accommodate us. David and I were allocated the Presidential Villa, separate from the rest on the other side of the island. It promised the most magnificent ocean view. Once everyone had arrived, the butlers informed us they'd drive us to our respective villas in little buggies. David and I jumped into the one headed for our villa.

The driver for our buggy walked over, examined some paperwork and enquired, 'Mr Cassidy?'

'Yes?'

'I am sorry, you are not going to this villa. Please come to another car with me.'

'Excuse me? There is obviously a mistake in your paperwork. My fiancée and I have the Presidential Villa.'

'Apologies again Mr Cassidy but Miss Magnusson will be taken to the Presidential Villa. You are in another.

'*What?*' David just about screamed at him. 'There has to be some mistake. Let me talk to whoever is in charge.'

Sam swaggered casually over to us. 'Um… actually… he is correct.'

'What the f… hell are you talking about, man?' David looked as if he would burst a vein.

'Best man duties, my friend. There have been a few little changes.' He peered over to where the others waited. 'Bridal party – Brandi, Greta, Adriana – over here!' The girls scurried over. 'You're not in the Private Beach Villa tonight. You'll be staying in the Presidential Villa.' They jumped up and down in excitement. 'David, you will be in the Private Beach Villa – please make your way to buggy number… three.'

David must have realised what was going on and why, but he didn't look any happier. 'I never asked you to do *this*.'

'I *know*. Lucky I'm so astute, huh?'

I stepped out of the buggy to try and appease David before it escalated. I pulled him aside, put my hands up to his shoulders and spoke gently, 'Baby, it will be okay. I can see why Sam is doing this. It won't be so bad to do something a little traditional. We can last one night without each other, can't we?' I tried to comfort him by caressing his back. I pulled him in for a hug. 'I love you, my handsome groom.' I rocked him.

He let out a heavy sigh. 'Darlin', I just wanna marry you. If it means having to be apart tonight then so be it – but never again, okay?'

'Oh you won't get rid of me if you tried.'

'Promise?'

'Abso-bloody-lutely!'

We both chuckled.

He leant in a little closer. 'You know, I might not let you out of bed for a long, long time after we're married.'

'That sounds just perfect to me.'

His mouth passionately lunged onto mine and his tongue caressed me with the heat and desire of a second date kiss. I returned every caress he gave and held him tighter with each one. A need rose in me to be so close as to merge into him.

'Come on you two. Plenty of time for that *after* you're married,' called out Sam.

David continued kissing me for a little longer and we rocked in each other's arms. 'Ah, my beautiful girl... I guess I'm gonna have to leave you for now. I'll be thinking of you tonight... don't forget how much I love you.' He gave me one last little kiss.

'I love you too my darling, my Sunset Eyes. You're my world now. I can't wait to marry you.'

He paused for a moment before he let me go, his affection radiating down to me. 'See you at the altar, my darlin'.'

I clasped his hands tightly before I let go and walked over to my buggy. The "thrill sisters" waited for me with anticipation. I climbed on board to a roar of giggles and screams. I looked back at the handsome man – the incredible man I was about to marry, who stood still gazing at me. I mouthed "I love you" as we rode off.

The Presidential Villa comprised of three floors of tropical luxury. The girls dived into the Champagne straight away announcing the official commencement of the hens' night. I wasn't quite so enthusiastic as I wanted to be clear-headed and fresh for the following day – *my wedding day.*

I took my suitcases to the main bedroom and unpacked a little. Eyeing the gigantic bed for our wedding night, it didn't feel right somehow for me to sleep there on my own. I decided to claim one of the others before joining my friends downstairs.

Well, one glass of Champagne won't hurt. The girls gabbled away, asking how I felt, what our plans were and still giggled over his hotness. Then Greta said something that pierced through to my soul. 'So have you thought about what your life is actually going to be like being married to *the* David Cassidy?'

I half laughed off her comment, saying he is the David I know and love, not the David Cassidy that is marketed to millions. Still, what she said was worth thinking about.

I stole out onto the balcony to finish sipping the last of my bubbles and to ponder my life. The sun had just slipped into the ocean and the sky slowly segued into a deep cerise. As I stared at the beauty of it all, sensations overtook my body as from a moving piece of music. The ocean seemed endless and the last red glows from the sun bled through the palm trees, reaching out to my wooden balcony.

Watching this stunning performance by mother nature reminded me of the awe I'd felt at Lundy Canyon. That memory gave me heart-rendering goosebumps. I sighed. It felt as if I stood on the brink of a brand new life, on this balcony over the sea. *Well, I am. But... What will it really be like...? A*

valid question. What am I giving up and what am I gaining...?
A husband for one. A loving, handsome, remarkably competent
husband at that. And he truly loves me.

I thought about our connection and how intensely we loved
each other. I felt secure in his feelings for me and I trusted him.
Perhaps that was a rare thing in this world, I wasn't sure. But I
knew it was very precious. *Yes, that is enough. What else matters*
really? My thoughts carried me to David. *Is he partying with the*
boys or could he possibly be staring out onto a similarly glorious
view with those eyes of his, pondering everything as I am? I tried
to visualise him and somehow send him a strong surge of love.

The magnificent glow began to fade and I suddenly thought
this too good a photo opportunity to miss, so dashed in to
grab my camera. Right on cue, Henry appeared at our villa.
He'd dropped by to catch us "running amuck" with his Canon.
On the tour he had taught me a little about aperture, ISO and
shutter speed and I'd gobbled it all up. I'm not sure if it was
genetic, as my father loved photography enough to construct
his own darkroom, but I loved capturing images, especially of
scenery – and odd bits and pieces. There was something truly
incredible to me about how you can precisely capture on film
what you see with your eye. It's really quite mind-blowing if
you think about it for long enough.

So I grabbed Henry to help me catch the fading red sky
seeping into the water. He took a few shots and I knew they'd
be outstanding. But I wanted to try also, especially learning
from the master.

After dozens of exposures we slipped back inside, away from
the swiftly cooling air to a sorority of raucous energy. Henry
told us to "carry on as usual", pretending he wasn't there. I think
he did manage to capture a couple of moments but he couldn't

help himself in joining the spirited conversations. Partying really didn't sync with my vibe so I paled into the background. I told them I was turning in, to which I received shouts of protests but I knew I left them in good hands with Henry as their entertainer. No doubt he would be in his element, gate-crashing a hens' night.

As I climbed the stairs Brandi called out, 'Just say *yes* to everything tomorrow.'

Late on the following afternoon, when the sun had only just begun its descent into a time between worlds, I walked down the aisle. As I caught sight of David, I felt my heart… and the whole world, halt. I wanted to savour that moment – it would never come again.

He looked divinely handsome in an ivory suit, with a white satin shirt and white rose in his lapel. He matched my dreamy Evelyn Neis gown perfectly. His intense gaze on me didn't waver. His eyes appeared to beam lovingly into my soul.

My father beside me wore a new formal suit Mum had bought for the occasion. I was exceedingly grateful he didn't wear his safari suit. Swedes do tend to be a tad quirky. However his mood was far from that. I think tears escaped from his eyes all the way.

The grotto they had adorned for us looked breathtaking. On the sides of the aisle, tropical cane chairs interwoven with vines of delicate white blooms formed two graceful rows. The view of the crystal sea rose to the fore. Tiki torches flickered behind the celebrant, continuing as a strand along the perimeter of the grotto to create an enchanting circle.

As we reached my groom, my father placed my hand in his. I had goosebumps from head to toe. David kissed my hand and enfolded our arms together. He did not take his eyes from me until the celebrant began to speak. His whole aura exuded serenity combined with strength. And I felt safe and complete, connected to him like that. An energy seemed to radiate between us; linking us in a bond deliriously sweet and solid as stone.

As the sun moved ever closer to its bed in the horizon, we exchanged our words of dedication to each other and placed circles of gold on each other's fingers. The celebrant, who had an inexplicable, almost ethereal vibe about her, blessed our union. We reached out to hold each other and our lips met in the sweetest kiss yet, which invited tears to run down our cheeks. As the flames of the tiki torches intensified against the deepening azure sky, we began our life together as husband and wife.

Our intimate reception bloomed with a heart-warming ambience. We celebrated in another open air lounge, strung with lanterns and dotted with tall vases of long-stemmed white roses. Red candles glided in a moat surrounding the platform and an ever so slightly curved bridge allowed entry. In a corner, a stylish pianist tinkled romantic notes into the velvety evening on a baby grand, while the scent of sweet blossoms permeated the balmy air.

We sparkled with happiness, and oh did we dance – swaying cosily with each other in between chats with our dear ones. I was cuddled and kissed countless times and felt incredibly blessed to have this circle of truly good people around me. I undeniably floated in an enchanted evening. A touch before midnight, David whispered in my ear and we left for our nest in paradise.

Chapter 26

How does it feel with your feet in the water?
Now is the time you want to get wet

The day we left Australia, a sombre cloud hung over the scene at my parents' house. We thought it best to say our goodbyes there as emotional displays at the airport may draw unwanted attention. A part of me felt torn but I tried to resolve my tears by reminding myself of the happy life waiting for me. Many promises were made of travels back and forth between the two countries. My girlfriends cried in unison and my mother handed me an envelope. My father held me so tightly I thought he would never let go. I had to free myself from his grip. We clambered into the car which pulled away with David and me peering out from the back window. I waved frantically against the window until they stole out of sight.

A message from Ruth waited for us at Adelaide Airport check-in advising she would meet us at LAX. She'd stipulated, "Be prepared for the press". On the plane I thought about our island paradise and the first few days of being Mrs David Cassidy. I wished we were back there now, basking in the sun and simply enjoying each other. It just hadn't been long enough. I had mixed feelings about what to expect in America. Of course I looked forward to my new life with David but a semiquaver of nerves taunted me. I didn't know why exactly but I was edgy.

Those silver wings truly did take us from one world to a completely different one. David's mum, Sam and Henry flew back with us so the paparazzi were treated to a real bonus. As we were about to exit the immigration area into the main area of LAX, they advised us the fan pool should be manageable with airport security and ours combined.

David and I both put our dark shades on. He grabbed my hand and asked, 'Are you okay, baby? Are you ready for this?'

I nodded.

'Just keep walking, keep a straight face, don't look at them and don't answer any questions… And don't worry, I've got ya.' He smiled reassuringly, gave me a quick kiss and we burst through the doors.

Instantly a thousand flashes shot at us, blinding me. I held on tightly to David, focused straight ahead and tried my best to ignore them.

Their shouting at us nearly unbalanced me. 'When are you getting married, Mr Cassidy?', 'How does it feel to be back home?' And to me, 'Miss Magnusson, are you looking forward to getting married?', 'Have you enjoyed your vacation with David?' And the constant pleading, 'Look over here, Miss Magnusson', 'Just one photo, Miss Magnusson?', '*Please*, Miss Magnusson?', 'Over here!' Behind all of this, the screaming of about a few hundred girls who managed to be out at this late hour, wailed like one continuous siren. Our security did an incredible job. They were worth every cent they earnt… or *dime*.

We raced to the cars Ruth had waiting for us. I honestly thought I would lose my footing as so much was happening all around me, it derailed me somewhat. I'm not sure why I had such a strong reaction this time as I'd seen it all before. I suppose the difference being this time it was also directed at me; I could no longer hide in the shadows. We leapt into the car and it sped off. My body refused to stop trembling.

David comforted me – his arm wrapped around me, his hand stroking me. 'It's okay baby, you did great.' He kissed me on my forehead. I was a mess.

The plan had been to have a quick catch up with Ruth at her office but David decided it could wait until the next day and we'd go straight home. With all the frenzy, we hadn't jumped in the correct car where Ruth had been waiting. David was pissed off he hadn't been able to say goodbye to his mother properly. He told me we'd go and visit her. This took my thoughts to Christmas looming around the corner and I grew even more uptight wondering how that would go here in the land of flashbulbs, *and* with David's relatives I hadn't met yet.

We reached the Encino house well after midnight. I gasped at the size of the keen group assembled at the gates – partly comprised of the paparazzi too, no doubt. The security guys in the car before us got out to ensure no one slipped through as we drove in.

'This is all for you, babe,' said David, 'they want a glimpse of "The One".' He winked.

I buried my face into his shoulder as he shielded me. Another round of flashbulbs exploded. We made it through and they shut the gates. Sam's car and the car with our luggage hadn't showed yet. My tremors didn't let up until we reached safety inside the house.

'That was some trip.' I wilted onto the sofa.

'I'm sorry darlin', this is gonna be tough on you. But just

don't give them an inch. I promise I'll protect you as much as I can.'

'I know, baby. Thank you.'

We didn't wait for Sam or our bags but simply flaked it in bed.

At the first splinter of morning the phone rang off the hook. It was Ruth. I heard her voice from the other side of the room. She wanted to see us; she needed to talk to us as we hadn't the chance the night before. David told her to calm down and have some coffee, and we'd meet her at her office. She told him it may be preferable if she came to the house.

We'd hardly had a chance to say good morning to Sam and gulp a few mouthfuls of caffeine when she arrived. She marched in, in full business mode, telling us everything the tabloids had been reporting and that today's paper already featured photos of us from the airport and of me hiding under David's wing as we drove through the gates at home. She ranted on about all of it, but I gathered the main points were that she was pushing for us to do our press conference as soon as possible and there hadn't been a good reaction from David's fans to the news that he'd become engaged. They of course weren't to know about the marriage until our press conference, as David had planned.

'You're going to have to tone it down,' she commanded.

'You're asking me to tone down my *marriage?* That's not gonna happen, Ruth.'

'No David, not your marriage, but you shouldn't be affectionate in public with Lisa and keep reminding your fans how much you love *them.*'

David didn't want to hear it. 'I have just got married and I love my wife, and the fans are just gonna have to dig it – coz this *ain't* goin' away.'

Ruth and David argued for a good ten minutes or so over this while I sat quietly looking for resolutions in my coffee. A hostile clump of nerves rotated in my stomach again. In the end, David agreed for us to do the press gig as soon as he and I had discussed it privately, but he wasn't going to "tone down" anything, as he put it.

Ruth organised a press conference for us at the LA Hilton by that afternoon. I had no clue within me how to handle this. David did his best to encourage me and said he'd try to do most of the talking, but they would definitely ask me questions. We went over and over what they might be likely to ask and attempted to prepare answers. He said no doubt they'd ask what it's like for me to be married to him, and for me to just say something simple, like "it's good". He also taught me a little trick he uses if he is ever nervous in interviews – to put on a really serious face, as it makes you look more authoritarian and in control.

When the moment arrived, I froze. They'd set us up on chairs, elevated a little by a platform from the twenty or so media people with big mics, in a significantly sized room. Giant spotlights glared at us with fierce heat.

David began in a warm tone, 'I want to tell you all… that I'm really happy to be able to say, that about a week ago I married the girl of my dreams, Lisa…' he gave me a half-smug glance, 'in a private ceremony in Australia.'

A constellation of flashes from Nikons fired off along with a barrage of competing questions. I kept hearing, "Mrs Cassidy? Mrs Cassidy?" and then realised they were addressing *me*. That was *my* name. It was the first time I had heard myself referred to by my married name and I found it something of a shock in this setting. I felt like a kangaroo in the spotlight of some scruff's ute, about to be shot.

'Mrs Cassidy, what's he like as a husband?'

I remembered our practice runs and blurted out, 'It's great.' An awkward moment of silence arose and I realised what I had said. I quickly added, 'It's great to be married and David has done well so far.' I sounded so corny and I was grinning from nerves like a lunatic on peyote buttons. But David smiled at me lovingly and strengthened his grasp of my hand.

More and more questions blasted at us and it became just one big blur. David answered most, and naturally breezed through everything. When he'd decided that was enough, he said so, thanked them and said goodbye. Though they continued persisting, once he'd made up his mind he simply ignored them and led me out of the room with his arm firmly around me.

I started shaking again like a crazy person. David held me and pressed his lips gently to my forehead. 'Come on, let's go get drunk.' That was the best idea I'd heard all day.

Chapter 27

Christmas arrived all too soon. We were invited to both Evelyn's, and to his dad and Shirley's place for the event. David wasn't looking forward to the latter. He thought we should visit his dad first and fly out to his mum's afterwards, where we could unwind and spend the night.

At his dad's, I met David's three half-brothers. They acted pretty chummy with me so I relaxed with them straight away. Shirley too was a warm, delightful lady. I could see why David had a great amount of respect for her. And his father, Jack? He must have written the book on charm. I knew David felt uneasy around him due to a number of unpleasant experiences from his past he'd shared with me. No wonder he had recognised the emotional control Judd put on me. I sensed from meeting his dad, what he'd be capable of, and it gave me a shiver. However he treated me like a princess and I was all for keeping everything nice.

A few uncomfortable moments surfaced when Jack became a little too friendly with me. As if he had to compete with David for some reason. He also had a few little digs over not being invited to the wedding. David ignored them and didn't bite back thankfully. I think he knew there was no point in arguing with him; Jack always made sure he won.

After copious amounts of food and wine, David excused us as we needed to go. Jack protested loudly but I'm glad David remained adamant. They all walked us out to our car, Jack with his arm around me, welcoming me to the family. He told David to make sure he brought me back again soon. No mention of wanting to see *him* again soon, however.

Evelyn's house had a cosy vibe, and felt more Christmassy too. We enjoyed a far more relaxing time in her company, but I began to miss my own parents. I had never spent a Christmas anywhere except at home, in that quirky little house in Croydon, where we always put up a real tree. This first Christmas in a northern winter was as far removed from home as possible. It seemed bleak instead of bright. Hardly any snow fell, although everyone promised it would still come.

As if David could sense how I felt, he put his arm around me and said, 'Why don't we ring my parents-in-law when we get home tomorrow?' I snuggled into him and felt safe.

Since we'd flown back from Australia, we had been spun into an insane world. The tabloids went nuts over our marriage, Ruth continued pressing David to "tone it down" and in between, David attended countless meetings over his upcoming album. We stuck together like glue. David wanted me with him everywhere he went and I wanted to be as close to him as possible.

Mail came in for us at Ruth's office – loads of it. David had always received a huge amount of fan mail but a surge poured in after our announced marriage. And a fair part of it was for me. David hardly read any of his fan mail due to time constraints. There were people to answer it for him and he suggested I do the same. But I couldn't help myself. I ended up regretting that move, as I received scores of letters from girls or women telling me they had slept with David or that they'd had his babies. Some told me he was still seeing them and threatened me if I didn't divorce him.

Then there were the letters that congratulated us and wished me, or us, the very best. In some of these, although they began nicely enough, the mood would change along with the handwriting – as it became messier, the message itself became crazier or even sinister. Oh yes, and numerous considerate fans even wrote to give me advice on how to look after my new husband and made considerable threats if I didn't take care of him well enough. Some truly bizarre people existed out there.

It became increasingly difficult for us to go anywhere apart from the studio, Ruth's office or friends' houses. David would have been recognised before but now I couldn't go anywhere either. And although we had been able to sneak off to quiet, unknown places in the past, these also became problematic. When we did muster up the courage to go out for a meal one night, a girl strode up to our table and started coming on to David. He politely asked her to leave us alone and a second later she lifted her top to expose herself, asking him if he'd like to play with her tits. All this happened right in front of me.

To say I didn't feel a lot of love from his fans is an understatement. And in turn, I didn't think much of them either. Sadly, my newfound confidence of the past few years seeped away through all the scrutiny. I became more and more paranoid. Through this, I think I subconsciously waged a war with his fans. I made a point of wearing the T-shirt my friends had given me with "The One" on it. I wanted to rub it in their faces. And I started acting like a smart-arse too. I finally managed to take on board David's advice of keeping a stern face in front of the media.

Often we were filmed or photographed with a haughty attitude or all over each other. The one thing I appreciated enormously was David's willingness to show loudly and clearly to the world how much he loved me. It pissed him off that his fans were hurting me. A couple of times he did take Ruth's advice; mentioning in interviews how much he loved and appreciated his fans, or giving some synthetic mushy statement to them, but his heart wasn't in it. I'm surprised we didn't actually give the finger together when shot by the paparazzi. 'Cause that's how we felt.

I realised David grew increasingly worried about me as I drew inwards, abandoning my cheerful self. There was nowhere I could go. I felt shut up at the Encino house, or the studio, or Ruth's. My world and freedom had shrunk to these places. He stood by me and took such good care of me, I felt so damn guilty for losing it. I hung onto him like anything, feeling as if I balanced on an edge, about to slip off at any second. The edge of sanity.

Every night before we fell asleep he'd wrap me in his arms and say, "I got ya, you're safe in my arms". That was the best place in the world to be.

Chapter 28

David's new album named after the title track, *Beautiful Girl*, was about to be released. He had changed recording companies to go over to RCA. They gave him a contract allowing him freedom to express himself as he wished, not having to abide by restrictive commands as previously with Bell. RCA decided to have a launch party and invite key people from the industry. Somewhere in the lead up, we realised this would be the first official function we'd attend together as husband and wife. Ruth advised me to stay in the background, which suited me fine.

However David held a different stance. 'Listen Ruth, Lisa and I are walking in together. I'm not having her somewhere ten paces behind me.'

'I understand your feelings David, but I just don't think you have to flaunt your *togetherness*,' she made quotation marks in the air, 'in the faces of your fans all the time. It alienates them David – can't you see that?'

'Ruth – you just don't *get it*. We are a solid couple and that's how we're going to present. Now, not you, or anyone else is going to change that. And the sooner you realise that's how it is and that's how it's always gonna be – the sooner we can all get on with it.' He patted her on the back.

On the way to the launch David told me we'd need to be apart for a bit of the time there as he needed to "take care of stuff", but he'd be right back by my side as soon as he could. I was down on myself for being so pathetic and insecure. *What have I turned into?*

I told him I'd be fine and he just held my hand tighter and said it was his job to look after me. *I love this incredible human being so much.*

We'd hardly stepped out of the car and the camera storm leapt into action. David gave them the smiles they wanted whilst holding firmly onto me. We walked alongside each other into the studios where hordes immediately surrounded us, wanting David. He spoke with them all, not letting go of my hand.

He leant over to me. 'Sweetie, I just have to go and prepare but I'll be back after the presentation. You stay here next to Ruth, okay?'

I attempted to give him a look of reassurance. Ruth spoke politely to me but I couldn't help feeling she'd begun to resent me a little. I told her I was going to the loo to freshen up my makeup.

I found my way to the rest room, reached the vanity basin and held onto it for a minute, closing my eyes and taking a few deep breaths. I sensed someone had crept up to me so I quickly opened my eyes. At the mirror beside me loomed a tall leggy model-type wearing a gold lamé mini-dress. It was so short that if she moved too much, I was sure you could see whether she waxed or not, and it was so tight you could have bounced tennis balls off her bottom. She began touching up her makeup. I dived into my handbag to search for my lippie.

The next thing, this tramp started talking to me, 'So you're David's latest squeeze, huh?

'I'm David's *wife*.'

She laughed with as much gusto as a kookaburra. I thought

she would wet her pants – if she had any on.

'Yeah, funny lady!' she continued snorting and laughing, 'like that means anything in this town.' She left the room still laughing and before exiting, imitated a gun pointing at me with her fingers. 'Pow!' And she was gone.

I had become so sensitive my whole body shook again. I hated this place. I hated being attacked all the time. *Oh god, I need to stop this. I must gain control of myself.* I took more deep breaths. It didn't seem to help. *Well I can't stay in the ladies' room forever.* I attempted some form of composure and stumbled back out. The room had filled to the brim in my absence. Luckily I spotted Ruth fairly quickly.

'Where have you been?' she practically scolded me.

'Long story, never mind.'

I stretched onto my toes to grasp sight of the front of the room, where David stood on a transportable stage. Ruth suggested we move closer. A guy on the mic next to David spoke glowingly of his career, and this new album being an exciting new beginning.

'A new beginning where we will come to know the *real* David Cassidy through the dynamic fresh material he has written for this LP.' He raved on for a few good minutes and told us the moment we'd all been waiting for had arrived. He called for someone to bring out the first pressed disc to launch the album.

And who should come out with it but Miss Lamé herself. The record was presented in a frame so large it looked like she didn't have anything on behind it. She strutted out on her nose-bleeding height stilettos and smiled flamboyantly, as if she were the object of every man's desire. She probably was at that moment.

She presented the framed record to David and a round of flashes fired from the photographers in the front row. Not only did she present him with the record, but kissed him on the lips while his arm nestled around her. She proceeded to whisper into his ear while he grinned saucily for the media.

Tremors overtook me again. I felt out of control. I apologised to Ruth, explaining I had to get out or I'd lose it, embarrass myself, and in turn be embarrassing for David. She understood thankfully and rushed me to the car. Unfortunately before I made it, tears streamed from my eyes. As luck would have it, a paparazzo hung outside and gleefully captured this.

The next day's tabloids ran with headlines such as, "Cassidy's Bride in Tears". The articles overshadowed the launch with how the role of Mrs Cassidy was too much for me. "Lisa Cassidy broke down at the launch of her husband's new album at RCA Studios yesterday. Mrs Cassidy left the launch in tears after being overcome with emotion. Some say she is having difficulty in coping with her new public role as the wife of heartthrob Cassidy, who is adored by millions of teenies around the globe."

I kept apologising to David and he kept telling me it was all okay. He was ever so understanding which made me feel guiltier still, telling me that all publicity was good for his album. I wasn't convinced. He felt sincerely sorry for what I had experienced and tried to reassure me, 'Baby you know how much I love you. All that façade is for publicity. You know I'm not gonna be led astray by some skirt that parades in front of me.'

I knew logically what he said was true, but some strange twist in my brain had attacked me along with Miss Lamé. David searched my face. I eventually spoke, 'I know honey, I know. It's just that it all happened so intensely and the things she said to me… I don't know… maybe I was hormonal…'

'Baby, there is nothing you need ever be jealous of. Please know that. I love *you*.'

I knew that. I started to cry again. Then cursed myself for becoming emotional yet again. 'Oh fuck. I'm so sorry, darling.'

David put his arms around me and kissed me on the forehead. He put his lips to my face and kissed my tears.

I gazed at my beautiful husband. 'I've got to find a way to be strong again.' I turned to stare out of the window as if the answer dangled somewhere there.

'Hey, Beautiful. If I could do it, then for sure you can. You're the wise one in this relationship, remember?' He smiled at me lovingly.

I laughed without meaning. *What a joke – me, the wise one.*

'And I'll do everything I can to help you. I do remember a time when it was the other way round and you were supporting me through a tough patch.'

I did remember. But I didn't think I was anywhere near as loving in my approach as he was with me. 'I'll try really hard darling, I promise.'

'You don't have to promise me anything. I already have the promise I want from you.'

Fuck, he's amazing. I have to, have to, have to snap out of this – for his sake.

As he stroked my back, he told me he was taking me out for dinner. He had organised for one of his favourite restaurants – a little Mexican place, to be open solely for us. 'Let's get a bit dolled up... well you more than me,' he laughed, 'you know, help us feel special.'

I kissed him, thanked him, told him what a wonderful husband he is and dashed off to try and make myself beautiful. I cursed my puffy eyes and tried to cool them with ice, and cover them with foundation. I desperately wanted to make myself as attractive as possible for him. I wanted him to be proud of me and not see this pathetic pit of emotions I had become.

I decided to wear the little red dress I had bought on Rodeo Drive. I took extra care with the finishing touches on my makeup, placed a little bit of highlighter above my cheek bones, and went to him. When he saw me, his face shone with affection and he immediately walked over and gave me an appetising kiss.

'That's my beautiful wife,' he purred. He planted soft kisses up and down my neck and then close to my ear. His ample cock throbbed against me, nudging me. Thankfully my emotional outbursts hadn't put him off. His hot breath in my ear gave me enticing shivers.

'I want you,' he whispered earnestly.

'Babe, I want you too but I just got dressed up.'

'How about I make you a little untidy?' he spoke softly. 'It's a good look on you.' His eyes glimmered with naughtiness.

He carried me to the bedroom, placed me gently on the bed and hitched my dress up to my waist. When he discovered the suspenders I had on underneath he almost hummed in delight. 'I know exactly what I'm gonna do with you, my sweet darlin'.'

His gaze on me didn't falter – his eyes glistened with the promise of pleasure, his lips lingered slightly open – with hunger. Slowly, and ever so precisely, he unclasped each of my suspenders. He slid his hands underneath me to grasp my panties. With one tug he had them just under my hips. He left them there and placed his hand on the heat between my legs. I was dripping for his touch.

He began rubbing me, deliciously; his eyes never leaving my face. Flickers of satisfaction sparked in his eyes with each stroke as he witnessed my pleasure.

I willed my voice to speak, 'I'm glad I please you.'

'Yeah? Let me please *you,* sweet baby. I'm gonna please you til you scream. Mmh, mmh.'

His eyes remained firmly on mine as he lowered his head. He disposed of my panties and in an instant his mouth found its way to my wetness. His tongue slipped into me and distinctly moved up and down, his eyes still watching me. I was determined to hold his gaze but my eyelids started trembling and I could no longer focus. I disappeared into a world filled with waves of pleasure – each thrust of his tongue. I felt the sweet burn growing, building… and the fire within me about to roar – he stopped.

I looked at him and he grinned. 'Not yet, baby.'

My panting became heavy – like a primal being. After watching my face for an endless amount of time, he returned to his task. His tongue played with me again until I writhed against the bed. I couldn't hold it any longer – and he stopped. Again the promise of more pleasure gleamed on his face.

I begged him to continue.

His expression began to almost glow as he spoke, 'I love you, my beautiful wife.'

He bowed his head once more and this time closed his eyes as his tongue *and* lips caressed me. His mouth devoured me and the only thing I could do – was scream.

We walked into the twinkling little restaurant, linking arms and laughing. We sat opposite each other, separated by a candle. David watched my mouth as I told him I loved him. He told me I looked so beautiful he needed to sit beside me. I felt happiness. Complete love for him and sweet happiness.

Over dinner we chatted about silly fun things like we used

to on his tour. When we'd finished our tasty veggie enchiladas, he ordered more wine. I saw he wanted to settle for a while longer and that suited me fine – I was having the best time I'd had in quite a while. And luckily no press, nor fans, were anywhere to be seen. After the waiter had poured wine into our glasses, David took my hand and said he wanted to talk to me about something. My paranoia kicked in immediately.

He could read me like a book. Gently he said, 'Baby, don't be uptight, it's a good thing.' He smiled deeply into my eyes and stroked my hand. 'I've been thinking about our house.'

'Our house?'

'Yeah. You know, where we live with Sam, in Encino?' he teased.

'Your house.'

He completely ignored me. 'Well, *our* house seems to have outgrown us I think. What do you think if we look for another place, our special place?'

'Umm…'

He continued, 'We both get along well with Sam but I think now that we're all grown up and married, we really should have our own place. Something we can make completely just ours. What do you think, baby?'

I still didn't know what to say. 'Well it's up to you…'

'No, it's not. We're a team. And I wanna know what my beautiful wife thinks.' He kissed the back of my hand.

Twinges of awkwardness gnawed at me but I figured I'd share my thoughts with him. 'I'm sorry baby, I really just feel a bit uncomfortable about this as I can't contribute financially.'

He stared at me. He drew close so our noses almost touched and squeezed my hand. 'I don't wanna hear that from you any*more*. No more talk of whose money. We're a team, I keep tellin' ya. Okay?'

I made a sound to the contrary and he kissed me. 'I'm gonna have to kiss you to shut you up, I can see.' He grabbed my face and stared directly at me. 'Okay?' He wouldn't let me go until I gave in. So I agreed to a mission of house hunting. It did make sense for us to have a marital home. I knew I would really miss Sam though.

Our conversation took my thoughts to my own life plan. I had no potential of earning any money and I had left my music studies behind me in Australia. I voiced my thoughts to David. He brightly responded with the prospect of me playing music and singing with him. I stipulated again I did not wish to be another Linda McCartney. I suddenly had the greatest empathy for her. She'd also been hated and ridiculed by Paul's fans. I had no doubt she would have been similarly attacked by them in one form or another.

He suggested I take up some other role as part of his business. 'What about promotions, publicity?' His voice became charged with enthusiasm. 'You'd be great in that area. I could arrange it through Ruth.'

'No, I don't think so.'

He looked disappointed.

'You know darling, I don't think I handle your business too well. Look at how I've been lately and your fans and I aren't exactly the best of friends.'

'I understand, baby. But that's all I know – this business. I don't know what else to suggest… what about trying for some parts?'

'I would love to do that… but not through the trails of your success. And whether we like it or not, I'm not blind to the fact that the notion of "Mrs Cassidy" carries with it a certain handicap in the entertainment industry. I really don't think anyone would take me seriously.'

He lowered his eyes. 'I've taken you down with me, haven't I?'

'I didn't mean it like that, baby.' I reached for his hand. 'You're the best thing that's ever happened to me.'

'Hmm... I can see that.'

'Don't, baby – you *are*. Lately I've just been off the planet. Ignore me. And you aren't anywhere near down. You've just turned the corner to a much more relevant career for you – the *real* you. You're on your way *up*, gorgeous man.'

His dreamy eyes smiled at me and he told me how much he loved me. I told him I loved him more – and that I loved how we could be so corny together.

'What's corny?' He brought his lips to mine. Our mouths enjoyed exploring each other until we realised where we were. David shrugged it off and kissed my mouth again. This was our private restaurant for the evening. Only one person came into the place during our special time together; a delivery guy with a dozen deep red, long-stemmed roses – for Lisa Cassidy.

On the way home in the car, he continued trying to think of options for me. 'Baby, I really think you should focus on something where you can use your creativity to the fullest – even if it's a hobby. Who knows where it could lead?'

It would be good to have an outlet... and it may just help me stay sane too. A fragment of a reminder flew into my thoughts over my passion for music. *No, I have shut that door. And it wasn't an easy thing to do.* Somehow, it was too painful to think about and I needed for that door to remain shut.

He wasn't quite yet ready to let go of the idea of finding a way for me to be creative within his business. But I truly believed I should do something on my own. I told him I'd bribe him with kisses which made him chuckle. Then the thought popped into my head to learn more about photography. Perhaps through Henry, or at least I could ask his advice.

'Okay, well just don't go spending too much time with that old fox or *I* will get jealous.'

'There is nothing you need ever be jealous of,' I murmured against his cheek. I pulled him closer to me. 'And I'm just burning for you, baby.'

'Well I'll just see what I can do about that when we get home,' his soft caramel voice hummed as he caressed across my waistline. 'In the meantime…' His hand moved lower.

Chapter 29

The thought of looking for our special home and learning more about photography boosted me. A few adventures had bubbled up and my world appeared brighter. David began our house hunt straight away and I phoned Henry who said he'd be happy to help with my shutterbug path. He put me onto a "great chick" for private lessons, as she'd have much more time and could also help with advice on business options. I couldn't help but notice a cheeky smile of satisfaction on David's lips when I told him.

House hunting was fun. Something about exploring houses excited me on a deep level. Ever since being a child, I'd sometimes spot certain houses from the back seat of the car and imagine what they might be like inside. Each room would tell a story and each house definitely had its own unique vibe, which I couldn't explain – I only knew that sometimes a house's vibe drew me in and gave me a good feeling.

David and I looked at everything from tiny quaint places to elaborate mansions. We both felt something in between would be best. David wanted to make sure we had a guest house for when the "Aussies" came to visit. We searched for quite a while but nothing really stood out, or ticked all the boxes. And if it suited us in a practical sense, it didn't sing to our souls. We needed to live with that song in our home.

As we drove home from Ruth's office one evening I noticed

a new place in the paper. I showed David and asked if he'd like to drive past. It was in Cheviot Hills, about sixteen miles south of the Encino house along the Ventura and San Diego Freeways. Despite the grey drizzly weather we asked our driver to take a detour for a peek from the outside.

Straight away we noticed that the place stood out as having a style of its own. It had a Spanish character about it many of the houses in the area comprised of, but it differed with a partly curved area on the second floor, similar to a turret. It looked just like a little castle. Although the weather was miserable, the windows glowed with an orange hue that warmed against the grey. We turned to each other, both feeling positive.

A guy ran out of the driveway heading for a car with a real estate sign on it, under the shield of his pamphlets. David jumped out and flagged him down. Luckily he had time to show us through. We wandered through each charismatic room and hallway, taking in the fireplaces, the curved walls, the intimate corners. The living area filled with light, extended almost right out to the pool, and several dark nooks captured romantic charm. We felt the vibe; we fell in love with it.

My thoughts turned to how much a place like this would cost. Though the real estate guy called it "very reasonable" compared to most houses in this upmarket area. David put in an offer. That night the guy rang to congratulate us. 2274 Montelemar Drive, Cheviot Hills was ours.

David fetched some Dom from the bar fridge and called Sam in, who made a sad puppy face at the news. We hugged him and told him he was to visit – *often*. A few glasses of Dom later and the three of us got it on, singing *Home On The Range* in three-part harmony. When we had the harmonies precise, David's face lit up and he gave the thumbs up. It felt a total groove to hit it spot on. Sam insisted he couldn't sing but I thought he sounded neat. We partied on and we did it well as per usual.

In the wee hours the phone rang. It was Mum. She had been worried as even the Australian tabloids ran stories on how I had "lost it" at David's album launch.

'I'm okay, Mum.' I skimmed over what happened. It thrilled me she had cared enough to ring.

It was so good to hear her voice after such a long time. I announced our exciting news and she asked me to pass on her and Dad's congratulations to David. She also told me Brandi had asked her to say "hello". As I listened to her, a part of me longed for the comfort of familiarity. I wanted to hear her voice for longer but I knew the call would be expensive so I said I'd let her go. Before I hung up, I told her she must come and visit us in our new home.

I rushed back to Sam and my darling husband. I felt his arm around me. My head flopped onto his shoulder and I let out a sigh.

The call from Mum reminded me of the envelope she had given me when we left Australia. It had contained a cheque for a thousand dollars – my parents' gift to us for our new life together. This was an enormous sum of money for them. I told David I now wanted to contribute this to our new house. He kissed me to shut me up.

David and I moved into our little "Cassidy Castle" as we came to call it, around a month later. Sam also decided to move out, into a smaller place. Boxes and chaos reigned absolutely everywhere but it I really dug the thought of setting up our own place – David's and my home together. I desperately looked forward to our new beginning and putting all the tears of my first months in America behind us.

Chapter 30

The life that spanned out before me wasn't as rosy as I had hoped. David was my rock, and I was his at times. Overall we loved each other well and we loved passionately. Our connection was always the most precious thing in my life. But continuous external factors put a great deal of pressure on us. The next almost five years in our little Cassidy Castle were a roller coaster ride of great proportions.

To begin with, David's new album didn't sell well. We weren't sure whether the fans didn't dig the softer, jazzier style of music, or whether they didn't like that the songs were mainly dedicated to me. He tried for a second album with RCA. This one was a little more upbeat but still in a different style to what the fans were used to. He quietly added a couple of new love songs he'd written for me, without stating they were my songs. I think the fans would have figured it out though. This album did a little better but not much.

David also tried for acting roles but it seemed they had all but forgotten him. After every audition he'd wait for the call, but the call never came. This brought him down to a low point and I tried my best to be cheerful and remain positive for him. I'd give him massages and create little fun surprises, including leaving love notes for him to find. He especially liked this one:

Hey there my sexy husband,

I'd like to steal away with you to the beach or somewhere secluded. We could hitch a lift from someone with a van, and sit at the back. I'd love to sit at the back with you, and touch you in the places that thrill you. Let you slide your hand underneath my skirt, whilst we are kissing with wet, hungry tongues.

It's hot at the beach and I'd enjoy looking at your smooth skin in the stark sun, the sweat trickling down your chest. And the sun would catch the highlights in your soft shiny hair. Your hair would tantalise me as I lay on my back and you kissed all the way down my body.

You'd ask me if I wanted a cool drink and I'd watch you as you walked over to the hot dog stand, the shades you wore giving you an extra enticing look. You'd come back with two OJs, taking a piece of ice from yours and running it along my cleavage. I would lie there not being able to wait until your soft lips touched my skin again.

My gorgeous husband, what do I love about you? I love the way your sunset eyes look deep into me, how your gaze is so loving and your smile so inviting. I love how you stand up for me, your stance and manner becoming threatening to anyone who dare attempt to hurt me. I love your passion for music, how you can pick up any

instrument and make it moan with delight, how
your voice of soft flowing caramel can melt me
by breathlessly crooning, then singing out with
dynamic strength.

I love how you care for me and your endless,
adoring attentiveness. I love how your euphoric
lovemaking to me is relentless, and even when I
think I've had enough, you give me more pleasure.
I love the privilege of seeing your face when you
come. I love the feeling of knowing I would do
anything you asked. I love how completely I can
trust you with my heart, my soul, my everything.

Yours forever,
Lisa

I also attempted to cook more often for him. Slowly I became better at it. Mum would send me recipes and I'd try them out on him. He loved how I expressed my care for him. But both in our own ways, we struggled with reality. We clung to each other like two vulnerable kids in a big scary world.

And I continued to be harpooned by his fans. Even though David's popularity appeared to be declining a little, the crazy ones hung in there. I received more and more threatening letters demanding I divorce him. A thread emerged, telling me they would ruin my marriage so the one who is the right Mrs Cassidy can take my place. The threats were firm, some saying they had "their people" within our circle. I had to stop reading them as they reignited my paranoia.

Then came a huge blow. David discovered that all through the years of his touring, during the time he'd made the most money, his finances had been mismanaged. He said it wasn't Ruth's fault; she simply didn't have a good head for finances. Other people within the business had basically stolen from him. I quietly thought she should have been on top of it. So while David's touring, record sales and merchandise had made millions of dollars, he ended up with only around fifteen thousand of it. A mere grain of sand compared to what he'd brought in. He, and consequently I, was broke.

How could this happen? He had his own goddamn plane for fuck's sake.

We scrimped as much as possible to hang onto our lovely home. David had wanted to fly my parents out to visit us from Australia but we had to scrap that idea. Ruth continually assured him of new television roles but she seemed to be slipping away – into a world of Valium. David never fired her. He'd go to see her and each time came back saying she wasn't quite there. She had given up the office to work from home. He knew she wasn't capable of keeping the promises she continued to make to him.

David had begun to drink more. Not just wine – he turned to Scotch. I had no interest in Scotch but also drank way more wine than was good for me. There was no more French Champagne; we resorted to good old Californian wine. We seemed to be okay together drunk, which I'm not sure was a good thing, as it kept us drunk. We were both mushy drunks and mostly ended up in bed doing weird things to each other, often unsuccessfully.

David became more and more of an insomniac and while I slept, he'd usually dream up some wild idea guaranteed to make us a ton of money. He'd wake me up, excited and animated, needing to tell me all about it.

David told me about the drugs he took in his teens. He'd tried it all. One night he asked, 'Have ya ever tried a joint?' I hadn't. Instantly he pulled one out of his top pocket and lit it. 'Try this, baby.'

He showed me how to inhale and keep it in for as long as possible. He added, 'But be careful, it's laced.'

I didn't care to know with what. But I thought I'd give it a go.

I breathed in the hot scratchy smoke but struggled to keep it in me as I coughed so hard I thought my lungs would burst. That was enough for me so David had the rest. I thought I'd hardly have any effect from one puff. Man, was I wrong.

We sat in our favourite romantic nook – a small corner room we called the "Bohemian Room". I loved its curved wall, featuring a tiny gothic-style window set high in the grey stonework. The fireplace adorned with wrought iron scrolls held hypnotising flames in its hearth. We'd laid Indian cushions all over squishy beanbag type seats and kept the space lit by candles on tall tiered holders. David often picked up and strummed one of the few guitars that always lay in there. The way his fingers caressed the strings, he seemed to arouse them to make music.

We'd been rapping before the joint but without realising it, we had both fallen silent. My eyes fixed onto a swirl on one of the cushions in front of me. Gradually it stretched forth from the cushion and reached out to the flames dancing in the fireplace.

'Look, honey! Look at *that*,' I shouted through fright. I stared at him, astounded he hadn't noticed what was happening in the room.

When we made eye contact, he laughed. He laughed so much it consumed him, making me spin into a worse panic.

The flames had begun to jump out from the fireplace and dance around the room. 'David! Can't you *see that?* I stood up and yelled.

He only laughed harder.

I felt the floor of the room sinking. I fell. Cushions lay underneath me but I didn't fall onto them – I fell *into* them. I had shrunk in size and found myself in the midst of dark grey fluffy material. The fluffiness became heavier and heavier until it completely absorbed me. I must have blacked out as when I became aware of the room again, I lay amongst the cushions.

My heartbeat dominated over any other possible sound and incessantly grew louder. The beat emanated from inside my head, nauseously booming. But it wasn't my heart – a light, like a strobe-light flashed inside my head and all my movements turned slow and heavy. Every inch I moved was intercepted by a spark of light.

I heard the beat again. It turned into music, erratic music. I lifted my head and saw David in the corner playing a guitar. Though he wasn't actually playing, but making sounds on it. A tiny part of me captured a thought – I had to focus. I had to be real. I looked at David and tried to call out to him but I only let out a moan.

It got his attention and he smiled at me. 'Hey, that's my beautiful wife,' he cooed as if he had only just seen me. 'That's my beautiful baby.' He put the guitar down and crawled over to me. 'How ya doin', Beautiful?'

He kissed me and his familiar strong hands caressed me. I started to feel calmer. His touch warmed me and his kisses tasted good. I remembered I had to be real.

I urgently tapped his arm. 'Baby... sweetie...' I squeaked between kisses.

'What is it, Beautiful?' he murmured dreamily with his eyes half closed.

'I need to tell you something,' my voice trembled.

'What do you need to tell me, gorgeous?' He continued kissing me dotingly.

'I need you to help me... I'm a little bit scared... just a little bit.' It felt so good to be able to say that, to vocalise that to him.

It seemed to make him more real too. He held me and stroked me. 'You're cold, baby... aw, baby. I'll look after you. I'll keep you warm with my love.' His words and arms were like a soothing balm.

I snuggled into him and we said little loving words to each other, but I don't think they were real words. We both knew them though, and we spoke our secret language of love. We drifted to a dreamy place... and back... and back to the dreamy place again.

Having that weed or whatever it was, certainly had been an interlude from our out of control lives but I'm not sure it was a pleasant one. And it definitely wasn't one of control. I hated not having a handle on myself so I didn't have any more joints. David would at times, and I'd leave him to it as I really couldn't connect with him stoned. I'd go off and take a few arty shots or even do a bit of cleaning as I simply didn't dig the vibe. Not that I behaved like an angel by any means, as my drinking became more frequent and heavy.

David and I coasted along in a hazy world. We plodded from one disappointment to the next and back to our hazy world, where at least the fear and worry over the messy events in our lives became softer, fuzzier.

Sometimes we'd go to parties and get smashing drunk. It probably wasn't the smartest thing to do as half the time I didn't know who I was talking to or what I said. David did the same. I am amazed actually, that we never fought with each other as we both had hot tempers and would get enormously pissed off at other people, but luckily never with each other.

At one party I threatened to punch out some up-himself actor David had known early in his career, who snubbed him excruciatingly. David felt quite hurt which unleashed my deepest anger. I leapt to respond – with aggression. Luckily David stopped me. I'm also glad the guy never knew I intended to come after him as that would have looked worse. I could just see the headlines reading, "Mrs Cassidy steps in to punch Hollywood bully for teen idol husband".

Another night we met up with some cats from the UK who remembered David from his tour. A few of them were in promotions and management, and offered to help David find work. He didn't think much of it as people made promises to him all the time they never delivered on, but he gave his details anyway. However a few months later he did receive an offer, although it was in the UK; playing in a musical at the West End. He would need to go for six months at least. Neither of us wanted to be apart but we knew we had to do this; we needed the money and we couldn't afford for us both to go.

This happened a couple of times over the next few years. David left for England and I stayed behind, trying to sell my shots but never getting anywhere with them. I'd also begun to write a journal, through which my passion for writing had reawakened. At school I had been a straight A student in English and even won awards. I thought perhaps I could write freelance articles for magazines back at home. Something along the lines of what it was like for an Aussie living in LA, under a pseudonym of course. But nothing came of that either.

Most of my time, I spent alone. My best friend was a bottle of wine. I couldn't travel back to Australia to see everyone and I missed them so. David was better when he worked, but each time he came home and a drought followed, he'd sink again.

He talked a lot about the earlier days when he'd been the heartthrob and what he could have, or should have, done better. I think another part of him felt he wasn't as capable as back then which simply wasn't true. I constantly tried to perk him up but without much success. Sometimes I truly believed the love we shared to be the only good thing in my life but even that I only had for short portions of the year. David kept assuring me he'd find work in America.

At times we'd hold onto each other so tightly and wonder whether being apart was worth it.

Chapter 31

And there would be no sun
And there would be no one to run to

Our lives coasted along, somehow surviving, and before we knew it five years had flown past. At least we had managed to hold onto our home. But was that even worth it? I encouraged David to talk to a counsellor of some sort as he hardly even smiled anymore. He remained reluctant, saying he had me to talk to, but I kept gently mentioning for him to just try it, suggesting that sometimes talking to an external person can be a good release.

Over time, he gave in. We searched for someone together who wasn't one of those kooky Hollywood types. Eventually we found a mature woman, Helen – a psychologist who sounded positive and realistic. David agreed to see her for a period of three months initially. A routine developed for us where every Friday he'd go to his appointment with Helen, while I prepared (what I hoped would turn out to be) a nice meal, put on a pretty dress and we'd enjoy an evening together when he returned. It was probably the first real routine we'd ever had. I wanted to believe somehow, slowly, things would come good. On one of these Fridays, our lives changed completely.

I had a veggie curry simmering in the crockpot and dashed

off to shower and dress as David would be home soon. I couldn't wait to see him, hug him and show him the shots I had taken of a stunning rainbow through the rain. For some reason I felt a real urgency to hold him.

I thought about him as I had my shower. I imagined the sensation of the water falling on me to be his touch and I poked my nipples into the stream one at a time. Particular times I'd made love with him and what a thrilling lover he was, arose in my thoughts. He always did it for me, made me zing every single time. It was just as hot with him now as it had been in the beginning. I told myself not to get too carried away in the shower, as he would physically be here soon. My mind played with an assortment of sensual plans. I wondered how long I could leave the crockpot going.

I dried myself a little, wrapped a towel around me and hurried to the bedroom to pick out a dress he'd like. As I walked in I thought I had either totally lost it or was in some kind of dream. A naked man lay in our now ruffled bed. I went into such shock I didn't say anything.

He casually said, 'Hi,' and continued reading a magazine. He didn't seem to pose any threat but I didn't know how to react – whether to call the police, or scream, or run, or all three.

'Who are you? What are you doing here?' I blurted out, clutching my towel to my chest.

'Look out of the window and you'll see,' he calmly remarked.

I walked over to the window but saw nothing out of the ordinary. 'What are you talking about?'

'Look harder.'

I peered to every corner of the garden I could see, but still nothing.

'Come back to bed darling, I miss your tits. Can't I stay a

little longer just this time?'

I spun around wondering why on earth he was saying this and at that precise moment David walked into the room. I certainly must have had a look of shock on my face because of what this jerk had been saying, which David obviously read as being from him coming in.

The guy jumped up from the bed in all his nakedness and ran to me saying he would fight for me if I wanted. I fled from him to David who looked at me as if I was something that had crawled out from the sewer. I immediately felt as if a sharp object had pierced right through me, seeing him look at me so distastefully.

'Baby, this is not what it looks like…'

David glared at me with hatred burning in his eyes, glanced over to the guy and took off.

I chased after him, begging him not to go. I tried to shout out anything I possibly could to make him believe me but it was all wasted. He left the house and sped off in his car, leaving me weeping at the front door still in my towel.

The jerk pushed past me with his clothes on, sang out, 'Bingo,' and ran for it. I had been set up.

I tried to think of what to do. Nothing, absolutely nothing, came to me. I had no idea where David had gone. I only hoped he would calm down and come back. I waited and waited. The sky grew pitch black and still I waited. Nothing. I didn't know whether to ring the police to make sure he hadn't had an accident, or to even report the guy breaking in. But I worried the story would reach the press. I needed some advice. But there was no one to ask. There was no one to reach out to. I kept willing with every part of my being that he'd come back. But he didn't. I finally cried myself to sleep at around four in the morning.

I woke with the dawn, feeling hung-over even though I'd had nothing to drink. The realisation of the day before hit me. I felt as if I'd been punched in the head, and the heart. I simply had to find him today. I had to reach him and tell him this is all wrong; it's not what he thinks it is and just make him understand.

I staggered to the bathroom and caught myself in the mirror. I looked like shit. I splashed water on my face. My eyes stung. As I dried my face, I heard the front door slam. I raced down the stairs as fast as I could. Half way down I caught sight of him and stopped in a jolt.

He looked like he hadn't slept. He stared up at me, still with hate in his eyes and then looked away.

I ran to him, 'Baby, please, let's talk...'

'I've got nothing to say to you.'

I tried putting my arms around him. He froze and stared at me, not acknowledging my hug in any way from his rigid state. He glared at the places where my arms touched him and looked at me in the same icy way. His words were slow and precise, 'Don't – touch – me.'

My eyes pleaded with him.

'Do – *not*.'

I lifted my arms from him. He pushed past me in a hurry to go upstairs. I followed.

'What are you doing?'

He didn't answer me. He pulled a large bag down from the top of the wardrobe and started throwing things into it. I couldn't believe what I was watching. His movements were sharp and intense.

Tears accompanied by small yelps of pain leaked from me.

He stopped for a moment and glared at me again as if to

say, "Don't you dare cry", and went back to stuffing his bag.

I couldn't stand any longer. I fell down against the door frame and wept uncontrollably. 'Please darling... Don't do this.' I didn't care that I was begging – the pain was unbearable.

David continued to ignore me. When he'd filled his bag, he stepped over me to leave the room and told me I would hear from his lawyers.

I cried so hard a half groaning, half screaming sound emanated from me. I partly rose. 'Nooooo... don't *do* this. Darling, pleeease... *pleeease.*'

I heard the door slam once more and fell again to the floor with the sound. My body shook with my wailing. This was so wrong, just so wrong. I could not accept this reality. I wanted my husband. I lay on the floor, shaking and sobbing until I was empty. I must have exhausted myself so much I fell asleep.

When I woke I looked like even worse shit than before but I didn't care anymore. *What the fuck am I going to do?*

My head pounded and every inch I moved, it hurt like crazy. I made my way to the kitchen and poured a little water into a glass. I found a bottle of pain killers in the drawer so I swallowed a handful, slumped into a chair and stared at the blank wall.

How the hell did this happen? How did they come up with such a precise scheme? What the fuck did I ever do to anyone for them to destroy my life? "The right Mrs Cassidy would take my place." *Bullshit!* I threw my glass at the wall. It hit so hard it shattered into a spray of shards, partly flying onto me. The sound was satisfying. However I was not going to clean that up. That wasn't *my* mess.

Instead I took a shower to wash off the glass. Some had cut me but I didn't care about that either. Only yesterday I had stood in this same cubicle with water caressing me, dreaming of David's touch. *David.* I started weeping again. It didn't matter, the shower wept with me.

After changing I thought I would ring Sam. His tone cooled when he realised it was me.

'Sam? Come on, it's me – *baby girl.*'

'Lisa I'm sorry, but I really don't want to talk to you.'

'But why? I haven't done anything.'

'Listen to me, Lisa. And then I need to hang up. David has given you the benefit of the doubt many times–'

'What are you talking about Sam? What benefit of the doubt?'

'Lisa, he knows about the letters you've written to your lover, he's known for a while. Only he thought because you have the skill of changing your handwriting, you would have done that. So he thought it wasn't you. I don't think he actually wanted to believe it was you. But then too many things added up and now… well you gotta know that you can't do that kind of thing. Especially not to my best friend. I can't talk to you anymore.' He hung up.

I could not believe this was the same Sam I had loved and been almost best friends with.

Letters? What the fuck was he talking about? What had gone on for a while? I couldn't fathom that someone, or some people, could be so cruel as to do this to me. I was lost, simply lost, for what to do.

There was only one thing to do – wipe out the pain. I bee-lined to the wine cellar; one bottle of French Champagne remained from the days when we had money. We'd been saving it for a rainy day.

'Well it's fucking raining now!' I screeched at the top of my lungs and popped the cork. I didn't even bother with a glass. I sat on the stone floor and drank it all. 'Here's to my fucking marriage! No, wait… here's a better one… here's to David's fucking fans. May you all go fuck yourselves and rot in hell, listening to *I Think I Love You* for all damnation. There!'

For a week I sailed through that cellar, drinking everything I could find. Then I found David's Scotch. Anything would do as long as it held back reality. *That* was unbearable and I just wanted it to fuck off and leave me alone. Fuck, fuck, fuck. In amongst all my swearing, I thought of Brandi. I never liked to phone Australia because of the cost but fuck that now. I had to ring her. I had no idea what time it was in Australia, let alone in LA. All I had been doing was drinking and sleeping, drinking and sleeping. Sometimes light seeped into the house and at others times it didn't. It made no difference.

I peered at the entries in my phone book. It took me a while to decipher the squiggles into the correct numbers. I heard ringing on the line.

'Hello?' a sleepy voice answered. It was *her*. I was so glad it wasn't her mother, or worse if Judd had answered.

I blurted out everything that had happened to me and all she kept saying along with me was "Fuck". I must have spent an hour on the phone to her. Everything she suggested was useless as I wasn't able to contact David. I had no idea where he was. In the end we didn't solve anything, but fuck it was good to talk to her. She told me to hang in there, that she loved me and she would ring me back soon. I hung up and cried.

Talking to Brandi had been such a welcome break from my misery but it also exhausted me. I dropped onto the bed and slept more soundly than I had in… well, since David had left.

I woke up sometime with light in my room. David stood

staring at me. I jumped up and tried to open my swollen, crusty eyes. I could only just make him out.

'David?'

'I'm glad you look like shit.'

More pain in my heart. And the jolt from sleep to this moment stung me.

He obviously wanted to talk. Not with me but at me. 'You know,' he uttered a little smugly, 'there were numerous opportunities for me… numerous temptations… where I could have taken a lover. But did I? No. I was the stupid faithful husband, who gave up hundreds of gorgeous girls. For what? For my – *wife*. What a joke.'

Through the slits that used to be my eyes I noticed he'd bleached his hair.

Anger stirred in my midst. 'Oh there were hundreds, were there? Well I'm sorry I kept you on such a ball and chain.'

'So am *I*,' he half chuckled. 'If I think of all the times I could have… all the times that we were…' I thought he was laughing but he had begun to cry. The words he'd been speaking had led him to a tender memory between us.

I felt the piercing sorrow of it as well. All my anger left me, seeing him so hurt. I had seen him cry before but not like that. I leapt to comfort him.

'*No!*' he yelled at me through his tears. 'Never again!' He wiped part of his face as his tears kept rolling down his cheeks. 'Never again am I going to let this happen to me. Never again am I going to trust you. I overlooked so many things – never again, *do you hear me?*' he was almost screeching. 'If you wanted to tear my heart out and shred it to tiny pieces well congratulations, coz you've succeeded. I *never* want to see you again. Take your money that your mother gave you and go back to Australia. I'm putting this house on the market.' He grabbed something from his side drawer and took off.

I fell back onto the bed, curled up in a ball and rocked. I rocked for some hours.

Later that same day I slowly meandered down the stairs. A horrid smell emerged from somewhere. I spotted the crockpot on the kitchen bench and lifted the lid. The veggie curry I'd made had gone mouldy. I threw the pot and all its contents across the kitchen.

During the next few weeks I tried to contact anyone I could think of in order to reach David. The office semi-managing him told me not to ring back, they had no business with me. And I received a similar response from anyone whose number I had. They either hung up or wouldn't take my calls. David remained totally out of reach. Even Henry wouldn't take my calls and my photography lessons had been cancelled. Then I received the divorce papers. He certainly didn't waste any time with that. I had to find another bottle of something somewhere for the courage to read them. Luckily I discovered one in a corner kitchen cupboard. It was red, which wasn't my preference but I was getting used to it.

The solicitor stated Mr Cassidy would be willing to agree to an equitable settlement of fifty/fifty, which they suggested I agree to as it was extremely generous. I drafted a letter, right there and then, saying I wanted nothing apart from the outfits he had bought me, and if they would be so kind, my engagement and wedding ring. I still couldn't believe this was actually happening. And my red friend gave me little comfort.

Chapter 32

The phone hadn't rung since David left so it startled me. I answered tentatively but my mood quickly lifted when I heard Brandi's voice. Her chirpy tone wrapped me in cosiness. And her news lifted my mood even more – she was coming to visit.

'What? Really? *When?* I can't *wait.*'

'Geez, *calm down.* Now don't get too excited – there's a condition to this trip you mightn't like.'

Anxiety snared me instantly. I didn't say anything further and let her speak.

She told me she wasn't quite able to pay for the trip on her own so her brother said he would help if he could come too. Apparently he had done well with the mining.

'You mean to tell me that Judd is coming?'

'Well… yeah. But we can get rid of him and have our "girls' time",' she tried convincing me, sounding *alltför* cheery.

It didn't sound ideal but I had run out of all options. And I certainly wasn't going to tell her not to come. They would be here by the weekend. I honestly couldn't wait.

I picked up a handful of timetables and route maps and worked out how to get from the house to LAX by bus. There I was, Mrs flipping David Cassidy on a goddamn bus. Not that anyone would have recognised me – I had lost so much weight and hadn't done anything with my hair in ages, or worn makeup. Although I did hide behind a pair of shades as big as saucers. My eyes still ached from all the crying I'd done and continued to do.

I found the correct terminal well in time for their arrival, plonked on a seat and watched the world go by. It had been such a long time since I'd flown anywhere. *The last time...* I quickly changed my train of thought so as not to cry. I tried to focus on the travellers and imagine what their lives were like, and what exciting places in the world they had been to.

Not long after, the Goodings siblings tore through the big doors leading in from the immigration area. Brandi looked outta sight. She'd turned *blonde*. She looked like Better Midler. And just behind her pranced Judd. He seemed a little less scruffy, if that was at all possible; a little polished even.

They spotted me and Brandi aimed her stilettos in my direction at full speed. *'Lisaaaaaaaaaaa.'* She gave me a huge bear hug and squealed her excitement. How I'd missed those squeals.

'Hey, Lisa!' called Judd, 'you've lost your *tits*.'

What was I saying about being "polished"? 'Hi Judd, I see you haven't changed.'

'Hey now, don't be mean to the *fi-nan-cier*.'

'Just shut up and get the bags,' ordered Brandi.

We caught a taxi for the way back, due to the amount of their luggage. We bundled into it with Brandi and me chatting in the back at a great rate. I had almost let go of a little pain, but every time a lull seeped into the conversation or I didn't have a distraction, that horrible cold empty sensation crawled within me, slowly carving pieces off my heart. *How is this pain so unrelenting?*

As we pulled up at the house Brandi looked impressed.

'Hey, neat digs,' commented Judd.

'Just ignore him, I think he's been watching too much Fonzie or something.' She flicked the back of her hand on his shoulder. 'Pay the fucking taxi, will ya?'

Normally I would have been so proud to show them around but the house resembled a junkyard. I hadn't been capable of anything, let alone cleaning.

'I guess it's the cleaner's day off,' laughed Brandi. She saw my face and quickly added, 'Hey it doesn't matter. We'll help you,' and squeezed me.

I didn't care anymore that Judd was there, I could handle him after what I'd been through. I showed them to their rooms and told them to have a lie down as they'd be jetlagged. More to the point, the trip to the airport had drained me and I needed a little nap myself. I grew tired so easily lately. I trudged to my bedroom, lay down on the bed David and I used to share, and cried a trickle more before falling asleep.

I must have slept for a couple of hours. As I woke up I heard music – guitar music. *Judd must be playing one of David's guitars.* That made me fume. I took off downstairs and thought I'd politely tell him not to play it, when I saw that Brandi had cleaned the place. All the broken glass, mouldy curry and everything else I had thrown around but couldn't face sorting. *What an angel.* I began to sob again.

'You're gunna have to learn to stop that.' She put her arm around me.

'Oh Brandi, thank you so much. It is so good that you're here. I've been feeling like I'm really losing my grip on sanity,' I blubbered.

'Come on now, we need a little party. What ya got to drink around here?'

I hunched my shoulders sheepishly. 'I think I've drunk it all.'

She laughed. 'Good girl!' Then shouted out, 'Judd, go and buy some grog from somewhere will ya? We're gunna have a *party.*'

Judd asked for the taxi number, jumped on the phone and took off.

'See? He's good for something,' Brandi chuckled.

I freshened up a little and soon Brandi and I tucked into some pretty awful wine Judd had brought back along with packets of chips. I hadn't eaten chips for years. But I guess eating *something* again was an achievement. We sent Judd into the other room to watch American TV and caught up thoroughly. Brandi wanted all the nitty-gritties on what had happened. She couldn't believe a section of fans could be crazy enough, or clever enough, to pull this off.

'There must be some crazy sick people out there.'

'Yeah, tell me about it.' This reminded me of a conversation I'd had years ago with David.

'But how'd this guy get in?'

'I have *no* idea. The only sign I saw was a vent from the air con that had been removed. But how he got in there in the first place is a mystery to me... Although, we hadn't been as tight with security as we used to be in the old days. It didn't seem vital anymore.'

'But couldn't you have shown David the forced vent?'

'Sweetie, everything you've suggested, I have gone through a thousand times in my head. David was so convinced I'd slept with this guy he refused to listen to me. I don't think anything I could have said would have made him see the truth in any case. Besides, he thought he saw the evidence. I don't blame him in a way. I've wondered at times how I would have reacted if it had been the other way round.'

'But surely he knew how much you loved him?'

'Well, I would have thought so. But I guess actually seeing something in front of your eyes counts for a lot. As they say, "A picture is worth a thousand words". And... he'd been on and off drugs, booze... I even found some Valium in a drawer. *And* all the stress he'd been going through. He was on the edge even *before* this had happened.'

'There's gutta be a way to reach David.'

'Well if you can think of something I haven't already, please tell me. I have written letters to his management, business contacts, friends, even his mother. Jack moved about six months ago when he and Shirley separated or I would have written to him too. All the letters to official people have been returned unopened and with the friends and family ones, there has been zilch response.'

'So maybe there still *will* be a response. Give it time. And I'm sure we could find Jack between us. I reckon *he'd* listen to ya.'

Dear sweet Brandi, she is such an optimist. Just like I used to be. I tried to let her words give me hope but I didn't hold out for it. The phone rang in the other room and Judd called out he'd get it.

'Unless it's David or Australia calling, I don't want to know,' I shouted.

'Okay, well let's make some Jack finding plans tomorrow, in the meantime, let's *party.*'

She told me that since she couldn't bring our friends over with her, she would do impersonations of them instead. She soon had me giggling by doing send ups of a few of the kids back in school. I couldn't help but laugh. I felt like I was at our high school reunion. She did one of Judd. She was great. He had to see this.

'Hey Judd, come here!' I called to him through my laughter.

'Coming, Lisa.' He finished the call by saying, 'So don't ring back now, ya hear?'

'Who was that?'

'Just some salesman.' Judd shrugged as he came in. He tried not to laugh while his sister did his tough guy imitation. 'Yeah, very funny,' he attempted to belittle her talents, 'more wine, girls?'

'Yes *please*,' we sang out.

I lost count of how many bottles we drank. Judd kept bringing one after another out and filling our glasses as soon as we'd had our last mouthfuls. We talked about what was happening in Australia and it led to all kinds of crazy shit. I don't think we knew what we were talking about in the end. When the light started creeping in from the split in the curtain we thought we'd go to bed.

The next few days nearly reached the scale of fun. Judd hired a car and we took off sightseeing. We drove around Beverly Hills rubbernecking at all the mansions and celebrity places. All the while Brandi schemed on how we could find Jack.

'Hey maybe we could knock on a few doors. I'm sure someone knows him in *this* neck of the woods.' She was a comic relief for me but I couldn't take her seriously. I existed in a different head space with them around, but underneath it all bubbled the unrelenting pain and chill that refused to leave me.

Each night we'd "party" just as we had on the first; til the light of dawn crept into the house. On the third night Brandi ended up so exhausted she flaked it on one of the beanbags in the Bohemian Room where we were drinking.

'Piker,' accused Judd.

I suddenly realised I was alone with him and a shiver passed through me. Before I could think about this too much he said, 'Hang there, I'm just gunna get something.'

He returned huddling a small bundle wrapped in a cloth. 'Here's a good party trick, right here.'

I watched him unravel the bundle, revealing a few small vials of amber coloured liquid and several syringes. He took one of the syringes and filled it with the liquid. He then picked up a tourniquet, rolled up his sleeve and fastened it around his upper arm.

I gasped; partly from the realisation of what he was about to do, and partly from the gross marks covering his forearm.

'Relax, sweetheart. It's all cool.'

'What the fuck is that? Where'd you get it from?'

He puffed up with smugness. 'I im-por-ted it.'

'You mean to tell me you got that through USA customs?' I shrunk back in disbelief.

He winked at me. 'You got it, sweetheart.'

'You're *crazy*.' I watched him push the stuff into his vein.

'Ooh yeah, baby!' He filled the syringe again, raised his eyebrows at me and offered it. I stared at the syringe and the tourniquet. I wondered if I could do it. Judd noticed my hesitation and proposed to do it for me.

'How does it make you feel?'

'Out of this world, baby. Try it, you'll see.'

I thought I certainly could use being out of this world for a while. I'd gratefully welcome a little relief from the pain, the anxiety, the excruciating sorrow. Just for a little while. I studied Judd's face. He looked a lot older than me even though there were only a few years difference between us. He stared back at me and didn't avert his gaze.

Looking into his piggy eyes, I saw the Judd from years ago. The cockiness and everything it led to with me. I began to remember how he snuck into the room I slept in, how he dragged me into toilets…

'*No!*' A voice from deep within me surged out. I wasn't going to run from one form of misery to another. 'You can keep it.' I killed that whim.

'Suit yourself, baby.'

Curiosity grew in me to see what effect this would have on him, expecting something similar to when I'd shared that laced joint with David. But I hardly noticed any difference. If anything, he seemed somewhat more mellow. And his pupils became little pins. *Very unattractive really.* He obviously needed to have someone listen to his melancholy stories and I was there. All his sentences could have ended with "poor me". I didn't exactly have anything better to do and I wasn't tired enough to sleep yet, so I listened and nodded in the appropriate places.

After about an hour of how sad his life was, he wanted to talk about David. At this point he did appear a little slower in his speech but I wasn't sure whether that was the alcohol or perhaps a combination of the heroin with it. I definitely didn't want to discuss David with him.

'You gutta let go, you know… yup… that's the… best… um, thing.'

I wasn't about to start listening to advice from Judd, so I got up to leave. He stood up too and started to sway. Perhaps the blood shifted in his body or his brain suddenly took the full affect, but his eyes noticeably drooped at that point and he gave a feeble laugh.

Underneath his breath he chuckled, 'Some wanky pop...
pop star lucked out in the... end. Just like the wanky salesman
he... he was. He won't bother Mr Judd Goodings any...' he
burped, '...anymore.' He took an unsteady step towards me.
'So don't worry... it's all cool. He won't bother you anymore.'
A slight sick smile wafted onto his face.

My heart sank to the icy cold pit of my stomach.

'That was David on the phone, wasn't it?' I shot at him. I
could tell the answer from his smirk.

My eyes enlarged with the realisation of what he'd done.
I leapt at him – hitting him, kicking him, screaming at him
and scratching him wherever I could. 'I hate you, you fucking
arsehole... *scum*. I've always hated you! You're nothing but a...
I can't even think of a bad enough word for you!'

I was so furious strength overcame me, enough of it to
physically push him out of the room. I almost pushed him
down the stairs, I was so livid. I physically dragged him to the
front door and threw him out. I didn't care in the least what
happened to him.

How fucking dare you.

I half expected him to pound on the door or to call out. But
I didn't hear a sound. *Good. Die out there!*

My mind raced at the speed of light. *David rang here? What
did he want? He wanted me... he had wanted me!* I couldn't
believe he'd wanted even just to talk to me. *What did Judd say
to him?* Thinking back, he must have been a reasonable time on
the phone. *David may even have heard me laughing... of course
he would have... and calling out to Judd.* That on top of all the
hurt he already felt. He was the one who had saved me from
Judd and he'd probably be thinking I've let him back in, and
into our marital home no less. *What did I hear Judd say? Not to*

ring here anymore? That was it. In a put on Southern accent.

I knew from within every cell of my body if there had been the slimmest chance of being able to reconcile with David, *that* would have flown out of the window with Judd answering his call. That was it. I knew it. I had no chance ever again with David. That would be totally unexplainable to him. I didn't sleep at all that night.

Brandi told me Judd could go and explain. I reminded her that David was unreachable.

'Well Judd can go and knock on every fucking door in LA until he finds him, *fuck him.*' She was fuming all right. But I knew that despite whatever Brandi thought she'd force Judd to do, it would be no use. My fate had been sealed.

I announced, 'I'm going to Paris.'

And that's exactly what I did. I still had a decent chunk of money left from Mum's gift, as I'd only used a little of it to buy presents for David – and a crockpot. I took out the remainder and bought a one-way ticket to Paris. I packed one bag and one suitcase, making sure I included all the treasured things; the romantic gifts and notes from David, and memorabilia. My closest companion, my camera, came with me too of course.

Before I left, I took out my lipstick and wrote, "I love you and I will forever", on every mirror and window of the house. I also left a letter explaining my side of the story, for what it was worth. I told the taxi driver where to head quickly, before my tears began to fall.

Chapter 33

Half of me is gone away
Gone, the love I've learned to cling to
Tomorrow I'll have to find a way
To live the rest of my life alone without you

My soul drew me straight to Montmartre – the area known for its bohemian artists until about the mid-seventies. However, creative types continued to hang out within the curves of its streets. I had no idea where my life headed. How strange, being on the threshold of a new life but not sure exactly what that might be. I was twenty-two, alone, and about to paint a picture on my blank Parisian canvas. I was scared, that's for sure, but I hoped with all my being that this would be a good beginning, despite it not being my preference.

If there is anywhere in the world to be with a broken heart, it is Paris.

I walked along the cobblestoned streets and in every direction, I saw a potential photograph. After overloading my eyes with numerous scenes, I wanted to gather my thoughts. A pretty little café stood on a corner, overlooking a square of diverse passers-by. That would do nicely. I decided to sit outside at one of the small round tables, in a red and beige braided wicker chair. My surroundings filled with colour and activity.

Strangely, this noisy bustle offered me a drop of peace.

'*Bonjour, mademoiselle*,' a sing-song voice called.

The waiter approached my *petite table*, arranged the ashtray just so and swirled a menu in front of me.

'*Bonjour monsieur. Je voudrais un verre de vin, s'il vous pla t,*' I requested.

'*Et quelque chose à manger?*'

'*Non, merci.*'

'*D'accord. Toute de suite, mademoiselle.*'

Not too bad for my first conversation in French. I had studied French in school and excelled at it. I suspected however, that actually living in France would turn out to be a completely different ballgame. The waiter brought me a glass of red wine. There had been my first mistake. I should have asked for "*un verre de vin blanc*", not just "*un verre de vin*". But it appeared one could drink red wine quite cheaply in Paris by the glass, so it was about to become one of my best pals.

I sat with my new friend and contemplated everything. What a whirlwind I had endured – again. This one brought devastation beyond the scope of imagination. The best husband in the world had belonged to me… but was taken from me and his love for me torn from his heart. I had felt safe in my cosy nest with him, felt safe in his arms… Just then an accordionist wandered near the café and began playing *La Vie en Rose* which set me crying into my glass.

Is that the only damn tune they know in this city?

A voice beside me said, '*Qu'est-ce que ne va pas, mademoiselle?* And a white hanky appeared under my nose. '*Vous* êtes *à Paris!*'

'*Oui, c'est vrai,*' I began, 'but I am alone…' I sobbed into the hanky.

'You are not alone *now*. My name is Chris.'

'Is that an Aussie accent?'

'*Mais oui!*'

That made me laugh a little. 'I'm Lisa Ca... Magnusson.' Even though it was unlikely I'd be known here, I thought it better to be sure.

'Nice to meet you, Lisa.' He kissed my hand. 'You have such a lovely smile, it makes you much prettier than the crying.'

'Well my, my, haven't you picked up the way of the French men?'

He chuckled. 'Ah, I have been here for almost seven years.'

He talked about being an artist and not having much luck selling his real paintings, but instead doing relatively well with creating charcoal portraits of tourists here in Montmartre's Place du Tertre. He asked me why I had been so upset and I told him the music of the accordionist made me sad as I'd just broken up with the love of my life. Saying those words caused my eyes to fill again but I managed to hold it together, continuing with how I'd only just landed, didn't have much money, needed to find work and needed to find somewhere to stay.

'Well it is not Versailles, but you are welcome to stay at my *appartement*. There are three of us there at the moment and people drift in and out all the time. It's not far from here, near the Petit Moulin.'

I considered his offer. I had barely just met this guy; he seemed harmless enough. He didn't look like a murderer but I suppose you can never tell. My instincts told me it was okay.

'*Okay,*' I announced.

'*Très bien!*' We shook hands.

I finished my *vin rouge* and Chris took me to the little apartment a few blocks away. It looked *très jolie*. I met Olaf from Germany, a musician who also lived there. The other resident, Monique, was presently out at her favourite *artistes* bar. Chris informed me she taught dance, her speciality being character dance.

My little room was exactly that – little. The tiny window peeped out onto the street which I appreciated. Before anything else, I placed a picture of David and me on the dresser. I gazed at his handsome face and wondered what he was doing.

Chris told me not to be concerned about rent until I found some work. *How kind of him.*

He also introduced me to a valuable network of people who hung around Place du Tertre. Most of them busily sketched people, mainly tourists, so I was no competition. The camera created my art. I took dozens of pictures daily, had them developed and sold them in a little spot alongside the others. I always sought out different, more creative angles, from which to capture the scenes of Paris and lesser known nooks. I'd go out in the fog and rain to take shots, and climb railings or lay down in the street for different views.

The rent was minimal for my little spot, although the developing of the photos ended up a tad costly. A waiter in the area knew someone with a darkroom who he put me on to. So I paid this guy, Marcel, much less for developing and it worked out well. And hence my career as a semi-professional photographer launched in Paris.

In my personal life, the pain I'd come to know continued as my foundation. Every night I had nightmares, where I'd wake up either crying or screaming. They were always the same. In the ones that made me cry, David would be holding me and I'd wake up knowing I could never have his loving touch again. And the ones that drove me to scream also began in David's warm embrace, but ghouls and grotesque creatures ripped him from my arms. David would reach for me and the ghouls just laughed, telling me he'd soon forget me, as I was replaceable.

Six months into my new life I was faring well in selling my photos. A few of the tourist shops also bought them, as postcards. I wasn't making a fortune, but enough to pay rent, contribute to the household pantry and even go to a colourful bohemian bar or two on occasion.

Almost six months to the day I had arrived in Paris, I received a letter from my parents. This wasn't one of their usual, "how are you / won't you come home" letters. This was an official letter from David's lawyers sent to me via my parents' address. Our divorce had been finalised.

Every now and then I spotted his face in a magazine with a story about him having a breakdown or a failed album. I could only make out so much of what the articles said as they were naturally in French. And I didn't want any of my new friends to translate them for me as I didn't want them to know anything of my past. Probably just as well I understood only the basics, so I wouldn't be analysing whether parts were media hype or based on truth. The divorce was of course publicised too but luckily without the details. At least I knew enough French to determine that.

One article concerning David did stand out. It told of Jack dying in horrible circumstances. He'd apparently left a cigarette burning and fell asleep. His apartment burned down with him in it. I knew David would be taking this really hard. I hoped with all my heart it didn't sink him even lower but on another level I knew it would.

As I walked among the fallen autumn leaves making swirls on the street one afternoon, I found a pretty little church. I wandered in. A figurine of a particular *Notre Dame* holding her baby stood on a small side altar. The statue appeared to be rather old and unfortunately the baby's head had been broken off. I wondered why they had never fixed it.

Her altar held dozens of candles lit before her. I started to visit her on a regular basis and tell her of my sorrows. It was the one place where I found peace of heart. Sometimes tears streamed down my face as I stared into hers. I always lit a candle for David and wished him peace and happiness. There in that little church I told him I loved him, where only the Lady could hear.

Chapter 34

I'm walking in the rain
Chasing after rainbows I may never find again

David released his next album about a year after Jack's passing. I noticed it in a record shop and picked it up. And yet, I didn't buy it as I knew I couldn't bring myself to listen to it. Every time I happened to hear his voice on the radio or somewhere, it would tug at my tears. As I read the song list on the album, I noticed he had redone one of the old numbers, *My First Night Alone Without You.* I remembered the words... *You who taught me how to live, to be myself and how to give. But now it's you who's giving up on giving... You've changed and now you're out of reach. And life tonight, just doesn't seem worth living.*

Time, and the years, simply drifted on and on. I had my share of attention from many guys in Paris but I never dated, only went out with friends occasionally, and certainly never hooked up with anyone. Marie, an older woman who sold fruit and flowers from her garden on the street always shook her head at me and called out, 'Lisa! *Vous êtes trop jolie pour* être *toute seule.* You are too pretty to be alone... Find a nice man that will make you happy.'

Except I knew there was only one man in the world who could make me happy. I never took off my wedding ring or my

230

beautiful marquise engagement ring. And I never could bring myself to visit, or even walk past, The Ritz.

Some years later, another article featuring David caught my eye. I'd become far more proficient in French by then so I understood most of it. One of the photos showed him reading a letter from a fan. It was a letter of apology she had taken upon herself to write on behalf of his fans. This is what it said:

Dear David,

In the early seventies, you made me happy along with all the other girls around the world. Like for them, you were my first crush. But I feel that all of us have let you down. We didn't play the part through like you did. We played our part of "first crush" when it suited us but we didn't follow through, and you stayed dedicated to us. I wanted to tell you, well if in any way I could speak on behalf of all of us, all your fans, how very sorry I am and beg your forgiveness.

You gave so much of yourself to us. You gave your life in fact. And we put so much pressure on you. We prevented you from having true freedom and having a real life. And we hated you for getting married. How could you do that to us? We also criticized other things you did and didn't do, like what songs you recorded. I am guilty of this. And I disliked you for not being the sweet person that your character Keith Partridge was.

When I saw you being cocky, I hated that in you. When you changed with getting older, I blamed you for that too, for not retaining your youthful looks. How ridiculous is that? How pathetic I was for thinking those things. Now that I myself am older, I understand the pressures you were under, the struggles you went through and what was stolen from you, financially and otherwise too. I understand that showing off and being cocky come from feeling insecure and it is perfectly understandable that at times you would feel this way. Gosh, everyone does sometimes but especially someone in your situation, as fame and being adored from afar doesn't help with building self-worth. It's a very precarious place to be.

I understand why you tried to kill Keith symbolically, why you wanted to be recognized for you and your own talents. I also understand that you did a lot of the things I hated because of the crazy world you were immersed in, but you had every right to do those things without being criticized by me or anyone else whose business it wasn't. And I feel especially ashamed for wanting you to always look like you did in your early twenties. That probably says a lot more about my own fear of getting older than anything about you.

So I most genuinely want to apologize – for all of it. I am so very, very sorry that you had to go through all this hurt for providing so much

*happiness to so many. And I am so very, very sorry
for even ever thinking any of it. You really did give
your life for us and for that I feel especially bad.
And if there was any way possible, I want to take
your pain now. Give me your pain – for some of it
belongs to me and I need to own it.*

*Yours sincerely,
Lisa Graham*

That was some letter. I understood why David would have
agreed to have it published. *What a kind person she is.*

I wondered though what she meant by him not retaining
his youthful looks. He always looked great to me. I examined
the photos again and in the five years or so that I hadn't seen
him in person, he did appear to have aged. His eyes especially
seemed somehow estranged and not like the Sunset Eyes I'd
loved, that used to gaze at me. He had also cut his beautiful
long hair.

A few days later it would have been our ten-year wedding
anniversary. I had now been away from him for just over the same
time we had lived together as a married couple. *Unbelievable.*
My love for him hadn't waned a bit. I loved him just as much as
I had back then, if not more.

I trekked to my little *eglise* to visit *Notre Dame* and lit
a candle at her altar for David. I spoke to him, 'My darling
Sunset Eyes, I hope you're well. It would have been our ten-
year anniversary today. I wonder if you remembered? Do you
even remember me, your "Beautiful Girl"?' I began to weep.
'My darling, I have never forgotten you and I still love you as

much as I did the day we married. In fact I love you more… I send you love, peace and happiness. I wish you the very best of everything in this world, whatever you need to fulfil your life. Be well my love, be well and be strong. Keep shining.'

I wept as Our Lady watched over me.

The next day a telegram arrived for me. It read, "David near fatal accident. Life at risk. Please come Mount Sinai Hospital ASAP."

It was from Sam. My heart stopped. My thoughts flew from being astounded he would send for me to a vile fear that David could die.

The guy who delivered it asked if I was okay as apparently I had turned white.

I showed him the telegram. I asked out loud, not particularly of anyone, how on earth he'd found me.

The guy said, '*Si un homme veut trouver une femme, il le fera. Même* à partir d'un *lit d'hôpital.* If a man wants to find a woman, he will. Even from a hospital bed.'

I took back my telegram, thanked the guy and began frantically thinking about how much money I could pull together for the fare. Still in shock, I wandered into our "lounge around" area where my housemates chatted. They noticed my distressed state.

'What's wrong, Lisa?'

I showed them the telegram and told them I didn't know how I would possibly get there. I definitely didn't have enough for the plane ticket. Chris asked who David was.

'He's the love of my life.' I burst out crying.

'Was this the guy you were crying over when I met you at the café, when you first came here?'

I nodded.

'Oh *chère* Lisa, if this is the love of your life you must go to him. I can help by contributing something. What say all?'

The most unreal thing happened – they all agreed to chip in for the fare. They thought between all of us, there may be enough. It dawned on me these dear souls had become my closest friends in the world. They cared about me; even though I'd been the "ice queen" most of the time and spoken very little about myself to them. Naturally I burst into tears again and promised them no matter what, I would pay them back.

I booked the first available flight to LA and sent a telegram back to Sam to let him know when I'd be arriving.

Chapter 35

You were the one, you were the only
You were Saturday night
No one else who held me ever felt so right

Sam met my flight at LAX. I chewed on some caution, unsure how to interact with him as last time we'd spoken he hadn't been very friendly. When he saw me he didn't smile at all. He simply said, 'Hi,' and led me to his car. He told me we were heading straight to the hospital and he'd fill me in on the way.

After a considerable and awkward silence, he must have found the desire to speak. 'I'm not sure whether you're aware of it or not, but the other day would have been yours and David's tenth wedding anniversary. So David decided he was going out to get drunk. He was staying at my place for a couple of days as he'd been quite down. I hadn't wanted to go with him as I didn't want to encourage his drinking. Now in retrospect, I wish I'd gone so I could've kept an eye on him. Anyway, it was getting quite late and he hadn't returned. I started to get worried that something had happened to him. So I rang the police. I gave a description of him and his car and was asked to wait on the line. Someone came on asking me who I was and what my relationship to David was. I told them and also said that I'm the closest person to him as none of his family is in LA. Then came the news. They confirmed that he'd been involved in a car accident and was being taken to Mount Sinai.'

Sam fell quiet for a moment and then continued, 'He'd been driving fast and well, he'd been drinking and... he'd wrapped himself around a pole.'

'Oh my god. How bad is he?'

'Well... he's not good.' Sam again had to compose himself before continuing. 'I saw him in Emergency and he was a mess. They thought he'd punctured a lung from the impact... and the lining, which caused... something else. They said it was probably the glass or a chunk of steel. The car was almost completely crushed. They said it was lucky he survived at all. He'd also suffered a cardiac event from the trauma and lost a lot of blood. He had to be resuscitated. They were thinking of a transfusion... and to operate to sort out the lung situation.'

I couldn't hold my tears any longer at this point. I told Sam to continue.

'I don't think I was really prepared to see him like that in Emergency. He was bad. He kept drifting in and out of consciousness, more out than in. At one point he recognised me and he looked like he wanted to tell me something so I bent down so he could whisper in my ear, as he really wasn't capable of making much sound. He managed to say one thing – "Get Lisa". I think he thought he was going to die...' At that point Sam lost it too.

'Oh, Sam.' I put my hand on his arm.

He tensed. 'But I'm not happy about it. I only contacted you as it was David's wish.'

'Sam! You've got to believe me that I didn't do anything. I was *set up*.'

'Yeah, David let me read your letter. He even wanted to believe you at one stage but I talked sense into him.'

'*What?* You had no right to do that—'

'I did so have a right... David's my best pal and he's gone through hell and back over this. I wasn't going to let you hurt him *again*,' he practically yelled at me.

I yelled back, 'What about what I went through, Sam? I went through hell too! And I was *innocent.*'

'The hell you were!' Sam was so irate he almost swerved into an oncoming truck. 'We'll talk about this later.'

'You're damn right we will.'

A small number of fans loitered outside the hospital. They recognised us as we walked in and whispered to each other.

As we approached the desk Sam leant in. 'And one more thing... as far as the staff here knows, you are his wife. Otherwise you wouldn't be let into Intensive Care.'

'Oh I'm sure I can manage to act that part.'

We met with the Intensive Care nurse who briefed me before I entered the unit. 'Please try and prepare yourself for seeing him. He has a lot of tubes attached and doesn't look the best due to a lot of glass shattering and some bruising. The surgeon has done his best to repair the pneumothorax – the air getting into the space between the lung and lining – that caused the collapse of the lung, and to remove the glass and chunks of metal that penetrated the lung. His cardiac condition is critical but we hope it will stabilise. All we can do now is sit back and hope he pulls through. Are you ready, Mrs Cassidy?'

I nodded.

We walked into a room where people lay unconscious in beds, with lights bleeping and obtrusive equipment surrounding them. The nurse led me to David's bed.

My stomach knotted and my hands trembled. When I caught sight of him, he looked so incredibly fragile. He did have tubes all over the place and a considerable one in his mouth. There lay the man that had leapt energetically over stages across the globe, singing with fire. The man that used to hold me so securely I felt safe from everything. Now he lay in front of me, hanging onto life by a mere thread. His beautiful face had cuts all over and he was horribly bruised along one side.

I put my hand on his. 'My darling David…' The tears simply poured in streams down my face. 'I've never stopped loving you. I never will. You have always been and always will be the love of my life. You must pull through this. You must. You have so much more living to do.'

My body started jerking from my crying and I stopped speaking as I didn't want to upset him. Although I knew he couldn't hear me. But maybe… We always had such a good connection between us… maybe… somehow he would know I was there.

I stood motionless watching him and loving him for I don't know how long. Eventually the nurse came and said it may be best to go. I leaned over and kissed him on his forehead. It felt like a privilege; one I felt partly guilty in taking as he had no choice in it. I told him again how much I loved him and that I would see him soon. I then left that awful room.

At the desk I told them I'd be there to see him again the next day and that I wanted to speak with one of his doctors. They asked me for a number in case they needed to contact me. I turned to Sam. 'Sam would you please give the number, I'm too distressed to think of it.'

Sam informed them, we walked away and he said he'd drive me to the house.

'What house?'

'His house… your old house… Cassidy Castle. He never sold it.'

As we made our way out of the hospital, we passed the pool of fans. *'Lisa,'* someone called.

I looked over and immediately one guy turned away from shyness, but I saw the girl who had called out. I recognised her. She had been pictured in the recent article I'd read in Paris; the fan who had written the apology letter. I stopped and she came over.

'Hi, I'm Lisa Graham,' she introduced herself.

'I know. I read your letter. It was very thoughtful of you to write that.'

'Oh thank you. That is so nice of you to say. It was *so* wonderful to actually meet David over that,' she glowed, 'and I just wanted to say how very sorry I am about him leaving – er, your breakup – or divorce rather.'

'Thanks Lisa. It was long ago now.'

'How is he?'

At this question I broke down.

'Oh I'm so sorry. I didn't mean to upset you.' She offered me a tissue.

'Thanks Lisa, I have a good supply of them. Look, let's just say we all need to send him our good thoughts and energy. I'm sorry but I have to go.'

'Of course. And I will ask everyone to do that. He'll be in our prayers. It was so lovely meeting you.'

A sensation of steel straps gripped around my chest and throat as Sam drove. My hands shook, my stomach churned and my heart sped uncontrollably. I couldn't even bring myself to talk to him, to defend myself.

When we arrived, Sam gave me the key – David's key to the house. I think my breathing stopped for an instant, but I felt blessed to hold it. Sam wrote down his current number and asked me to let him know if the hospital phoned, and to ring when I wanted to go back the next day.

I got out of the car and walked up the curved stone driveway. When I felt the familiar click of the key in the lock, I hesitated to open the door. My head told me it would be okay to enter but another part of me remained sickly nervous in wondering what I might find. I turned on the lights and my anxiety engulfed me with an urge to throw up. I ran to the toilet. My stomach had nothing in it but nevertheless I went through the motions several times. It was horrid.

After lying on the cold bathroom floor a little I hauled myself up to take a tour of my old home. Everything appeared exactly as when I'd left. To my amazement, even the "I love you" messages I'd left in lipstick all over the place were still there. After some *five years*. This was like walking back in time. However, mess lay about everywhere – discarded bottles of wine, dishes randomly left, his clothes scattered. I decided it must be my karmic turn to clean up as I had been incapable of doing that when I had my own breakdown here. Besides, I wanted to clean up for him. I picked up one of his shirts and held it to me. His sensual scent made me giddy. I breathed it in, relishing it.

The anxiety within me still managed to twist my stomach in waves while my veins quaked. I certainly could have used a drink but I was determined not to. Instead I threw myself into the cleaning.

My thoughts repeatedly flew to David and I imagined holding and comforting him. *Hang in there,* I said over and over in my head to him. But another thought persisted in interrupting my doting headspace. That Lisa kept popping into my head. *What is it about her? Have I seen her before…? Before that apology article somewhere?* These thoughts continued to bug me and I wondered whether my collection of scrapbooks I'd filled with clippings from David's tour were still in the house. I put down the mop and decided to look.

If I remembered correctly, they had been put away in one of the spare bedrooms in a cupboard. I approached the white louver doors and opened them carefully, as if they held an ancient secret. And there they were – piled neatly on top of one another right on the middle shelf, exactly as I'd left them. I pulled them out and sat on the floor flicking through them.

That brought the tour back to me as if it had been just the other day. David looked so sexy in his jumpsuits. I spotted a pic of the black one with the sparkly swirls and remembered how he had sung the first few lines of *Could It Be Forever* to me from onstage with that cheeky smile of his. I had been so elated, realising at that moment he really did have feelings for me. Fuck, I had been excited. *Mon dieu* – what a time it had been.

Browsing through the pages of different scrapbooks I found an article on how a small number of fans had managed to climb up on stage to David during one of his concerts. He had been terrified. It was headed, "Teenies break through barriers to reach their idol". And bingo – a picture of Lisa from years ago with two others jumped out at me. It was definitely her. Lisa undeniably gave the impression of being ring leader, or aggressor.

So I *had* seen her years ago after all and it had stuck in my mind. I wasn't sure why it had bugged me so much. *This is her but so what?* I read the print under the photograph, "Cassidy fans (Left to Right), Shelley Granger, Linda Graham, and Richard Stein". I read the line a second time. Lisa's name had been written as "Linda". *Is it a mistake?*

I studied the picture again, and their faces. Suddenly a vile realisation crept over me. The guy in the picture, Richard Stein, I had seen before too... in my *bed*. *This is the guy who broke in and pretended to be my lover!* I examined his face thoroughly. Without question, it was him. *Creepy little arsehole. I bet that was him outside the hospital tonight also with Lisa... or Linda.* The guy who had turned away his face.

My first thought was to let him have it, if he turned up there in the morning. But I began to wonder what all this meant. *Did Linda change her name to Lisa? Why...? To emulate me?* I gathered she was the "right Mrs Cassidy" who was supposed to replace me. *Does she think having my name will somehow make her more appealing to David?*

She certainly thought of a cunning way to meet him that worked. *Apology my arse.* And I then remembered she'd said to me she was sorry David had left me. *How would she know that?* In Paris I had made sure to get my hands on every American tabloid that talked about our divorce and absolutely none had given any details on our split. I had felt extremely grateful to David that he didn't drag my name through the dirt.

I couldn't wait to confront those little gutter swipes. I'd bet my last dollar they'd be at the hospital the next day. And I would do it together with Sam.

I dashed back downstairs, finished the mopping and the rest of the cleaning. The place looked good. It was even cleaner than when we had lived there together. I thought I'd better try and grab a little sleep so I stepped softly into our old bedroom and crawled into the bed we had once shared. His exquisite scent was there too. I cuddled his pillow and tried to will some sleep to come to me.

Chapter 36

First thing when I woke, I rang Sam and frantically told him to come straight over; that I wanted to go and see David, and I wanted to talk to him. Sam asked if the hospital had called.

'No, but I want to go and see him anyway.'

'Lisa, visiting hours aren't for quite a while yet. I really don't think–'

I practically screamed down the line, 'He's my husband and I want to *see him*.' A silence fell between us as we both realised what I'd said. My voice lowered and I emphasised, 'Sam I really want to talk to you about something.'

He promised to come over as soon as he could.

♪ ♪ ♪

Sam bounded in the moment I opened the door. 'I notice you still wear your wedding and engagement ring.'

I truly wanted to bang his head against a wall. '*Sam.* You just don't get it, do you? I still *love* David. I have never done anything to intentionally hurt him and I never will. Now will you listen to me?'

Sam sat while I told him what I had discovered about Linda Graham and her side-kick. I showed him the clippings. He didn't seem convinced.

'Okay, let's say that these two did come up with this sick scheme. What's confronting them going to do? They'll just deny it and try something else or fade into the distance of the fan world.'

I stared at him. 'Yep, well, maybe. But maybe, just maybe, with you beside me, you might just see one tiny look on their faces that gives them away... or one tiny bit of evidence that proves my innocence. Just one tiny piece is all I need because if you believe me then I know David will, if he...' I didn't want to go there. 'It may be a long shot, but I just want one chance, however miniscule, to prove to David that I always loved him and would never hurt him... just one chance...' I crumpled into tears.

'Let's go.'

All the way to Mount Sinai my head kept churning over what I could possibly say to Linda. I felt certain she'd be there – along with that creep. It was critical that I say the right thing and not blow this.

As we arrived at the hospital, we observed their little group huddling a short distance away from the entrance. 'Okay Sam, come with me and pay attention.' We walked over and I greeted Linda.

'Hi, Lisa. It's so lovely to see you. How are you?' she returned.

'Yeah, I'm okay.'

I scanned the group. The creep was there, busy looking at the ground. I took that to be a good sign. He stood close to another guy and three girls lurked with them.

'And who are your friends here?'

'Oh how rude of me. I should have introduced them to you. This is Cindy... and Sue... and Rosie... and this is Ricky and Simon.'

Ricky hardly glanced towards me and persisted in staring downwards but I noticed that he and Simon held hands. It dawned on me this was going to be sweet and I felt my posture elevate.

'Do I detect a little romance here?' I directed my attention to the boys.

'Oh aren't they cute? They're quite inseparable,' chimed Linda.

'How nice.' I looked directly at Ricky. 'Do we know each other, Ricky?'

He gave a quick peek somewhere in my direction, bowed his head again and muttered, 'No.'

'You're sure we don't know each other?'

He kept his sight firmly on the ground and shook his head. 'Nope.'

'And Simon here is your boyfriend, and you're gay?'

He cast his eyes at his wiry companion who seemed annoyed with him for not answering. Simon eventually rolled his eyes and said, 'Well, ye-ah!' in his face.

'Then all that makes it impossible for you and I to have had an affair together, now doesn't it?'

Little Ricky had begun to squirm and act a little defensively. 'I don't know what you're talking about.'

Linda appeared a little uncomfortable too.

'Oh really? I see. So you don't remember breaking into my house and jumping into my bed just before my husband came home… to make it look like we were having an affair?'

'You're crazy,' he half laughed, looking over at anything except me.

'Well you know what? Sam and I have come to pick up

David as he's being discharged today. You are all his fans. So here is a lifetime opportunity to come and meet David Cassidy as he's being let out of hospital. Come on, let's go.'

They all remained motionless and silent.

'No? What's the matter, Ricky? Don't you want to fight for me anymore? Aw come on, Ricky. David would *love* to see you again.'

At that point Ricky turned on his heel and walked off, giving me the finger high in the air. Simon looked like he may throw up. Either that or he was about to give Ricky a big serving. He hesitated but set off after him. I guess poor Linda had no choice but to follow. She didn't say a word but scuttled in the same direction, her accessories trailed behind her.

I called out, 'It was lovely to meet you *Linda*. I'll make sure David sends you an autographed photo of us.' I folded my arms and turned my head to Sam.

'Oh, baby girl I... What you must have gone through...'

'Yeah, no shit? Come on, I want to see David. I can't bear the thought of him in there like that, and alone.'

Chapter 37

We bee-lined inside to the desk near the ICU and I asked to see David. A different shift of staff greeted us and it seemed they weren't aware of his name. I gave it again and the girl looked on her list or whatever it was and said, 'I'm sorry but there is no one by that name in the ICU.'

The realisation of what that meant stabbed me like a blunt knife ramming through the last ten years. I dropped to the floor and screamed. A raw raspy sound rose from some primal place inside me. I observed this happening from a distance and at the same time my own voice generated the screaming. I could not accept this as reality – I simply could *not*. I would not have anyone telling me I'd never hold him again, that I'd never again see his beautiful eyes.

Sam lifted me up and put his arms around me. He didn't say a word. He just held me. I felt him crying.

Somewhere far, I heard a voice calling, 'Mrs Cassidy, Mrs Cassidy.' I sensed a hand on my shoulder. 'Please Mrs Cassidy, come and sit down.'

'I don't want to sit down!' I screamed, 'I just want my *husband*.'

'Mrs Cassidy, I'm dreadfully sorry…'

My tears convulsed out of me hearing those words.

'Mrs Cassidy, please listen to me… there's been a dreadful mistake…'

'Mistake? Wha…'

'Your husband has been moved to the High Dependency Unit. The nurse on the desk has just returned from vacation and was not aware of the patient list. I am so very sorry to have caused you this distress.'

'You mean… My husband isn't… My husband is okay?' I would have given her absolutely anything she'd ask for if this was true.

The matron asked me to accompany her into a small room where we sat on a sofa. I took Sam with us. She proceeded to tell me David had been moved to another area as his overall condition had further stabilised, but was still somewhat serious.

'He is conscious at times but we need to keep a very close eye on him as things could change at a minute's notice. Please understand that we are doing everything we possibly can for him.'

'But what are his chances… of surviving?'

'I'm sorry Mrs Cassidy, but I cannot give you even an estimate. Patients who have been in similar or worse conditions have survived and yet others who have been in better conditions have not. It's a very individual thing and you can simply never tell.'

'Can I see him?'

'Well yes, but it would have to be only you. I don't mean to appear harsh but you really can't stay very long as we don't want anything exacerbating him too much. I'm sorry. I do hope you understand.'

She led me to another area which looked equally as drastic as the ICU. Bleeping monitors and intravenous drips dominated in a subtly lit space. David's bed was at the far end. As we approached, I saw he was still wired to machines but the large tube from his mouth had gone. The nurse said she needed to check his underwater seal drain, whatever that was. She lifted the blanket to reveal a huge tube inserted into his massively bruised chest.

I gasped.

Immediately I put my hand to my mouth to silence myself. She told me the tube had been positioned through his ribs and stitched into place. It ran through a "liquid sealed drainage system" to let the air bubble out of the pleural space, which apparently is the space between the lungs and ribs. Blood also drained from it. It looked horrendous. I resolved not to cry.

After she'd put the blanket snugly back into place, she left me alone with him. It broke my heart to see his beautiful face strewn with cuts and bruises. At least he looked peaceful lying there, and not just battered about. I put my hand on his and lightly kissed him on the forehead.

He let out a sigh.

'Darling David,' I whispered to his forehead, 'I love you so much. You've got to hang in there. Be strong baby, be strong.'

His voice was a feather of a whisper, 'Lisa… mmh… my Lisa.'

'David? Oh, David…' My tears flowed through my words.

'Lisa… I love you… my beautiful girl… Please… please don't leave me.'

'I've got ya baby, you're safe in my arms.'

Chapter 38

2000

All my feelings come together
All of me is here

The regal blue curtain slowly opened and I held my breath. My knuckles had turned white from squeezing my hands together. This took me back, and I was surprised at my level of nerves for how his performance would go down. David was nervous too, I could tell.

I took his hand in mine. 'He'll be fine,' I whispered.

'I know, baby.' He flashed his gorgeous smile at me.

The MC jumped onto the stage and announced, 'Ladies and Gentlemen, Marryatville High School takes great pleasure in welcoming you to their First Year Students' End of Year Concert. And we're kicking off tonight with one of our most promising talents. Ladies and Gentlemen, please put your hands together for Arch Cassidy and his band, *Heart Rock Canyon!'*

Instantly a group of girls at the front jumped up and raised a banner with "Marry me Archie!" in glittering letters.

David laughed. 'Some things never change.'

His face filled with elation as he watched Arch rocking it out on stage. I was extremely proud right next to him.

'He takes after his father,' I whispered into David's ear. He squeezed my hand.

On the final chord, Arch surged his arm into the air and the audience erupted with applause. David clapped hyper-energetically and whistled, then grabbed hold of me and kissed me. We both couldn't wait to see him to congratulate him and tell him how well he'd done. But we thought we'd better not be rude, and should watch the other kids' performances too.

The next band had a gimmicky theme and was set up in a boat. Ironically, they were called *Rock the Boat*.

David turned to me. 'Darlin', remember one night on the Thames when we nearly rocked the boat?'

'Yes, *nearly* but we didn't quite get there.' I put on a pouty sad face.

He leant so close to my ear that I felt his breath, and his soft caramel voice whispered, 'I'll sort that out tonight, beautiful girl.'

Afterword

Back in 1974, I *was* one of the girls outside The Town House in Adelaide. David was somewhere inside but for some reason he never summoned me up to his room. I wonder how it would have played out if by some wild chance he had. If his book, *C'mon, Get Happy* is anything to go by, he may have wanted me to kneel in front of him in his favourite sexual position. Would I have done this? I'd like to think I would've had the intestinal fortitude to decline that offer. If I *had* done it, it probably would have been the catalyst for a seriously dysfunctional sex life and years of therapy. Perhaps I had a lucky escape.

Did he really think the only thing all those girls wanted from him back then was just sex? Maybe a few of them might have wanted the big DC as a notch on their belts but I daresay the majority would have thought that maybe, just maybe, if they performed whatever sexual act he desired, there might be a chance they'd end up being "The One".

I would really, *really* love to know what happened to some of those girls. What emotions they were left to deal with after their encounters in the inner sanctum of the Cassidy world. Were their illusions of Him shattered, or did they somehow twist things around in their heads to make it all less bitter to swallow, if you'll pardon my pun. If you are one of these women – *please*, write a book.

In early 2013, David Cassidy auctioned off tickets to one of his shows including a "meet and greet" with him, to raise money for the American Alzheimer's Association. Despite the prize being in New York and me being in Australia, I thought I would bid.

A thrill of significant proportions grew in me with the prospect of actually meeting my "first love" in the flesh. Another part of me wondered whether I really wanted to go there. What if he didn't live up to the version of him I had in my head? What if he was rude to me? What if, by meeting him, I killed off something inside me that was so precious to me?

I gave myself a bidding limit. As it drew close to the end of the auction, I went over. I went way over. I got caught up in the competition with another bidder. I didn't know whether s/he was bidding against me in real time or had put on a top bid that kept outdoing mine. The thrill became stronger. The urge to win intensified and I kept bidding. Then something made me stop. I wanted to put on one last bid. A curious thought occurred inside my head, telling me it might be best not to win after all, but still urged me to make a mark in this auction. Maybe I wanted to make a difference for David even in some small way, in return for the contribution he had made to my life. Whatever the reason, I went for it. I put on quite a substantial bid.

Only a few seconds to go. My inner-self reaffirmed what I wanted; to bump up the bid significantly, but not to win. I held my breath. The auction ended – I came second. Perfect. I walked away happy and decided to instead go and see the artist who had the second greatest impact on my life – Julie Andrews. You could say I gave up David for Julie in an odd way.

For me, contentment is simply the fantasy. I could never

forget my first love and choose to remember him in the way I had made him up from his image. And if needed, I can always pull him up from the depths of my mind to swoon over on a rainy day.

Acknowledgements for use of Lyrics

257

I Am A Clown – Tony Romeo (Sony/ATV 55%)
© 1972 40 West Music
Used by permission of Sony/ATV Music Publishing Australia Pty Limited
(ABN 93 080 392 230) Locked Bag 7300, Surry Hills, NSW 2010, Australia
International copyright secured. All rights reserved.

I Am A Clown – Tony Romeo (EMI MP 45%)
© 1972 EMI Sosaha Music Inc
Used by permission of EMI Music Publishing Australia Pty Limited
(ABN 83 000 040 951) Locked Bag 7300, Surry Hills, NSW 2010, Australia
International copyright secured. All rights reserved.

I Think I Love You – Tony Romeo (EMI MP 100%)
© 1970 Screen Gems-EMI Music Inc
Used by permission of EMI Music Publishing Australia Pty Limited
(ABN 83 000 040 951) Locked Bag 7300, Surry Hills, NSW 2010, Australia
International copyright secured. All rights reserved.

Point Me In The Direction Of Albuquerque – Tony Romeo (EMI MP
  100%)
© 1970 Screen Gems-EMI Music Inc
Used by permission of EMI Music Publishing Australia Pty Limited
(ABN 83 000 040 951) Locked Bag 7300, Surry Hills, NSW 2010, Australia
International copyright secured. All rights reserved.

I'm On The Road – Barry Mann/Cynthia Weil (EMI MP 100%)
© 1970 Screen Gems-EMI Music Inc
Used by permission of EMI Music Publishing Australia Pty Limited
(ABN 83 000 040 951) Locked Bag 7300, Surry Hills, NSW 2010, Australia
International copyright secured. All rights reserved.

Roller Coaster – Mark James (EMI MP 100%)
© 1973 Screen Gems-EMI Music Inc
Used by permission of EMI Music Publishing Australia Pty Limited
(ABN 83 000 040 951) Locked Bag 7300, Surry Hills, NSW 2010, Australia
International copyright secured. All rights reserved.

Only A Moment Ago – Terry Cashman/T P West (EMI 100%)
© 1970 Colgems EMI Music Inc
Used by permission of EMI Music Publishing Australia Pty Limited
(ABN 83 000 040 951) Locked Bag 7300, Surry Hills, NSW 2010, Australia
International copyright secured. All rights reserved.

About the Author

'The day I stop seeking out the magic dust in life is the day I stop living', is author Léa Rebane's motto. Léa has worked in a constellation of roles and projects throughout her life, ranging from manager of a school for aspiring young performers to facilitator of community health groups. Creating diversity, and a little adrenalin, keeps Léa inspired and optimistic. For her, these are the shields for dodging the downpours that life tends to squirt us with from time to time.

Léa has previously been published in various Adelaide newspapers, as part of an anthology of birthing stories in *Inside, Outside, Upside Down* and as a commissioned writer. In 2003, Léa received an *Outstanding Achievement in Writing for Publication* through Para West Adult Campus and has studied through Adelaide TAFE's Professional Writing Unit.

Léa lives in South Australia's lush wine region – the Barossa Valley, with an assortment of dogs, peacocks and alpacas. She currently works in Aboriginal Health and as a restaurant reviewer on breakfast radio. Often she is found leaping onto the boards in amateur theatre, which she says keeps her *almost* sane.

CPSIA information can be obtained at www.ICGtesting.com
Printed in the USA
BVOW04s1511191014

371297BV00001B/18/P

9 780646 922140